AN IDIOT IN
LOVE

AN IDIOT IN LOVE

A NOVEL

DAVID JESTER

Skyhorse Publishing

Skyhorse Publishing books may be purchased in bulk at special discounts for sales promotion, corporate gifts, fund-raising, or educational purposes. Special editions can also be created to specifications. For details, contact the Special Sales Department, Skyhorse Publishing, 307 West 36th Street, 11th Floor, New York, NY 10018 or info@skyhorsepublishing.com.

Skyhorse® and Skyhorse Publishing® are registered trademarks of Skyhorse Publishing, Inc.®, a Delaware corporation.

Visit our website at www.skyhorsepublishing.com.

10 9 8 7 6 5 4 3 2 1

Library of Congress Cataloging-in-Publication Data is available on file.

Cover design by: lillithc

Print ISBN: 978-1-5107-0001-7
Ebook ISBN: 978-1-5107-0005-5

Printed in the United States of America

To Yiota

Contents

1

Kerry Newsome

My ignorance of the opposite sex, and of relationships, became apparent when I was eight.

Kerry Newsome was in the year ahead of me. She was a nine-year-old underachiever with the charm of a fairy-tale stepsister. I had seen her on the playground a number of times, and she had giggled her way through a handful of awkward conversations with me, but I rarely gave her a second thought.

That all changed during one confusing recess. I was kicking a battered soccer ball around a chalked, concrete playground when one of her friends interrupted me.

"Kieran!"

I turned to see Laura Bell hollering at me, anxiously shuffling on her feet as she did so. She beckoned me over and I reluctantly scuttled her way.

She stood near the boundary of the playground, where a five-foot metallic perimeter shaded a view of the thick woodlands beyond.

"Kerry wants to see you," she said with a wink and a smile.

I made a point of looking around the playground.

"She's behind the bike sheds," Laura inserted.

I frowned at her, unsure what she was suggesting.

Her mild manner changed to frustration as I remained standing. "Just go, would you?" she pushed.

Laura had judging eyes that bore the hallmarks of prepubescent psychopathy and windowed the mind of a future dominatrix. I didn't want to obey her, but I didn't want to disappoint her. I found myself following her sternly pointed finger and drifting toward the rear end of the school where a shaded corner housed three bike sheds and an unused, dilapidated janitor's shed.

Kerry was waiting by the side of the bike sheds with her hands on her hips, chewing her lips as she surveyed the playground with anticipated disappointment and annoyance.

She often wore her golden-blonde hair in pigtails, but Peter Armstrong—an effeminate, mini-metrosexual who passed his recesses playing Hopscotch and skipping games with the girls—had spent his morning braiding her golden locks into three long strands that swung pendulously down her back.

Her hazel eyes twinkled with delight and she ambled toward me.

"Laura said—"

Kerry grabbed my hand and quickly turned away, not interested in anything I had to say.

"Where are we going?" I asked, careful not to trip over the heels of her scuffed black shoes as she pulled me across the playground.

"Come on," she urged without explanation.

The side of the furthest bike shed was bordered by a thicket of outstretched bushes. A thin, wood-chipped alleyway led to the rear of the sheds and a secluded spot used by the older, more delinquent juveniles.

Cigarette butts littered the ground like a carpet of discarded cancer. I stepped through the slalom of filters—blackened and soggy from the rain—and found a patch of bare mud to rest my tattered sneakers.

Kerry didn't seem to mind the ashy assault course. She waded through the butts with tiptoed glee and rested her back against the shed, her hands tucked behind her backside. She eyed me with a sly smile.

"What do you want?" I asked, wondering why I had followed her this far.

She giggled, looked away awkwardly, and then exclaimed without lifting her eyes: "You show me yours and I'll show you mine."

I let a smile creep onto my face. I didn't know she was interested in *that*—if I had, I wouldn't have been so reluctant to follow her. This was what my school days were made for after all; this was the reason I became excited at the thought of going to school.

I looked around to make sure no one was looking—no movement in the bushes, no eyes peeking through the many holes in the back of the shed.

"Okay," I said, with a *prepare yourself for this* inflection.

I pulled it out and beamed a broad, dimpled smile.

Slowly, preparing herself for what she was about to see, she lifted her eyes from the ground.

"What the hell is that?"

I looked down at my hand. I turned it this way and that, examining the grasped item.

"What's wrong with it?" I said, worried. "It's perfect."

She shook her head as she stared at me, disbelief in her eyes. "A soccer sticker?" she spoke slowly.

"Not just any soccer sticker," I said proudly. "It's Andy Cole. Leading Premiership goal scorer, record breaker, signed from—"

"I'm not interested in bloody soccer!" she spat, annoyed.

I looked around, visibly aware she had dragged me to the middle of nowhere. "But you said—"

"I didn't mean *that!*" she spat.

"I have Teddy Sheringham, but it's nowhere near as—"

An exasperated sigh stopped me short. "You're useless!" she said, throwing her hands in the air. She barged forward, knocked me aside, and trudged angrily back toward the playground.

That's hardly fair, I thought to myself as I watched her stomp away. *I never got to see hers.*

The playground can be a fickle place, and in an instant, Kerry's affections turned sour. For the rest of the week, she shot cold, despicable glances my way and more than once I heard her giggling with her friends and turned to see their eyes on me.

I didn't know what I had done wrong, and my ignorance worked in my favor—less than two weeks passed before Kerry's affections turned my way again.

I found her waiting for me outside the school gates one morning. The bell had already rung, the children had already flooded into the building, and I was already late, but that didn't stop Kerry from waiting for me.

"Where have you been?" she demanded to know, devilment in her eyes.

I was breathless, having run the last half mile. "I missed the bus," I blurted out. I tried to squeeze past her, eager to get into the building, but she stepped in front of me.

"I've been waiting for you," she said, crossing her arms over her chest.

"Okay," I nodded and smiled. I waited in the momentary silence and then tried to duck past her, but she blocked me again.

"I'm late because of you," she accused.

"Well . . . that's . . . I don't think—"

"Stop blabbering!"

"Sorry," I hung my head.

"Come with me," she ordered.

"Again?"

"Kieran!"

"Sorry."

I followed her around to the back of the bike sheds. She had more of a purpose in her step than she had two weeks ago; she practically dragged me through the gap leading to the rear of the sheds and the cigarette graveyard.

"What is this about?" I wondered.

She didn't answer me. Instead she shoved me, the force in her push strong enough to send me sprawling against the wooden facade. A small gasp escaped my lungs as I collided with the solid surface. I opened my mouth to complain, but I stopped when she dove forward and pressed her lips against mine.

I mumbled an objection, but she didn't move. Her eyes were closed, her concentration on the kiss.

The lingering taste of sweet cherry confectionary had stuck to her lips; it pressed into my mouth and I salivated. I had overslept and, as a result, had skipped breakfast. She was making me hungry.

After a minute which seemed like an eternity, Kerry pulled away from me with a superfluous *muaw* sound.

When she smiled, she exposed a small gap between her front two teeth. She was showing that gap to the world now with an ear-to-ear grin. "Well?" she wondered.

I paused, unsure what to say. I had never kissed a girl before; I had never wanted to. I didn't even want to now, but it was done. I tried to remember how it went in the movies and on television, but

if the screen didn't fade to black after the kiss then my parents usually pulled me away and told me it was time for bed.

"Thank you," I said slowly, gauging her reaction with each syllable.

The smile stayed on her face fleetingly, fading when she realized that was all I had to say. "Thank you?" she asked, seemingly
offended. "Is that it?"

I didn't want to tell her the truth— that it had been uncomfortable, sticky, and generally unpleasant—but I felt too awkward to
convincingly lie about how good it was.

"Well?" Her hands were on her hips, the expression of contempt
that had blossomed in her during the last two weeks back in her
eyes. "Kieran!"

I licked my lips. "Have you got any more of that candy left? I
haven't eaten all morning, I'm really hungry."

I watched fury build on her little face. It crossed over her lips
and left them snarled and menacing. It cut to her nose and flared
her nostrils as they drew in rapid, annoyed breaths. It passed to her
eyes, which burned with a deep ferocity, and it ingrained in her
brow, which raised and furrowed.

She stammered through a number of replies, her head twisting
from side to side, her eyes burning into mine and then into the
wood behind me. Then she gave up and let out a protracted sigh,
her head low.

Subconsciously, I had covered my privates during her aggressive
state. When she calmed down I removed my hands and breathed a
sigh of relief.

"I'll tell you what," she said after a moment's silence, the calm
now completely restored. "I'll give you all I have left," she produced
a half empty pack of candy from her pocket, "*if* you kiss me again

during lunchtime. A longer kiss this time, *and* you have to enjoy it."

I didn't like those terms, but I didn't want to upset her any further. We made a deal and I wolfed down the candy before I even made it to the school building. I wiped a mess of sticky cherry residue from my mouth with my sleeve and hurried to my classroom, nearly thirty minutes late.

I had hoped to slip in unseen, but the class was silent and in the process of reading. All eyes, including those of my teacher, turned to me.

"You are tardy, Mr. McCall," Miss Henderson said, looking up from the copy of *Robinson Crusoe* she had been reading aloud.

"Thank you," I beamed proudly.

"It means late."

"Oh. Sorry."

"Sit down."

"Sorry."

"And stop apologizing."

"Sor—okay."

I sat down with an apologetic sigh and held my breath until Miss Henderson started reading again.

Sitting next to me, pretending to follow the words in the book, was my best friend Maximilian Chester House, a child whose name held more potential than his intelligence or personality. His father called him the MC, while our teacher likened him to a brand of coffee, and my father often said he was an idiot with a smart man's name.

Our parents had been friends for years; we lived three houses down from each other, were born within two weeks of each other, and obviously went to the same school. He was a friend of convenience, and the best friend I had.

"Where were you?" Max whispered.

"Me? Where were *you*?" I demanded, checking to make sure our teacher hadn't heard my outburst. "You said you'd come and call on me. You were supposed to wake me up for the bus."

"I got a ride in. My mom didn't go to work this morning, so she drove me here."

I released an exasperated sigh, my face undoubtedly a picture of disgust. I glared at Max, telepathically forcing my anger and my questions into him. He turned back to his book, ignorant of my mind tricks.

"Why couldn't you give me a lift?" I asked, resorting to words.

Max simply shrugged. "Never thought of it," he said genuinely.

"You're a dick," I told him.

"Piss off," he spat back.

"I hate you."

"I hate you too."

"I should never speak to you again."

"Fine by me."

"Fine!"

I looked away sheepishly, the final *fine* had been too loud and our teacher had stopped reading. I quickly buried my head in a nearby book and hid my face until she started again.

"Do you have anything to eat?" I asked Max, licking the remnants of sugar from my lips. The sweet treat hadn't sated my hunger—if anything, it made it worse.

"I thought you weren't talking to me."

"Don't be a dick."

Max sighed and lowered his attention from the book. He glanced at the teacher to make sure she wasn't looking and then produced a bag of Twizzlers and sneakily passed them across.

"Anything else?"

"Not for you, no."

"What's that supposed to mean?"

"I have some chocolate," he whispered in an irritated voice, "but that's for recess, my mom didn't give me any money today; we bought those on the drive to school."

"Oh, I see," I said. "*I* couldn't buy anything on the drive to school, you know why?"

"They'll do for now, won't they?" He gestured to the licorice.

"Gimme the chocolate and I'll forget you ditched me this morning."

Max seemed to deliberate over this.

"Come on," I pushed. "My parents are back tomorrow. I might be able to charm my way to some extra pocket money. I'll give you everything back, and more."

"More?"

"You'll be swimming in candy."

Max smiled at the thought of this—not only was he convenient as a best friend, but his stupidity allowed me to get away with a lot.

"Okay." He gave in and handed me a Snickers and a bag of M&Ms. I set the treats up on the desk in front of me and lowered my head, preparing for a morning of indulgence while the teacher's eyes were buried in a book.

"I feel sick."

Two hours into the lesson, I felt a curious bubbling emanating from my stomach, coinciding with intermittent gurgling sounds.

"You shouldn't have eaten all that candy," Max said, not looking as sympathetic as I had hoped.

"Maybe *you* shouldn't have *given* me all that candy," I retaliated, sticking out my tongue, which had been dyed blue from a luminescent Jolly Rancher I had taken from another friend.

I felt my stomach kick out in disgust, not liking the action. I held a hand to my mouth and swallowed a noiseless burp. "I think I'm going to be fine," I said without conviction.

The sickness subsided partially and I felt relieved when the school bells chimed for recess.

Outside, I embraced the fresh air like a prisoner on the steps of freedom. I tilted my head to the skies and took long, deep lungfuls. Each breath helped the sickness subside, pushing the bile and vomit down with every oxygen-enriched mouthful.

"What are you doing?" I heard Max ask, his inquisitive voice breaking through the background noise of playful pupils still scattering themselves over the playground.

"Breathing," I muttered softly.

"But—"

"Go away, Max."

"Okay."

Feeling confident that I wasn't going to unleash a breakfast of sugar onto the school steps, I lowered my face with a contented, soothed smile. I expected to see Max still standing in front of me, but instead I found myself face to face with Kerry Newsome. I cursed under my breath at the sight of her, the memories of our proposed meeting rushing back to me.

"What are you doing?" Her arms were crossed over her chest. An unamused, questioning look in her eyes.

"Waiting for you, I guess."

She nodded slowly, deciding if she was going to believe me. Then, without warning, she grabbed my hand, turned, and set off, dragging me down the stairs at a brisk pace.

She broke into a stride after a few paces and before long she was running, pulling me behind her.

I felt my stomach groan as I bobbed along the coarse ground. It lifted and heaved with every step my weary feet made on the cold concrete.

As we brushed past a group of startled pupils tossing stones onto a messy Hopscotch board, I felt something rise inside me. It bubbled past my stomach and lurched through my throat. I closed my eyes and waited for my breakfast to make a quick getaway when a foul smelling gust of air trickled into my mouth and looked for an exit.

I opened my mouth and let out the burp along with a *thank you* to the vomit gods for biding their time.

Leaves and twigs pricked at my skin as Kerry wasted no time dragging me down the thin passageway that led to the back of the bike sheds. Three older boys were leaning against the sheds, smoking hurriedly in the spot where Kerry had kissed me earlier.

"Oh, it looks like someone's already here." I turned to leave, but Kerry roughly grabbed the back of my collar.

"Stay," she ordered.

One of the boys grinned, another looked unsure, the third looked away. All were older than Kerry and me; they were in sixth grade, three years above me and two above her.

"I think we should leave," I whispered to Kerry, hoping she would pick this moment to finally listen to something I said.

"Just ignore them." Kerry put her hands on my shoulders and pushed me back gently. "Now, I think you owe me something."

I looked at the boys and then at Kerry, my eyes swapping between four people who scared the shit out of me. "I don't think—"

"Get lost, kids."

Much to my delight, one of the boys interrupted us. I felt Kerry backing away from me and had an urge to shake the older boy's hand.

Kerry's hands promptly went to her hips. She glared at the boy who had dared try to intimidate her. "Aren't you Adam Tickle?" she asked.

I giggled, unable to suppress it.

"Something funny, kid?"

Tickle, I thought with a smile. *Hilarious.*

"No, no, not at all."

He stared at me momentarily and then turned to Kerry. "What's it to you, kid?"

"Don't you dare call me *kid.*" She thrust a finger at him and I was sure I saw him flinch. His friends saw it too; they finished their cigarettes and watched him intently.

"I'll call you what I fucking like—"

"Don't you swear!" Kerry was angry now.

I felt my legs lift and back away of their own accord. As I was edging away from the confrontation, Kerry was edging closer.

"I know you," she said. "I know your *dad*, I know your *mother.*"

Mr. and Mrs. Tickle, I giggled again.

Four pairs of eyes turned toward me. I looked away, coughed, and sheepishly whistled.

I felt my stomach kick, an anxious lurch that released more noxious gas.

"Leave us alone or I'll tell them you've been smoking and swearing at little girls and boys," Kerry warned.

The older boy looked defeated. He turned to his friends in vain hope, but none stepped forward. He turned back to Kerry, ready to fight back, but the malice in her eyes told him that not only was she telling the truth, but if he tried anything else, she would scratch his eyes out.

He muttered something in annoyance and skulked away, motioning for his friends to follow him.

"Bunch of cowards," I said, when I was sure the last of the boys had disappeared from earshot.

Kerry didn't waste any time in getting what she wanted. Without saying another word, she wrapped her arms around my neck and lowered her head until her forehead touched mine.

I wet my lips nervously, closed my eyes, and prepared.

She locked onto my mouth with sloppy suction. I had time to prepare, and I had the earlier kiss as a reference, so the sloppy embrace wasn't as much of a shock as I expected, but just when I thought the kiss should be finishing, I felt something wet poke through. A slimy tongue tried to get in on the action.

I tried to force my lips together but the slippery muscle wormed through the gap and, after glancing off my teeth, forced its way into my mouth.

I felt the tongue slide inside and I thought of the creatures from the film *Alien*. I had seen it less than a month ago and had only just stopped having nightmares. I tried to force that image out of my head and endure the kiss, but it wouldn't budge.

I saw their long tentacles, dripping with thick pus. Their thick, scaly skin rippled with the gleam of a million beads of slime. Their bulbous eyes—

I managed to duck out of the kiss just as I unleashed a wave of vomit, but I didn't have enough time or speed to move away from Kerry. The digestive rejections of a breakfast of sugar and additives hit her like a thick neon wave from a toxic waterfall.

Kerry, caught in a split second of shock, merely closed her eyes and pinned her lips together as the wave washed over her. It soaked and clung to her hair. It dripped down her nose like droplets from a shower head, running rivulets over her lips.

I avoided her face for the second wave, but only succeeded in covering her shoes and legs with the orange colored, sweet-scented vomit. It splashed onto my own shoes, as well, tiny specks of orange decorating the black leather like pixels on a broken screen.

Damn, my mom will go mad, crossed my mind before the third wave scattered over the cigarette-covered ground. Kerry managed to jump back to avoid it. She clawed clumps of vomit from her face, scooping them and flicking them onto the floor as annoyed noises escaped her sticky lips.

The third wave was the final wave. I could feel a rumbling of finality in my stomach. I actually felt better and that put a smile on my face.

Strands of sick hung from my mouth like spaghetti. I wiped them away with the back of my sleeve and lifted my head to look at Kerry. She was red with anger; under the glaze of the vomit, she looked pearlescent.

I could tell she wanted to say something, but nothing coherent escaped her mouth. A lot was said and I thought I picked up a few swear words, but there was nothing tangible.

I lowered my head in shame and waited for her to finish, which she did with a flurry of expletives—some of which I had never heard before and tried to remember for later—and then, after a momentary silence, she demanded, "Well? What do you have to say for yourself?"

I shrugged, still looking at my shoes, trying to flick the spots of vomit from the top of one with the bottom of the other.

"Don't you have something to say to me?" she demanded, her voice cracking as it rose above the hustle of the busy playground. "What's the matter with you?"

"I'm quite hungry," I said honestly.

She ground her teeth together, her eyes flaring at me with a flaming ferocity. "Is that all you have to say for yourself?"

I shrugged again, then, sensing the lecture was over, I asked: "Can I have that candy now?"

Kerry glared at me. Her eyes darted back and forth. She opened her mouth, suppressed a scream, and then slammed it shut again. Her jaw worked aggressively as she tried to pulverize her own teeth. Then, following another loud grunt, she threw up her arms, exasperated, and stormed off, mumbling curse words under her breath.

The story of my sickly exploits slowly passed through the school. The boys would gather in hordes, asking me to recall the tale as they listened with eager grins, interrupting with cheers at the end. The girls were equally fascinated, but weren't interested in hearing about the story from Kerry. She had been coated in vomit, had dripped from head to toe in *boy cooties*, and before long she became a social pariah.

She lost her friends, became bitter and isolated, and whenever I saw her, whenever I said hello or passed by, I noted nothing but hatred and revenge in her eyes.

A few weeks after the incident, I was desperate to reconcile with her. I felt bad for what had happened.

During lunch, when all the students rushed out onto the playground, I found Kerry sitting hunched over on one of the benches in the cloakroom. I waited until the last of the stragglers left with their coats and playthings, and then I saddled over to her, sitting a few feet away and gliding my backside along the wooden surface until I was close enough for her to notice.

I had expected sadness in her eyes—she was sitting alone and looking pitiful after all—but a fire still burned there and I had added extra fuel just by showing up.

"Hey Kerry," I said unsurely, trying to avert my gaze from her eyes in case she turned me into stone.

She didn't reply, but I was sure I heard a small growl.

I plastered on my best smile and stared at her forehead, trying to feign sincerity while keeping my gaze away from hers. "I was just wondering if you . . . I don't know . . . maybe wanted to come outside and play?"

Again there was no reply. She still stared.

"It's a nice day, well, it's not raining. I mean . . . you can borrow my coat if you want. You can warm up pretty fast playing soccer, if you *want* to come and join me and my friends for a game that is. I mean, I know you don't have any friends anymore and I—"

"I don't like you, Kieran McCall," she spoke slowly.

"You'd like my friends. And I'm sure you'd like me if you got to know me." I wasn't giving up.

"Go away," she growled.

"Look, I'm sorry about throwing up on you, but you tried to kiss me, what do you expect?" I paused; she looked like she was ready to pounce. "Not that I have a problem with you, you're very pretty and all that, but I don't like kissing in general. I don't even like to kiss my grandma, and she's *family*. Although she smells god-awful. My dad says it's just old age, but I'm pretty sure it's piss."

"Go away, McCall," Kerry said again, her voice deeper and more gravelly. The anger was building and it had a great deal of frustration for company.

I still didn't want to give in, falsely believing I was on a roll. "If I let you kiss me again, will that help? You don't have to give me any candy or anything; I'll do it out of the goodness of my own heart. What do you say?"

"Go away."

"What if I let you throw up on me?"

"What?" A twinge of surprise tickled the corner of her face and then disappeared.

"It's disgusting I know, but hear me out." I edged closer. "I threw up on you and I got treated like the hero while everyone hates you."

"Everyone *hates me*?" She looked hurt by this.

I lowered my eyebrows and looked into eyes that seemed genuinely hurt. "I thought you knew? Why else did you think they were ignoring you?"

"I just thought—"

"It's not important," I quickly interrupted. "What I'm saying is, if you throw up on me then you'll be the hero and I'll get just enough hate to stop *me* being the hero, but because of the first incident—when I threw up on you—it won't be enough to turn *me* into a complete Billy-no-mates like *you*." I finished with a grin, pleased with myself. "What do you say?"

She punched me.

It was the first time I had been punched in the face. I was surprised. I was annoyed. I was hurt. After the initial shock, I removed a protective hand from my face to tell Kerry these things, and then she punched me again.

Years later I would laugh along with friends when I told them that my first kiss had been with the first girl to beat me up, but at the time, the only thing I could concentrate on was protecting my face as I rolled onto the floor while she straddled me like a horse. Her surprisingly powerful fists hammered into every part of my body.

There were no teachers nearby and no students to cause a commotion and bring attention from an elder, and as I didn't know how to fight or even if I should hit a girl—my mother had always told me not to, but a situation where my life may depend on it had never cropped up—I just lay there and took the punches.

The fight was one-sided and lasted for a brutal five minutes. I like to think Kerry stopped out of sympathy for the blubbering wreck beneath her, but the truth was probably that her arms were tired.

When she finished beating the living shit out of me, she crawled off my torso and pulled herself back up onto the bench.

I watched her through a gap in my arms. She stared at me and I could see the flame in her eyes had died. Something else lingered there—pity perhaps.

I slowly pulled myself to my feet and dusted myself off. I wiped the remnants of tears from my eyes and allowed a few drops to trickle down my cheek. Meeting Kerry's pitied gaze, I told her: "There was no need for that."

She sunk her head into her chest. I heard a muffled groan. "Get lost, Kieran."

She didn't need to tell me twice. I hobbled out of the cloakroom and onto the playground. My body ached, but apart from a few scratches on my cheek and a minor cut on my lip, my face remained intact.

I expected Kerry to boast, and I was prepared to allow her that honor. She was a girl but she was tough. My friends would mock me for a while but eventually they would agree that, given the chance, she could beat them up as well. But Kerry didn't tell anyone. She remained an outcast for the rest of the school year.

2

In Lenny's Footsteps

After Kerry Newsome had kissed me and then tried to kill me, I became even more wary and unsure of the opposite sex. For most of my youth, I thought girls were *icky* and weren't to be touched or befriended, and my friends, being of the same age, mostly agreed.

There was one exception though. His name was Lenny and he became a lady-killer at the age of eight. At seven years, three-hundred and sixty-four days old, Lenny was just as repulsed by the opposite sex as the rest of us, but after a "word" with his dad on his birthday, all of that changed.

His dad was drunk and clearly unsure about which birthday it was as he told his son: *Grow up, be a man. Kiss girls, play the field!*

Surprisingly, Lenny's dad was not insane. Lenny took heed and, during his eighth birthday party, he put aside his childhood tendencies and turned on the charm in front of a mixed sex crowd that included several unsuspecting females from our class and the neighborhood.

Lenny wasn't a particularly good-looking boy, but he was the only one in a class of fifteen boys, and a neighborhood of five, that cared or dared to get a girlfriend. After three weeks he had three on the go.

I struggled to understand what Lenny saw in these giggling, whispering humans that smelled of fruit-scented shampoo and played with dolls, but I tried my best.

At first, Lenny wasn't popular with boys our age, but after becoming a huge hit with the older boys in school—walking around the playground with armfuls of girls won him some acclaim—we decided that we liked him as well.

"I could ask Kerry Newsome out," Max said. He looked around uncertainly, received a few worried stares, and then slumped his head against his chest. "Or not," he repealed, disheartened.

Together with our friends Olly and Peter, Max and I loitered near the school building. Olly lay across one of two benches with Peter and Max on the other. I stood, watching the playground with my hands stuffed into my pockets.

"You talk about her a lot," Olly said, tilting his head over the back of the bench and looking at Max through an inverted world.

Like Max, Olly and Peter were in the same class as me. I enjoyed their company more than Max's but they lived farther away so I spent less time with them outside of school.

"I feel sorry for her," Max said unconvincingly.

"It's Kieran's fault," Peter said.

"It was an accident," I argued.

Peter shrugged. "That's what *you* say."

I hadn't told anyone about being beaten up. When I realized Kerry wasn't going to boast, I told everyone that the marks on my face were from running into a door in the cloakroom. It was the first thing that came to mind, and at the time I wasn't sure it was going to pass, but they believed it instantly. I was so annoyed with the laughter and mockery that I almost told them the truth.

"Who's that with Lenny?" I asked, noticing him arm in arm with a girl I didn't recognize. She was taller than him, her left shoulder dipped awkwardly so she could slide her arm through his.

"Penny Collins," Peter explained. "Sixth grade."

"Sixth grade?" I blurted.

Peter shrugged. "The kid's a player."

"Of what?" Max wondered, ever the innocent.

We all laughed, but the truth was I didn't know what he was talking about either and Peter had only learned the word the previous week.

"Numpty."

"Idiot."

"Why you always gotta pick on me?" Max wanted to know.

"Because it's so easy," Olly replied, his head still lolling over the final wooden slat on the weather-stained bench.

Max bolted upright, glared at each of us in turn, and stormed away. "Pricks," he muttered under his breath. A few feet away from us he turned and declared, "I'll go and play with my *real* friends," before disappearing amongst a cluster of kids trading soccer stickers.

We all watched silently as Max introduced himself, received a distasteful look from each trader, and then skulked away when one of them shouted, "Get lost, shit for brains," in a voice loud enough to cover the entire playground. He ambled back our way and threw himself down on the bench with his arms grumpily folded over his chest.

"Your friends busy?" Olly wondered.

"Fuck off," Max spat to a chorus of laughter.

I joined Max on the bench. "So how did Lenny end up with her?" I asked Peter.

Peter shrugged again. He was so nonchalant his parents often said that one day his heart would stop out of sheer apathy.

"We need to find girlfriends," Max said.

"I hate to admit it, but the muppet is right." Olly shifted upright. The blood had rushed to his head and his face was red, but he didn't seem to mind. "Everyone is going out with everyone. Just this morning Dipstick Denny asked out Dorothy from fourth grade."

"Dorothy?" Max clenched his face in disgust. "She's ugly."

"Dipstick ain't no prize."

"Who's left?" I wondered.

Olly held up his hands with his fingers spread, pulling down each appendage as he reeled off the names: "Laura little-eyes. Cow-shit Lizzie—" He was a lazy underachiever who was bottom of the class at nearly every subject, but Olly excelled at nicknames and insults. He seemed to spend all of his time thinking them up; when it came to Max, he had a never-ending list.

"She doesn't smell of cow shit anymore," Max cut in, "not for—"

"Shut up, slipper-fucker," Olly warned. He continued to count: "There's Little Miss Mental in fourth grade—"

That was Kerry. I cringed whenever he called her that. I was convinced I had been the one to send her that way.

"—Billie Blow-job—"

A mild-mannered girl with an unfortunate way of eating ice pops.

"—Sock-Tits Tabby—"

We thought Tabatha Williams was the first girl in the class to develop breasts, then one of those breasts fell out when playing basketball.

"—Piss-stain Pepper—"

It turned out to be splash-back from a malfunctioning school faucet, but Olly didn't do take-backs.

"—and Spadeface," Olly finished, looking somewhat pleased with himself.

"Spadeface?" Max enquired.

"The new girl."

"Lisa I think her name is," I said.

"Why Spadeface?" Max wondered.

"Because she looks like she's been hit with a fucking spade, why else?"

"I think she's quite pretty," Peter jumped in.

A chorus of *oooo* lifted from the group and Peter turned a light shade of red.

"Well, you said we needed girlfriends, she's mine," he said confidently, "or she *will* be."

"What about you?" Olly asked me.

I shrugged, I didn't know. I wasn't so sure I cared either way, but I had convinced myself that I needed to hook up with someone.

"Laura little—*Laura*, I guess." I liked the way she smelled, but most of all I was sure she liked me. She was my best bet.

"Kermit?" Olly turned to Max.

"Erm," Max pretended to ponder this. "I'll try for Kerry," he said, as if he was being forced to. "If I *have* to pick one, might as well."

"Which leaves the rest for me," Olly said, puffing out his chest and patting it like a proud gorilla.

"All of them?"

"Hell, if Lenny can do it, why not me? It'll be easy."

Olly soon found out that he lacked Lenny's charm and was made to eat his words when the girls rejected him one after another. He might have had more success had he not insisted on saving time by waiting until they were grouped together before asking them.

"We know what you call us."

"Yeah, we heard you talking about us."

"You're a prick."

"You're a dickhead, Oliver Harris."

"And how many times do I have to tell you, it was water!"

Olly decided to take another leaf out of Lenny's book. He went up in the grades and tried to hook up with a girl from fifth grade. While he was trying his best not to insult his potential suitors, Peter almost instantly won over the new girl.

Lisa Jones had only been at the school for three weeks after her parents moved to the area from the city. She needed friends and hadn't succeeded in making any, so when the opportunity arose to slide into a clique, she jumped at the chance. Peter was surprised, to say the least—when he first asked her, he had been so nervous that he covered her in spittle and then nearly choked on his own saliva, but she was desperate and he was the first to ask.

Max had less luck with Kerry, which wasn't a surprise. He tried to talk to her and she ignored him, completely blanking him as he broke into a full-scale monologue that lasted an entire recess.

He didn't give up. The next day he tried the same tactic; she walked away from him. He tried again the next day *and* the next, and after a week of trying she finally spoke to him, but only to warn him that if he pestered her again, she would bite his nose off.

During the second week, on the day that Olly was shunned by an entire grade of ten-year-old girls for calling them "frumpy Barbie-Fuckers," Max followed his parents' advice and bought Kerry a box of chocolates. *Whoppers*. Kerry ate the candy with gusto and told Max to get lost while showering him in chocolate spittle.

Peter, having been dating for three weeks and considering himself a Casanova, offered Max some advice on the third week. Unfortunately for Max, he took it. Kerry slapped him, hard. He stayed away from her for the rest of the week, deciding to play it safe and study his prey from a distance.

About that time, I made my first move on Laura. We were in the same class so I often spoke to her, but I rarely said more than a few words. Since the challenge to make her my girlfriend, I decided to pay more attention to her, which turned me into a gibbering idiot around her.

It took me a week just to say something coherent, and even then it had been something completely irrelevant. I pulled it back in the second week and things were back to normal between us: she would say hello, I would reply in kind. Not exactly a sign of undying love, but much better than telling her I hated the taste of cheddar cheese when she asked to borrow a pencil.

I didn't know how to ask girls out, and Peter was no help. "It just sort of happened," he told me. "I guess I'm lucky that way, girls like me—Lisa *loves* me. She practically threw herself at me." Max tried to help, but the giant red handprint on his face suggested he wasn't best positioned to offer advice on how to talk to girls.

"Those guys are idiots," Olly told me. He had pulled me to one side, leaving Max and Peter alone to argue over who was better at talking to girls. "Don't listen to either of 'em. They're a pair of fucking muppets."

"So what do I do?" I wondered. "How do I talk to her?"

Olly casually shrugged his shoulders. "I don't know."

"But you said—why did you drag me over here then?"

"Advice."

"What advice? You didn't bloody tell me anything."

"Believe me, mate, not listening to tweedle-dee an' tweedle-dick-head over there is better advice than anyone on this playground is gonna give you." Olly paused, pondered, and then said: "Except Lenny that is, that kid's a stud. What'd *he* have to say?"

"He told me not to worry, said it was easy, and she'd fall into my lap."

"Sounds a lot like what Peter said, huh?"

I nodded, looking visibly subdued.

"Who knew Lenny was retarded?" Olly looked thoughtful for a moment and then he planted a firm hand on my shoulder. "Suck it up mate, what's the worst that could happen?"

I thought about Kerry Newsome using me like a punching bag in the cloakroom. I didn't think Laura had that mean streak but she looked like she could do more damage than Kerry if she did.

I gulped and tried to look composed. "You're right."

"Of course I am, now get to it, Laura's over there," Olly pointed across the playground to a small group of girls by the basketball nets. Laura was there, leaning on the pole, playing with the hair of a friend while another girl tied braids in hers.

"In class, when she's alone," I said. More girls meant more possibilities for getting the shit kicked out of me again.

That afternoon was art time. The class were given paints, brushes, and large canvases, split into groups of two, and told to create. It was an ideal opportunity for the pupils to mess around, and it was the perfect time for me to make my move on Laura.

As usual I had been paired with Max. He was gathering paint-brushes and supplies like a hoarder at a garage sale.

He was always excited at art time; his parents were strict and rarely let him make a mess, so in times like these he really let loose. Our corner of the classroom would look like a war zone before the afternoon was out.

"I'm going to paint pirate ships, and sunsets, and islands full of treasure and—"

"Great," I said, cutting into his ramblings.

His eyes were wide, his pupils dilated. He held brushes in both hands; his arms—bent at the elbows, pointing toward a piece of A3 paper stretched over our desk—were waving up and down.

"And—and—and—and," he stuttered quickly.

"You're not going to pass out are you?"

"—and lions and tigers and trees—"

I peered across the room at Laura. She was standing over her canvas, surveying the white paper. She gently grasped a brush in her right hand and pressed it to her neck; a stray forefinger stroked the hairless flesh around her jaw. She chewed gently on her bottom lip, nibbling a dried flake of skin that clung to the fleshy fibers.

"—and birds and fish and horses—"

Laura had teamed up with her friend Jenny. Jenny was popu-lar with the boys, or at least with the boys who thought enough about girls to *make* her popular. She was one of the first to go out with Lenny and still spent a lot of time following him around. He seemed to like her, but these days there wasn't a girl that Lenny *didn't* like.

"—and Spiderman and Batman—"

I quickly thought about what I was going to say and real-ized I didn't have the slightest idea what to say or where to start.

Remembering Olly's words—*what's the worst that could happen?*—I forced images of being beaten up by Kerry Newsome out of my head and sauntered over to Laura and Jenny's table.

"—and spaceships!"

"So . . ." I stopped a few feet short of their table and dug both of my hands into my pockets. Standing on my tiptoes, I tilted over to glance at their blank paper, making sure I had their attention. "What you girls got planned?"

Laura was smiling and I reciprocated. I liked her smile, it made me smile. It was broad, wide, and unashamedly happy. It was like a clown's smile, only I didn't wet myself when I saw it.

Jenny, on the other hand, wasn't smiling. She was staring at me with her eyebrows arched upwards, one hand on her hip. "Not sure, what about you?" She looked over my shoulder and nodded toward Max.

I turned around. Max was frantically waving his hands and springing up and down on his heels. A high-pitched screeching sound steamed out of his grinning lips. He sounded like a boiling kettle.

"Oh my god," I muttered softly.

"He looks happy," Laura noted, probably adding "*and dangerous*" in her mind.

I turned back to the girls and looked sheepish. "He gets excited," I said. "Bless him."

They exchanged a smile.

I slumped my head downward, staring at my feet as I nervously tapped them into each other. "So, I was thinking," I began, deciding to wing it. "Would you mind being—do you *want to be*—" I coughed, I couldn't say the words. I looked up briefly, but shot back down again when I saw they were staring expectantly at me.

"Do you want to be my girlfriend?" I forced the words out, then I waited.

The brief silence that followed seemed like an eternity. I had taken a step back in case she decided to swing for me. I was envisioning her standing on top of the table and yelling, "*Everyone, you'll never guess what ugly little Kieran McCall just asked me,*" when I received a reply.

"I'd love to."

That had been roughly what I wanted to hear, but not quite, because it had been spoken by Jenny.

I looked up to see her wide-eyed stare waiting for me. Her hand had gone from her hip; the *what do you want* look had disappeared from her face. She looked happy.

"Oh."

"I never knew you liked me," Jenny declared.

I tried to smile but it didn't look convincing. I didn't really want a girlfriend so I wouldn't have minded about looks, or even personality to an extent, but Jenny scared me. Her eyes had an intimidating bossiness that I didn't like.

I wanted to say, "*I don't like you. You're mean and you scare me.*" I wanted to tell her I was talking to Laura and would have never thought of asking her out. I wanted to say many things, but what finally came out of my mouth was, "Of course I do."

She shook her arms excitedly and made an "*oooo*" noise. For a moment she reminded me of Max and I thought things might be okay. I didn't much like Max either but I still considered him a friend; maybe Jenny could be the same. Those thoughts didn't stay with me for long.

After a drink on New Year's Day, my father had told me that women were great until you married them. He said that a cloud of darkness falls over them the minute you say "*I do*" and they're never the same again. I thought it was just the drink talking, but then I saw that darkness cover Jenny.

The smile faded from her face. The excitement and delight disappeared. She glared at me with all the enthusiasm of a scientist at a Creationist Conference and said: "We'll meet up at recess. Be quick, don't mess about, I can't stand people who mess about. Got it?"

I stood still and silent, not sure how to react. I was wondering if the brief smile on her face had been imagined while trying to recall if I had said "*I do*" at any point.

"Don't stand there looking like an idiot," she blared. "Go back to your own table."

"Oh, okay. Sorry." I turned and trudged back, wondering what had just happened.

"And I want a present," Jenny called after me.

I turned back, incredulous. "What? What present?"

"Something nice."

"But I didn't get you anything, I don't have anything to give you."

"Well, you should have thought of that earlier."

"But—but—but."

"Just get one, Kieran," Jenny said, turning her back to me.

Defeated and deflated, I slumped down next to Max, who was hacking away at the paper. "I've got a girlfriend," I said, my voice trickling out of my mouth like it didn't want to leave.

Max didn't take his eyes off his painting. "Laura?"

"Jenny."

"I didn't know you liked her."

"Me neither."

When the teacher called an end to the lesson, I practically sprinted out of the classroom, leaving Max to clean up the mess he had made in his merriment. The canvas looked like Salvador Dali had had a stroke. My only involvement had been to poke random dots on the paper whenever the teacher was looking.

I was too miserable to paint, too worried to enjoy myself. I had thought things through though, and I had a plan.

The way I saw it I had two options. Option 1: I tell Jenny that I made a mistake and face the consequences, which would probably be painful and could possibly be humiliating, but was the right thing to do. Option 2: I pretend I was as interested in Jenny as she thought I was and be prepared to have her as my girlfriend until the day came when she finished me.

I decided to plump for option 2. I understood that the day may never come when she was tired of me, but I was sure I'd do something to upset her or change her mind between now and eternity, and if not then I was prepared to get married and write off this life as a lost cause. I'd cross my fingers and pray for reincarnation on my deathbed.

My eyes drifted over Jenny's coat-peg in the cloakroom. A short white duffel coat with fur trim hung over a Barbie branded backpack.

I hesitated, stopping short at the sight of her belongings. I shot a glance over my shoulder. I could hear the rumbling excitement of a class of schoolchildren preparing for a fifteen-minute break, but none of them were in sight. Unlike me, they had all participated in the painting; there were brushes to clean, pictures to show off, hands to wash.

Feeling indecisive but knowing I had to act quickly, I dug through my own backpack and pulled out a notepad. There was a split second where what I was about to do seemed logical and felt like a good get-out clause, but for each millisecond after that it grew exponentially more ludicrous. I only paid attention to those first thoughts, ignoring the niggling doubts that grew inside my mind like a rapid cancer.

My pencil case was full of pens, felt tips, crayons, and pencils. In class I spent more time doodling fanciful drawings than I did writing, so I liked to be prepared.

I pulled one out at random, scribbled on the top corner of a sheet of paper and stuffed it back when it came out dry. I did the same with another two pens before I found one that worked; it was red, but it would do.

I ripped the top sheet off the pad and folded it in half.

Through the door, around the corner from where I sat, I could hear the sound of doors closing and cupboards shutting. Wood on wood, metal on metal. The noise of taps gushing water onto paint-covered hands.

The class was finishing up; they would be out soon.

I panicked. I quickly scribbled a short message in large, bold letters on the top sheet of paper, tore it off the pad, and stuffed it into the front compartment of Jenny's bag.

The classroom door opened, the noises increased.

I quickly jotted down another note. Messier, shorter, bolder. Cramming scrappy shorthand onto a small pre-folded piece of paper. I stuffed that into Laura's bag and then quickly tried to seal it back up again. A strip of flesh from my thumb caught in the zipper. I moaned in surprise and pulled back, feeling a tear as my skin ripped away from the metallic zipper.

My thumb instantly turned red, a white perforated line appeared across its tip and was quickly filled as the blood seeped through. I hissed through gritted teeth and squeezed my hand, trying to ease the pain. The blood trickled through my clenched fist and dropped into Laura's bag. A couple of drops dripped out of sight, one hit the folded paper.

Cursing under my breath I quickly closed the zipper and stuck my thumb into my mouth, catching it just as another drop of blood fell from the paper-thin wound.

Lenny was the first to enter the cloakroom, and as usual he was followed by a line of females.

"That nice, Kieran?" he asked, motioning toward my suckled thumb.

"Shut up," I mumbled back with a mouthful of thumb. I brushed past him, heading outside.

A startled scream made me turn around. The noise was feminine, and instantly a part of me hoped that Jenny had been sucked into a black hole or had stepped into a one-way dimension, but the attention seemed to be on Lenny. Everyone was looking at him, and while this wasn't unusual, the horror on his face was.

He was standing over a backpack, peeking inside. The color had drained from his face. He had something in his hand, something he had removed from his bag.

I moved closer, nudging a fellow pupil out of the way to get a better look.

Lenny stood upright. I could see the object of his horror; it was a small, white fluffy animal. He gripped it tightly, like his life depended on its safety.

A line of crimson ran down the animal's back, from its small head to its fluffy tail. It was so stark, so red, that it looked terrifyingly out of place on the pristine toy.

Max was standing a few feet in front of me. I hurried up to him and nudged him in the back, preparing to ask him what all the fuss was about, but just as Max turned around, Lenny pulled another blood-stained item out of his bag. A letter. My letter.

"You've gotta be kidding me," I mumbled.

Lenny read the letter, looked up at the gathering of his fellow pupils, and then fainted.

In the playground, I stood on constantly shifting feet and tried to look innocent. "I don't understand, why faint? It's just a letter."

The commotion had died down. Almost simultaneously the room of children had shouted for a teacher. Suspecting the worst, three of them had rushed in.

Lenny was roused before they even got to him; the kids were told to *get the hell outside* seconds later.

"Didn't you hear?" Olly seemed to light up whenever a potentially morbid subject sprang into the conversation. "His cat was murdered," he said with the intoned mystery of the Crypt Keeper.

"Murdered?" I said, taken aback.

"Oh, it's such a sad story." Lisa wriggled out from under Peter's protective arm. Peter looked offended but tried to shrug it off with a stretch. "It happened a few weeks ago, maybe a month, I'm not sure. When was Susie's birthday again?" She turned to Max as she delved into another subject. "Because it was around that time, maybe a few months later."

"March, or May," Max loved this sort of inane conversation, no doubt the reason Lisa asked him and not Peter, who barely liked to talk at all. "It definitely wasn't June," Max said with a broad *I know things* smile. "Or *was* it?"

"Not important!" Olly snapped, throwing his arms wildly in the air. "Look," he grasped me on the shoulder, "someone ran over his cat. He was upset, *very* upset."

"He loved that cat," Lisa added.

Peter looked sternly at his girlfriend, apparently only just realizing that she had also fallen for Lenny's charm.

"He was heartbroken," Max uttered.

"Diddums," Olly stabbed, cruelly.

"Don't be mean," Lisa warned.

I sighed deeply. "Can we get to the point?"

"Okay," Olly said, shooting a frustrated glance at Lisa before turning to me. "So the cat gets run over, he thinks it's murder."

"It *was* mur—"

"Shut your face, I'm talking here!"

"How *dare* you—"

"Peter, deal with your girlfriend, would you?"

After a few squabbles, a lot of shouting, and some random offerings from Max, I finally learned that Lenny had found his cat dead on the road one morning. It had been run over the night before. No one came forward to admit flattening the feline so Lenny decided she had been murdered.

His mother tried to talk him out of going to the police and asking for a manhunt, but his dad, in another slice of drunken wisdom, affirmed and expanded on his beliefs. He told his son that a serial animal murderer was stalking the streets and poor little Fluffy was his latest victim. It seemed apparent that Lenny's dad was either insane or a total dickhead, but Lenny loved his father and, unfortunately for him, listened to everything he said.

While Lenny hunted down the killer, his mother bought him a small fluffy toy as a memento and replacement. Things had been going well for Lenny; he had stopped crying for his lost pet and he was well on the way to doubting his father's theory about the perverted pet killer.

"It makes you wonder, don't it?" Olly said, looking philosophical, "there *must* be a pet serial killer out there. First it kills Loverboy's cat and then it taunts him. I mean, did you see the blood on that little toy? Sick man, *sick*."

The others sounded their agreement. I gulped down a large slab of saliva and guilt. My heart sank even further when I recalled what I had written in the letter, scrawled in glaring red ink:

L, It was a mistak. It was ment 2 b u, nt her.

It was supposed to be Laura's bag. The letter was supposed to go to her, not Lenny. But I couldn't tell anyone that now. I didn't think there was a law against writing letters but who would believe me? I'd look like an idiot; I'd probably get the blame for making Lenny pass out, if not from the teachers then certainly from the kids. They'd hate me if I was responsible for scaring him.

I just have to play innocent, I thought. *Stay cool, don't tell anyone, don't even—*

My eyes widened. My heart practically jumped out of my chest. I remembered the second letter, the one I had written for Jenny. It had been in the same handwriting, I had used the same pen, the same notepad.

I turned my head anxiously, scanning the playground, looking for Jenny. I couldn't see her.

"Where's Jenny?" I asked, still scanning the concrete field.

"Oh, I forgot about that," Max jumped in. "She's your *girl-friend* now," he said, rolling his tongue mockingly around the word *girlfriend.*

"Really?" Olly said, shocked. "You picked *her*?"

"Where is she?" I said, growing increasingly impatient.

"You miss her already?" Lisa asked, without a jot of sarcasm.

"Something like that."

"She'll be hovering around Lenny as usual, she's obsessed with him," Olly said. "You picked a winner there, mate."

Olly *did* pile on the sarcasm, but I thanked him anyway and quickly walked back toward the school building.

I took a deep breath before pushing open the door to the cloakroom. I imagined Jenny standing on the bench, the letter in one hand, a megaphone in the other, surrounded by teachers and organizing them into a mob to get back at me.

When I entered the cloakroom, there were no angry teachers with pitchforks. No shouting; no calls for blood. Jenny was sitting quietly on one of the benches, alone.

"Hey—" I squashed up my face, looked to the ceiling, to the floor, to Jenny's watery and expectant eyes. "Sweetie," I continued, happy with the choice of word, regardless of how dirty it made me feel. "You okay?" I sat down next to her and hovered an arm above her shoulders. I had seen this sort of thing done on television when adults were trying to soothe other adults, but quite a few of those television programs ended with the soother and the soothee kissing or hugging, and I didn't want that. I pulled my arm away and scooted an inch away from her, just in case.

"I'm worried about Lenny," Jenny said. She looked up at me and did a double-take, her eyes saying *I could have sworn you were sitting closer.*

"He'll be fine, go outside and play, get on with your life. Lenny would want it that way."

Jenny looked genuinely confused. "What the hell are you talking about?"

I shrugged. They never asked that on television.

"I think I'll just sit here for a while," Jenny said, lowering her head.

I had to get her out of the cloakroom; I had to get my letter back.

I eyed the Barbie backpack; it was directly opposite her, a foot or so away from her feet.

"Someone wants to see you outside," I said, in lieu of anything else.

"Who?"

"Max." As usual Max had been the first name in my head. That had never served me well in the past. It was often the reason I ended up with him as a partner, and certainly the reason he ended up as my best friend.

"Max?" Jenny asked. She was either shocked or disgusted, I couldn't tell, but I could sympathize; Max had a way of doing that to people.

"Yeah, he has something to show you, said it'd cheer you up."

Jenny stared at me with doubtful eyes. I tried to smile earnestly, but with each passing second I was sure my face would break and the words *I'm lying* would be spelled on my forehead in anxiety-riddled acne.

She nodded and stood. I allowed myself to breathe again.

Halfway to the door she turned and asked: "You just gonna sit here?" with a hint of surprise.

"Just gonna have a think," I said, nodding slowly to add a somber tone to my words. "A think about Lenny. Life. You know."

"Hm," Jenny sounded unconvinced. "Okay."

She disappeared out of the door and I stood immediately, moving for her backpack.

I pulled open the zipper and yanked out the letter. I thought about tearing it up there and then, I thought about hiding it. I even thought about eating it, but before I could do any of those things, the door swung open and Jenny's head popped around the corner, her eyes beaming like a bird of prey on the prowl.

"Shit," I mumbled. The letter was still in my hand, the bag open in front of me.

"I knew you were up to something." She let the door slam behind her and she stormed forward. "What is that?" she gestured toward the letter, her eyes hot, her face angry.

I thought she was going to hit me. I sensed another cloakroom beating.

She snatched the letter from me with one hand and then shoved me back with the other. I stumbled over a backpack and crashed to the floor, protected from the fall by my elbows, which crunched under my own weight.

I looked up dismally, watching Jenny open the letter. I thought for a moment that I should have eaten it as soon as I had it, but then reasoned that she would have probably ripped open my stomach and retrieved the letter anyway.

"It's you?" she said, waving the note accusingly.

"No, not me," I said, keen to worm my way out of the situation. "Someone else, I'm helping them. I mean, not *helping* them, *I'm, I'm*, I'm trying to show them—yeah, that's it—I'm trying to show them that animal murder is wrong, and that you shouldn't—"

"It says your name, Kieran," Jenny turned over the letter and thrust her finger at the hastily scribbled word at the bottom.

"*Another* Kieran," I said.

Jenny glared at me, as if she were trying to bore holes into me with her eyes. She sighed heavily, lifted the note to her face again, and, keeping one eye on me in case I tried anything, she read: *"I don't like you, I made a mistake. I don't want to go out with you anymore."*

I pulled myself up from the floor and slowly rubbed my right elbow, which burned with a steady pain. I cleared my throat and grinned at Jenny. "Okay, it was me."

"No, *you don't say*," she spat sarcastically.

"But it went to the wrong person. I mean, not *that* one, that one was supposed to go to you, cause I really don't want to be your boyfriend. You're nice I'm sure, but not my type, I'm not even sure I *have* a type but if I did," I paused, scratching my head and gauging a reaction—there wasn't one. "Well, it wouldn't be you. It wouldn't really be Laura either but the letter, the *other* letter, was supposed to go to *her*, not Lenny. I didn't kill his cat, I didn't even know he *had* a cat, and as for the blood, well." I held up my thumb, the blood had been sucked dry. "Well, there *was* blood there before, there isn't now. Never mind, just please don't tell anyone," I finished.

Her anger had turned into realization, more of the fact that I was too stupid to be a taunting serial killer than anything else, but it was better than nothing.

"Please," I repeated, sensing trouble in the silence. "I'll be your boyfriend."

"Don't worry," she said softly, the anger completely gone now. "I won't say anything,"

"*Phew*, thank you." I wiped an imaginary line of sweat from my forehead. "I don't have to be your boyfriend though, do I?"

She shook her head and handed me the letter. "This has made me realize how much I like Lenny. I want to be his girlfriend again."

I folded the note, tore it through the middle several times, and then scrunched up the pieces before sticking them into my pocket. It would have made more sense to do it over a bin, something I realized when picking a few stray pieces up from the floor, but I managed to get the majority in my pocket regardless.

"So, some good came of all this then," I declared happily. I scuttled toward the door, eager to get out before she changed her mind. "What are you going to tell Lenny about the animal murderer?" I asked.

Jenny shrugged. It seemed she wasn't going to tell him anything. That was good enough for me.

3

Lizzie

Every summer, without fail, my parents took me on vacation to a fairly lame family campground. It usually rained and we seemed to spend the majority of the vacation crowded into a small camper, watching a tiny pixelated television and eating microwave meals.

We had nothing to do except play board games and wait for the rain to stop, after which we would move on to the arcades, walk the beaches, or play in the park.

The arcades were cheap, claustrophobic, and rang with the incessant noises of luck and misfortune. The beaches were stony, dirty, and rife with seaweed. The local bars stank of fake tan and tears and were packed with middle-aged women beyond their prime and older men too drunk or decrepit to chat them up. The poorly maintained parks were months away from becoming death traps. The gift shops stacked items designed for local use—plastic footballs, buckets and spades, kites—which weren't made to last beyond purchase. Bingo halls oozed with the melancholy of despairing tourists with nothing better to do and, in the onsite club, the finger of an apathetic bartender perpetually hit rewind/play on a hi-fi haunted by the ghosts of discos long since dead.

It was the epitome of a classic family vacation: it was miserable, gloomy, and depressing. I loved it.

I saw everything through rose-tinted spectacles and adored it all. Through the ages of five to ten, I looked forward to those vacations more than Christmas. I loved to fly my kite in the fields, come home to the *ping* of a microwave, and chow down while watching the television fire a blizzard over whatever was on.

I loved to blow my parents' money on the arcade games and penny-slots. I liked the rocky beaches, the pier, which was cold and windswept even in the height of summer, and the sweet shops that stamped a local logo on every product and sold it for twice as much.

I made friends in the parks, vowed to be their friend forever, and then promptly forgot their names the instant we left, and I played bingo with old people who tried to give me candy and persuade me they were young once.

It was a highlight of my childhood, but I had no interest in it when I was eleven and another trip to the campground was arranged. I wanted to stay home; I wanted to play with my friends in the fields by the house. Two weeks felt like a really long time, and I didn't want to miss anything.

I had no choice in the matter and that put me in a bad mood on the two-hour car ride. I gave my parents the silent treatment the whole way; they were delighted with the break.

We left just after dawn and, when the car pulled into the campground, it was still pleasantly warm outside. The sun belted down beats of bright hot light through the back window. I shaded my eyes from the glare as the car weaved through the mass of campers and pulled up alongside the one we had rented.

My dad jumped out of the car first, desperate to stretch after a couple of hours behind the wheel. My mother was still half-asleep and took her time. I darted out before her, eager to show them both that I was still annoyed.

"I'm going for a walk," I said, quickly regretting it.

"Oh, you're talking now, are you?" Dad beamed at me. He had tiny wrinkles on his chin, his forehead and his cheeks, and they stretched with individual grins when he smiled. His stubbled beard—flecked with differing stages of gray, white, and silver—reflected the sunlight and glistened at me.

"I—I—no," I stuttered defiantly, storming off.

A boundary of trees and thickets lined the campground; I cut through these and entered onto a small park that sat at the edge of a large empty field.

A carpet of gravel chips covered the floor of the park, with patches of softened tarmac under the equipment.

A set of swings in the center of the park was the only fully intact piece of equipment. The climbing frame in the corner was rusted and looked unstable. The rocking horses next to it hadn't rocked for many years. Three rungs had been plucked from the center of the monkey bars, denying even the most limber of primates a fighting chance. The sandpit was more stone than sand; the slide was streaked with what looked like mud, but could have been something much worse; the merry-go-round didn't *go* at all.

A small blonde girl was sitting on the swings. She had turned her head sideways to look at me as I surveyed the broken park. She wore a smile that stretched from ear to ear. I could almost see her iridescent eyes twinkling under the glare of the sun.

Despite—or perhaps because of—my experiences with Kerry and Jenny, I had yet to warm to the opposite sex. I had never found my first crush, had never experienced something I still wasn't sure was real, but when I set eyes on the little blonde girl, swinging gently back and forth, her hair lifting and relaxing in the faint breeze, I knew things were about to change.

"Hello," she said. "My name is Lizzie, what's yours?"

I tried to reply but the words caught in my throat. I coughed, cleared, and repeated as best I could: "Kieran."

She continued smiling, her eyes never leaving my face. "Do you want to swing with me, Kieran?" she asked pleasantly.

I took a seat on the swing next to hers; she watched me while I tucked myself in between the chains. Then she turned to face ahead, out over the expansive fields, which stretched to the horizon.

"It's a lovely day, isn't it?" she said.

I grunted in reply, unable to take my eyes off her. I wanted to talk to her; I wanted to tell her everything about myself. I wanted to ask her an infinite amount of questions, to find out everything I could about her. Where did she come from? What school did she go to? What grade was she in?

We swung side by side for a while. Every now and then she would glance at me and pick up the pace with a smile. Then she would giggle when I tried to match her swing for swing.

I didn't know what she found amusing but I was captivated by her laugh and I giggled along with her, happily watching her features explode into delight.

I wanted to stare at her without interruption but didn't want to come across as weird. I tried to get as many looks as I could, sneaking sly glances when she wasn't looking, admiring her smile, the dimples on her fair cheeks, the shine in her glistening hair, the brightness in her eyes. I turned away when I saw her head moving to me, not realizing that she was trying to sneak the same covert looks at me.

I felt so comfortable with her. So happy. It didn't dawn on me that we had been sitting in total silence for ten minutes until she spoke again.

"How old are you, Kieran?"

"Eleven," I said, locking eyes with her. "You?"

"I'm eleven as well."

"Okay."

"Isn't that weird?"

"It is, yes," I said, happy to believe it was because she said it was.

We swung side by side in silence. The bright morning faded to a dull afternoon. A thick veil covered the sun and the merriment it had brought. A grayness descended on the horizon that my new friend loved to adore.

"I have to go." I felt her swing stop and jolt as she suddenly jumped. She stood at the base of the swing set, one arm wrapped around the support pole, her body leaning toward me. "Goodbye, Kieran."

I didn't want her to go, but I was still bathing in the joy of meeting her and I was sure I'd see her again. "Goodbye, Lizzie."

She giggled one last time, then she turned and ran away. The quickening gloom of the depressing afternoon rained shadows behind her as she cut into the trees and disappeared.

I walked back to the camper with a skip in my step. The day had drawn cold and depressing, but I still felt a warm glow bathing my skin.

My parents were hovering around the kitchen when I strode through the door and greeted them with a fresh face.

They looked at each other. My father's eyebrows were raised. My mother shrugged her shoulders with a *meh* expression. "Dinner is ready soon," she told me, brushing past my dad and busying herself by buttering bread.

"What's got into you?" Dad quizzed, remaining still and keeping his eyes on me as Mom danced around him with muted sounds of frustration.

"Nothing," I replied with a smile.

I slid past them both and strode into the main room. I picked up a magazine and plonked down on the sofa, which wrapped around the back of the camper like a tartan scarf.

Dad followed me. He sat down with a loud exhalation and turned to stare at me. After twenty seconds of uninterrupted comical glaring, he joked: "If you're on drugs you can tell me, you know."

I lowered the magazine and laughed a muffled response. "If I was on drugs I would *never* tell you."

"Why not?" he feigned surprise and hurt. "You'd be missing out. We could share. I have a cupboard full back home."

"Really?"

"Sure. Uppers, downers, lefters, righters. I got the lot."

I raised my eyebrows and lowered my head, gesturing that I wasn't impressed with his attempt at humor.

"Well, if that's the way you're going to be," he slapped his thighs with both hands and stood up. "It's your loss. No drugs for you. Just don't come running to me when you're all desperate and shaking for your fix."

He left a smile over his shoulder and then disappeared back into the kitchen, greeting my mother with an unwanted hug from behind before getting in her way when trying to help her with dinner.

The smile that Lizzie had put on my face remained there through-out dinner. I ate with glee, keeping one eye on the gloomy day outside the window and my mind on Lizzie. She occupied every thought I had for the rest of the day, and that night I struggled to sleep.

She made me feel comfortable. I had yet to feel myself around girls, but with Lizzie I felt at peace. I was content. It was as if she oozed an anti-anxiety drug I had breathed in when I sat down next to her.

I hadn't been talkative, I hadn't been charming, but conversely, I hadn't acted like a complete idiot as I had the tendency to do.

As I struggled to sleep that night, tossing and turning in a bed that squeaked and resisted every move, I decided that from that day, I would never act like an idiot in front of a girl again. I decided that now I actually liked girls, and now that I had experienced my first crush, things would change for me. I thought Lizzie had lifted the spell.

On that peaceful night, when the moon cut through the plastic window like a flashlight through a water bottle, I thought I was becoming a man. I thought things were going to be okay from then on.

I couldn't have been more wrong.

I woke with the sun beating a spotlight onto my pillow and spread-ing bright warmth over my face. I closed my eyes and squinted out the glare with an unappreciative moan.

I cursed myself for not closing the curtains, and I cursed the day for waking me. I was up and staggering to the toilet, my eyes half closed, my bare feet slapping sullenly on the cold bathroom floor, before I realized that I needed that sun; I needed that glare.

If the sun is out, maybe Lizzie will come out, I thought.

The thoughts of running into Lizzie brought delight to my face. I hurried through my morning urination and dashed out of the bathroom.

"Breakfast?"

My mother was standing in the kitchen, my morning stumbles having woke her.

"Erm, no thanks."

"You going back to sleep?" she asked, still half-asleep herself.

"No."

"Then sit down, I'll bring you your breakfast."

I peered around her shoulder at the room beyond; my dad was spread-eagled on the bed, his legs enjoying the sudden extra room as they kicked invisible footballs under the duvet. On the wall above the bed, I glimpsed the large decorative clock: *7:43.*

A little early for Lizzie to be outside playing.

"Okay," I relented. "I'll get dressed first."

I threw on my clothes from the previous day and sat down to a bowl of cereal and a slice of toast. My mother sat with me, drinking coffee and looking like she needed a few extra hours in bed.

"Why do you keep staring out the window?" she asked, watching me dig into a slice of toast with peanut butter.

I shrugged. "Nice day, I guess."

She stared at me with raised eyebrows, daring me to express any physical tells that I was up to something.

"They fitted new swings and stuff in the park," I said, deciding she would see through the vagueness of my original answer. "If it stays sunny, I'll get to play with them later."

She took a long and thoughtful sip of her coffee, staring at me over the rim, her eyes cutting through the steam. "Is that why you were so happy when you came back yesterday?"

"I wasn't *that* happy," I said, hoping to play down my mood.

"You didn't stop smiling all day."

I filled my mouth with the remains of my toast to buy some time, letting a few thoughts wash over me. "I met another kid there, we had fun."

"Another kid?"

"Another kid," I nodded.

"A boy kid?"

"Does it matter?"

She smiled broadly, failing to hide both delight and amusement. "Well, if you want to bring *her* over here later on . . ." she allowed the sentence to trail off.

I imagined bringing Lizzie over to meet my parents. My mother would probably be okay, but I doubted my dad would let up. The stupid little references: "*Does your* girlfriend *want something to eat?*" "*Does your* girlfriend *want a drink?*" "*Kieran, ask your* girlfriend *if* . . ." And then his jokes: "*Did you know Kieran wets the bed?*" "*Maybe you can replace his cuddly toy; he's getting too old for that,*" and "*So, did he tell you he used to be a girl?*"

"No," I said. I didn't want to scare Lizzie away. "Maybe another time."

Mom shrugged, still grinning.

I watched the clock over the next couple of hours. The time drifted languidly.

At eleven, I eagerly rushed out of the camper. My dad was just surfacing; he moaned with surprise as I brushed past him. I muttered a goodbye and dived from the elevated camper and onto the grass below.

In the trees, at the exit to the park, I paused and composed myself before stepping out.

I looked around expectantly. Lizzie wasn't on the swings. She wasn't on the slide. She wasn't on the climbing frame or any other piece of broken equipment.

My heart dipped but didn't sink entirely.

I sat on the same swing as the previous day and stared at the view that had enticed Lizzie. The horizon was clear and shone like a shimmering topaz, broken by the penetrating rays of heat from the sun that bobbed on its surface.

I thought about what I was going to say when Lizzie came:

Hey, Lizzie. Nice day, isn't it?

Too boring.

So, where do you live?

Too forward.

Do you want to go out with me?

Way too forward.

Lizzie, hey, I was waiting for you.

Too desperate.

I swung back and forth gently.

The sun had climbed the very tip of the horizon before I finally turned around. Lizzie wasn't there. No one was.

A rustle in the trees had alerted me, but the wind—picking up and fighting against the beautiful day—was to blame. The smile had dripped from my face. The warmth had ebbed from my body. A light chill cut through me.

The sun was dipping down in the skies behind me; the wind was getting feisty with the trees. I gave up waiting for Lizzie and lurched solemnly back to the camper.

I couldn't hide my disappointment from my parents and they sensed something was wrong. I didn't want to tell them, but before the night was over my dad had figured things out.

"Your girlfriend didn't show, huh, son?"

I shook my head, looking beyond him at the television where three unrecognizable actors swam amongst a mass of gray and black pixels.

"Did she tell you she was going to be there?"

Again I shook my head. "Where else would she be?" I asked him. "It's the only place to go for kids on the resort."

"She could have spent the day on the pier. At the arcades. Shopping. Maybe her parents dragged her to the club or to a restaurant."

I brightened up a little and turned to face him. "I never thought of that."

"Of course you didn't. You head out to that park tomorrow and I'll bet you'll find your little friend waiting there for you."

"Okay," I said happily, "I will. Thanks, Dad."

For another night I went to bed happy, and for another morning I woke up excited to get out of the camper.

I rushed to the park again, found my spot, nestled into the sun-drenched sky, and waited.

She didn't show.

I waited the next day and the next. Lizzie didn't show at all.

I stopped off at the park every day during the two-week vacation, but Lizzie, the little girl who won my heart and the first girl I fell for, never showed up.

4
Teenage Dreams
Part One: Katie

I thought the feelings I had for Lizzie would open doors for me. I expected my return to school would be a return to a world of new opportunities, a world where I adored the opposite sex, had multitudes of crushes and perhaps, eventually, got myself a girlfriend.

It didn't happen.

I returned to see the same faces on the same girls I had known since nursery school. They didn't appeal to me. My short-lived adoration of the opposite sex stagnated.

Then, in middle school, the doors didn't just open—they imploded in a sticky mess of hormones and desire.

First there was Katie. She lived a few miles away and had gone to a different primary school. I laid eyes on her during the very first day of school. The teacher had been babbling tediously and our eyes had met across the room.

She had thick shoulder-length hair that bounced with a springy vibrancy when she moved. The dark locks framed her cute features: deep dimples, chubby cheeks, big eyes. Her skin was heavily tanned, beyond the powers of the English sunshine, which made the whites of her hazel eyes stand out like bright lights at the end of a dimly lit tunnel.

On the fourth week, I decided to make my move. I had correctly assumed, albeit very late, that Katie was waiting for me to do just that.

I planned to let my friends ask her out for me. I hadn't told any of them that I liked her, but it was obvious to most of them. Unfortunately for me, the friend I chose was Max, perhaps the only person in the class who hadn't realized I fancied Katie.

In class I wrote Katie a note and nudged Max. I gestured for him to give it to her with a swift nod.

He looked across the classroom and then glanced briefly at the note. His immediate reaction was one of surprise and horror, but then he seemed to come to terms with himself. He shrugged, muttered something under his breath, and then handed the note to Chris Peterson, the school bully.

The next few seconds were a bit of a blur; my heart was pounding too fast for my brain to keep track. I don't remember what was said or how he reacted, but I do remember the beating he gave me on the playground afterward.

"Why the hell do you think I would want to ask Peterson out?" I asked Max after the beating.

He shrugged. I could see his eyes scanning my forehead from left to right. "What's a Hama?" he asked innocently.

"I think it's an O," I shook my head. "It doesn't matter, it's not important!" I snapped, instinctively rubbing my forehead where the words had been ingrained in sloppy black ink. "The note was for Katie!"

"Oh," realization dawned. He looked down at the concrete slabs underneath his feet, then back up to my wounded, graffitied face. "She's pretty."

I threw my hands in the air and groaned heavily. "You're fucking hard work, Max."

He didn't seem to know how to reply to that one, so he remained silent.

Over the years, me and the other kids in my class had assumed that as we were growing older and maturing, Max was staying the same. We thought he was retaining the same level of innocence, ignorance, and general stupidity he had possessed since an early age. It didn't become apparent until later that Max was actually getting stupider.

I watched Chris work his way around the playground. After beating me and holding me down to draw on my forehead, he had gone to join in a game of soccer. I glared at him through lowered, bitter eyebrows as he hacked and slashed his way through the field of players.

"Did you think I fancied *him*?" I asked, gesturing angrily into the distance. Chris had scored a goal and was gesticulating wildly and proudly to a group of spectating girls.

Max shrugged. "Not my place to judge."

Olly had also joined me in middle school, but when I asked him to put in a few good words with Katie, he told her he had seen me undressing in the changing rooms and promised her she would *not be disappointed*.

"I don't care how old she is," Olly insisted. "Girls love that sorta thing," he said defiantly.

"Clearly she didn't," I said.

"Maybe she's a lesbian," Olly offered.

"I don't think—"

"You should get a tattoo with her name," Max cut in, ever the idiot. "Break the ice as my mother says, *then* you can show her your massive cock."

Peter, Olly, and I all stared at Max in open-mouthed wonder.

Three girls from the grade above us had been skipping nearby, and even they turned to look. Max stared back, oblivious.

"Never get a tattoo," Olly said, shaking Max out of his head. "My dad knew a guy who got one once; he wanted Elmo boxing Tyson on his back, paid a small fortune for it. The tattooist was a pro, forty years in the business, thousands of happy customers. Poor sod had a minor stroke ten minutes in, didn't know where the fuck he was, couldn't remember anything. The guy ended up with Maggie Thatcher riding a Space Hopper."

"Bullshit," I spat, sensing shenanigans.

"I shit you not," Olly assured. "The tattooist reckons he had that image in his head for weeks, said he was glad to get it out."

"Is that really true or is this like the time you saw Lord Lucan in Tesco?"

"It was either him or his double."

"In *Tesco* though?"

Olly simply shrugged. "He's gotta do his shopping somewhere."

I stared at him unsurely for a moment, shrugged off the insanities, and changed the subject: "I'm not getting a tattoo."

"Maybe you should," Peter piped up, attracting everyone's attention. "If I had gotten a tattoo of Lisa's name maybe she wouldn't have dumped me."

The group sounded a collective sigh.

Lisa had used Peter to adapt to her life at a new school and a new environment. He became increasingly obsessed with her; the few times he wasn't with her he was talking about her.

It had taken Lisa a couple months to find a new group of friends, not realizing that if not for Peter, and his reputation as a boring idiot, she would have befriended them a lot sooner. She broke up with him four months in. She hadn't really been interested in him, but he did have pity and familiarity on his side, so they had spent the next two years in a yo-yo relationship until Lisa eventually decided she had enough.

"Would you forget about her already?" Olly said. "You're thirteen now, you're nearly a man. Grow a pair of balls and find *another* girl to play with them."

Peter looked appalled. "Lisa *never*—"

"Well, then why are you complaining so much? Shut your mouth an' find a girl that will."

Peter *harrumphed* and pressed his lips tightly together, his talking done for the day.

My friends had failed me, but I still refused to meet the situation head on. I went to Katie's friends.

Christy was my first port of call. During the lunch break, after scrubbing my skin clean in the school bathroom, I found her wandering around the entrance, her eyes on the floor.

Katie and Christy had been best friends all their lives. They lived near each other, went to the same schools, and were even born in the same week.

I tracked up to her with my hands in my pockets. She wasn't a very pretty girl and she wasn't very interesting to talk to, but I liked her. Partly because of her connection and proximity to Katie, mostly because her friendship with Katie reminded me of the one I shared with Max.

"Hey Christy, what you up to?"

"I'm looking for a contact lens," she said, without looking up.

"I didn't know you wore contacts."

She looked up at me, confusion in her eyes. "I don't," she said with a frown, as though I was insane for stating such a thing.

Christy reminded me *a lot* of Max.

I decided to skip the questioning, not sure where it would take me. "Can I have a word with you about Katie?"

Christy shrugged as if to say *I'm not going to stop you.*

"The thing is," I began, looking away awkwardly, joining Christy in her search for the lens. "I like her; I like her quite a lot actually."

Christy lifted her head, smiled at me, and then lowered it again. "That's nice," she said to the ground.

I pushed on, "Could you do me a favor?"

She glared at me. "I'm not looking for your bloody contact lens as well," she warned.

I shook my head. "No, I want you to ask Katie out for me."

"You as well?"

"Me as well—" I paused, confused, surprised. "What do you mean: *me as well?*"

Christy lifted her head again. "Well, she's already got a boy-friend, hasn't she?"

"Has she?"

My mind suddenly conjured up a show reel of Katie. Images of her flashed before me at hyperspeed. Katie in class. Katie smiling. Katie laughing. Katie leaving school. Katie blowing me a kiss.

That last one hadn't been real, but it was in there nevertheless.

I had never seen Kate with another boy. I had seen her in brief conversations with some, but nothing more than passing greetings. If she had a boyfriend she hid it well.

"She's with the little fat boy," Christy said with her simpleton smile.

I had definitely never seen Katie with a little fat boy, but now I could see nothing else.

"*Little fat boy?*" I asked.

Christy didn't reply. Instead she turned around and pointed. I followed her outstretched arm; it led to the school gates.

I didn't see what she was pointing at straight away, but then two shapes materialized. The wall at the opening of the gate jutted upward like the rook on a chess board, two people were leaning against its stone face, locked in an embrace.

My heart sank when I realized that one of them was Katie. She was pushed up against the wall, her arms around the neck of the boy in front, her long hair in his grubby and unappreciative hands. Her lips were locked tightly onto his, exchanging tongues and saliva.

My body and heart sunk. The pleasantries on my face ebbed away as every facial muscle sagged. An instant feeling of loss and regret struck me. I felt terrible.

Then I realized who the lucky boy was and I felt even worse.

"That's Chris Peterson," I said.

"Yeah," Christy said softly, looking admiringly at the kissing couple. "He asked her out earlier. She likes the bad boys. I don't think she used to be that interested, but she saw him beat up some little kid this morning and she fell for him." Christy turned back to me, my face now flushed with anger and embarrassment. She didn't seem to notice. "Sweet, huh?"

Teenage Dreams
Part Two: Trinity

I expected something to happen when I turned thirteen. I wasn't quite sure what, but something was surely going to happen.

It was a big age. It was the official ascent into adolescence. The day when I stopped being a boy and became, well, not quite a man but certainly something less boyish.

Part of me imagined that at sixteen, a mystery man would show up with an ID card, a pack of cigarettes, a condom, and a wink. Two years later, at eighteen, I thought the same man would bring along a crate of beer and a note that congratulated me on becoming an adult. At thirteen, that man would have nothing to bring me—pubic hair and acne had already been going strong for a year or two—but I thought it would be decent of him to show up.

Nothing happened. At least not for me.

After a summer that ended far too early, I went back to school with all the apathy that the first day after summer usually brought. Then I saw Trinity Adams and that apathy disappeared.

She had also turned thirteen in the summer, but she had changed dramatically. Her breasts, previously only slightly noticeable under her shirt, were now huge. They bobbled around underneath her uniform when she walked and I found myself entranced by them.

When she smiled at me, I nearly melted. I thought she was the most attractive girl I had ever seen; the truth was she was average at best.

The other boys in the class noticed her as well, and immediately swallowed their conversations when she entered. Their eyes turned to her, following her across the room, fixed on her bouncing breasts.

I turned to Olly, who was also following her with his eyes. "Is it me or did she get very attractive over the summer?" I asked.

"Nah, she's still ugly," he said confidently. "Great tits, though."

Chris Peterson had been sitting on a corner table with his arm around Katie, but when Trinity walked in, he dropped his shoulder, shrugged Katie away, and rushed to guide Trinity into her seat.

I knew that if I wanted to make Trinity my first girlfriend, which I did, then I would have to act quickly before she was also tainted by the hand of the chubby bully.

I waited until recess to make my move. All around the playground, I could see clusters of boys nudging each other, daring one another to go and talk to her.

"Ask her for a suck," I heard one say as I shifted past.

"I'd love to bounce on those babies."

I watched her exchange a laugh and a smile with two girls. She didn't seem aware of the stares, but her friends were, and they studied the playground with cautious eyes.

I could feel my heart race as I closed in.

The two girls said something to Trinity and then moved away. It was amicable; they were all still smiling, but Trinity was alone now.

I coughed, cleared my throat, closed my eyes tightly, opened them again.

I tapped her on the shoulder and wore my best smile.

She turned, smiling. "Hey," she said pleasantly.

I had it all prepared. I had thought about what to say all morning and had rehearsed it a number of times.

I prepared to rush through it all, to get it all out there before Chris or anyone interrupted me and tried to steal her away.

"Hey, Titty," I said with a smile. "I just—" I paused. The smile dripped slowly from my face.

Trinity. Trinity. I thought slowly. *Please tell me I said Trinity.*

She wasn't smiling. She looked shocked.

Keep it going, move on, she might not notice.

I forged another smile and forced myself to continue. "I was wondering if you wanted to go out with me. To the movies or something. I know tits not much—"

I did it again.

I gulped down a thick glob of saliva. Trinity had noticed the slips.

"—*It's*, sorry," I said, coughing into my hand. "I have a little—" I waved a hand around my chest to indicate a cold. Then I looked at her breasts.

I was still waving at my chest and staring at her breasts when she cleared her throat exaggeratedly.

What am I doing!

Stop staring! Stop staring!

I pressed my hand to my chest and held it there with my other hand, as if restraining it from further stupidity. "I'm so sorry," I said, my face flushed with embarrassment. Hers was a red shade of annoyance. "I didn't mean to. I don't know what, I mean; I'm not even like that. I'm a good guy, I don't even like, I mean they're lovely an' all, if not a little big—"

Fuck. Fuck. Fuck.

I didn't want to look at her face. I knew she was angry at me, but that left only one option. My eyes fell to her breasts.

"I'm so sorry," I said, speaking slowly and staring at her chest as if it was the last chance I'd have to see it. "I—I—I—" I paused, shrugged, and turned around. "I'll see you later," I walked sullenly back across the playground. A few boys looked my way, wondering if I had succeeded in asking her out or copping a feel.

I sulked back to my friends, meeting none of them in the eye, staring at my shoes with a melancholic smudge across my face.

"I made an idiot outta myself," I muttered softly.

Olly put a heavy hand on my shoulder and squeezed. "Don't worry, mate," he said, leaning over so that his mouth spoke directly into my sunken ears. "There'll be plenty of tits to go around soon enough. This is the golden age for us; this is when things start to get interesting." He grabbed my chin and lifted it up, forcing me to look out over the expansive playground. "You see all of these ugly bitches," he said, wiping his free hand across the landscape, "all of them will be fuckable soon enough. The world is our oyster, mate, so stop sulking and eat up."

For a thirteen-year-old virgin who couldn't talk to a woman without annoying her, Olly seemed to know what he was talking about. I didn't believe him at first but then I began to notice all the other girls in the same way I had noticed Trinity. None were as well endowed, but many were prettier.

6

Teenage Dreams
Part Three: Penny

There were a few girls on my radar in the final year of middle school, but all were minor crushes, none kept me awake at night.

There was Andrea in the grade below: blonde hair, blue eyes, golden tan. She had a strong accent and giggled loudly after every sentence. When I first heard her I thought she was putting on a voice for comical effect. I even laughed along with her to show her that her impression of an annoying idiot was amusing, but the voice never went away. I decided to enjoy her from afar instead, putting enough distance between us so that I could at least pretend she didn't sound like an anguished feline.

Cherry was in Andrea's class. She was shy and somewhat timid but she had a smile that could soften the hearts of murderers. Unfortunately, it was hard to get her to speak. She greeted everything with a shy shrug and often turned away when people spoke to her.

Ali was new to the school. She wore a burka, with only her dark eyes, like shiny black holes, on show. I think I liked her because she was different; because she was the same age and, unlike the others, I hadn't known her since nursery school. And also because she reminded me of a ninja, and I loved ninjas.

Kelly and Penny were two girls I had known since nursery school. They were fairly uninteresting throughout primary school but had blossomed at age twelve. At thirteen, they were full-figured adults, at least in my eyes.

I never asked out any of the girls I liked, shying away for fear of a repeat of the Katie or Trinity incident. I rated them regardless and found Kelly usually came out on top, with Penny hovering in second.

That all changed one summer, and it began with the boy who had cost me my first crush at the school.

Chris Peterson had maintained his role as the school bully over the course of the first year and into the second. Katie had broken up with him after a few short weeks and had since worked her way through the male population of the nearby high school, but he had wormed his way into the arms of other girls desperate for macho boys.

After Katie, Chris had dated Gail Clemens. He had been her first boyfriend, but just a week later, she dumped him to date a sixteen-year-old high school dropout. Then came Patty, who picked Chris up at the end of the year, was with him for a day, and then immediately jumped up to dumb high school boys.

Olly called Chris a *gateway idiot*, but never to his face. I related this joke to another kid, and then another, keen to spread the insult around the school. I had been telling a third when Chris overheard.

I had finished class early and was killing time near the gym, just outside the changing rooms. Chris came in from outside with a menacing glare on his chubby face. He had seen; he had heard. I was doomed.

He bounded straight for me, his eyebrows lowered, his nose flaring like an angry bull. I knew there was no point running; he would catch up to me eventually.

I took a step back, my hands raised defensively. "It's not what you think," I told him.

He grabbed me by the throat and shoved me against the door. My spine and skull clattered against the wood, bright blue stars danced in the corners of my eyes.

"Then what the fuck is it!" he demanded.

I mumbled something back, still a little dazed.

"What?" he spat.

"Depends," I said, coughing the word out. "Depends on what you heard." I tried to smile, but he didn't seem impressed.

"What the fuck did you say?" he spat every syllable, the corners of his mouth frothing.

I was thinking the same thing, struggling to believe that I had just tried to be smart to a kid who could crush me and currently had a hand on my throat.

"Nothing," I replied with a strained voice.

I tried to softly pry his hand from my throat, not wanting to apply too much exertion and indicate a desire to fight back, but keen for him to know I didn't want it there.

"I fucking heard you."

"Then why'd you ask?"

I felt those words coming out of my mouth but I didn't react quickly enough to stop them. I wondered if I was concussed, or possibly brain damaged. If not, there was a good chance I would be soon.

I saw his eyes widen. I would have gulped if his hand wasn't making it impossible.

"What'd you just say?"

"Something very *very* stupid."

"You bet it was stupid," he said slowly.

I could feel my face darkening through lack of oxygen, could sense my life ebbing away. It occurred to me that I was going to die pinned up against the girls' changing room by a fat idiot.

I gripped his hand with more pressure and managed to pry away his little finger.

"What are you doing?" he said, staring at my busy hands in bemusement.

I had worked the nib of a forefinger away. "Trying to save my life," I replied without looking up. The little finger clasped back when the forefinger lifted. "*Shit,*" I gurgled.

He let go.

I breathed deeply.

He punched me in the stomach before the breath had time to complete.

I coiled up instantly, my head near his groin. I thought of headbutting him like a ram, but quickly let that thought slip. If I didn't kill or cripple him, he was just going to hit me back harder.

I expected more punches. I only hoped that he would at least have the decency to drag me outside and let me enjoy the sunshine while he beat the shit out of me.

Instead he laughed, opened the door behind me, and shoved me backward.

I toppled into the girls' changing rooms and hit the floor with a thud, quickly assuming the fetal position.

Chris disappeared in a fit of hysterics. He expected me to be caught, called a pervert and shamed by a room of girls, but no one had heard; no one had seen. The door faced a walled partition, which housed a number of empty footlockers and aspirational posters. The main changing room was around a corner a few feet from my head, and beyond that a raised partition led to a line of showers, the noise from which had helped drown out the crashing door.

I crawled on the slippery floor and climbed to my feet. I checked the doorway to make sure Chris had gone, sighed with relief when I saw he had, and then straightened up my collar, which had tightened against my throat.

I stopped with my hand on my top button. I sensed movement out of the corner of my eye. My heart froze, my skin prickled with goose bumps. I thought someone was sneaking up on my peripheral, about to expose me.

My heart kicked into gear with a bang, beating faster than it had ever beaten before. Then it relaxed. Softened. The movement had come from a mirror, ahead and to my left, directly opposite the changing area.

In the tall, slightly smeared glass, I could see waves of pink flesh shuffling around amongst the lockers, benches, and clothes pegs.

Instantly I felt a reaction in my pants. One very common for a thirteen-year-old but not acceptable in school. I ignored it. I didn't care. I was entranced.

In the steaming glass, I saw the waddling bodies and pristine flesh of an army of girls as they conversed, laughed, giggled, and dressed in the misty changing room.

A small voice at the back of my mind was screaming at me to turn around and leave; the consequences of being caught were too big. That voice was drowned out by a million screams telling me to stay, fuck the consequences.

I saw classmates like I had never seen them before—all fleshy and bouncy—as they walked to and fro, clueless to my voyeurism. I saw Kelly striding around in her underwear and Katie standing topless, her lower half obscured by an unfortunately placed bag.

The one who caught my attention the most was Penny, standing near her peg, rifling through a small sports bag. She was completely naked.

In that instant, standing next to my number one, Penny—my former number 2—went straight to the top of my list. To my young, inexperienced eyes, everything about her was perfect, and she was naked, which was always a bonus.

I watched Penny dress without blinking, growing impatient when other girls, some naked, crossed her path and the steamed mirror's line of reflection. When she was fully dressed and waiting for the teacher to give her permission to leave, I ducked out of the changing room and into the hallway.

I was happy to have escaped without being seen. I had a beaming smile on my face and an erotic image burned into my mind. I had never seen a girl naked. I had caught a few glimpses of topless girls in magazines and in films, but nothing else. I was delighted to get that part of my growing-up out of the way and ecstatic it had happened without incident.

I was still smiling when the screaming began.

The girls had flooded out of the changing room. Some dispersed down the corridor to their next lesson, others loitered.

I was watching them file out one by one, thinking, *I've seen you naked, and you, and you,"* as they emptied the changing room. A bespectacled, pale girl named Elly was the first to look at me, the first to point; the first to scream.

They all started after that. Elly was the only one screaming but they were all pointing at me, and most of them were laughing. I followed their taunting fingers, but before my eyes lowered that far, I realized what they were pointing at.

My top was still riled up. My shirt was twisted and wrapped around my midsection. After skidding across the floor, my trousers had also been pulled up by the waistband, which in turn had lowered the zip. And there, taking advantage of the gap in the top of the zip, bursting through like a newborn into the world, was an underpants-shaped bulge.

I was so shocked, I didn't even correct it. I just stared, praying that the world would end at that exact moment or I would wake up and discover it was all some horrible nightmare (which, admittedly, had followed a fantastic dream).

The world didn't end, and the laughing continued. In the embarrassment, the bulge was rapidly dying, but I covered what was left regardless and trotted outside, keen to get away from the taunts and the laughter.

Word spread around school and I tried to persuade my parents to move to America, but they weren't interested. I also tried to convince them I had Leprosy and needed to take a year or two off, but they weren't buying it.

I was a laughing stock at school, but it could have been worse. The rumor mill chewed me up blue and spat me out red—some stories said I had been caught having sex with a teacher, most seemed to say I was masturbating. The convolution meant that Chris never recounted the story of pushing me into the girls changing room because he didn't find the connection between that and whatever version of the story he had heard.

The girls knew, of course, but it didn't seem to cross their minds that I had been spying on them. Thankfully the story died before the year was out.

I tried talking to Penny after I was sure the incident wouldn't be mentioned, but every time I looked at her, I saw what I saw in that mirror. I couldn't look at her or talk to her without my brain jumping up and down like a little kid, screaming: *I've seen you naked, I've seen you naked.* I knew where those thoughts led and was keen not to go down that road again.

7

First Love

A few months before my sixteenth birthday, I finally had my first girlfriend.

It was summer vacation. I was fifteen and had just finished my last year of school. I was going back after the summer to join the sixth form, but my days as a mandatory pupil were over. I had completed my exams and had achieved passes in most subjects.

I wanted to celebrate. I wanted to spend the summer getting drunk with unruly friends on street corners. I wanted to chat up girls in clubs and pubs. I wanted to lounge around all day, eating junk food and playing computer games.

My parents had other ideas.

"I'm fifteen," I told my mother firmly. "I can't go to the campground; it's for old people."

"You used to love it when you were a kid," she said, ignoring the *old people* comment.

"I'm not a kid anymore, things change," I told her.

She seemed amused.

"He's right," my dad butted in, peering over the top of his newspaper. "Look at his face, for example. He used to be cute."

"Ha-ha Dad," I said, with as much exaggeration as I could muster.

He grinned with pride and ducked back behind the paper, his part in the argument over.

"Everything has been booked and arranged," my mother said sternly. "You're going."

"*UN*-book it, *UN*-arrange it," I pleaded.

"And what else do you plan on doing all summer?"

I shrugged and glanced instinctively at the computer console at the foot of the television. "I don't know."

"Well, when you find out, you let me know, won't you? In the meantime, we're going to the campground. Get packed."

I maintained a visage of disgust all the way to the site but I warmed to the idea by the time we arrived. I didn't want to admit it to my nearly sixteen-year-old self, but the thought of spending a couple of weeks on arcade machines and cheapened theme park rides stimulated me.

It was raining when we arrived, the sun had been out all morning, but over the last thirty minutes the clouds had darkened with the contents of an afternoon shower. I helped my parents take the suitcases into the camper and tried to get comfortable inside the confines.

The last time we had been to the campgrounds was three years ago; it had been one of the wettest summers on record and had rained for the entire two weeks. We were desperate to leave after just six days, but my parents didn't want to admit it to each other or to concede defeat to me, so they had persevered.

I stared out of the window and glared at the sky. "It's going to rain for two weeks again," I said.

"You brought your trunks, didn't you?" Dad said as he lugged the final suitcase into the camper.

Technology had come a long way in those few years, but the television in the camper hadn't. The picture had degraded beyond the realms of sight and it emitted a constant whining crackle. The alternative was a portable television approximately the size of a paperback book, apparently designed with Borrowers in mind.

I turned to my mother who was shaking raindrops from her coat. "What am I supposed to do?" I asked her. "It's pissing it down—you said it wouldn't rain."

"That's what the weatherman told me." She hung up her coat and picked up mine, casually discarded on the kitchen unit.

"No sun, no television," I complained. "What am I supposed to do?"

"We have a television," Dad said joyously, holding up the portable.

"I hate that thing."

"Good, cause I want to watch golf." He sat down at the dining table and lifted his feet onto its surface.

"Read a book," my mother offered.

"All day?"

She shrugged and looked out of the kitchen window. "It's just a shower, it'll end soon, then you can go to the park."

I stomped my feet and let out an annoyed grunt. "I told you this was a bad idea," I said grumpily.

"Hey," Dad said calmly, without looking up from his television. "I've told you before, if you talk to your mother like that, I'll kill you when you're sleeping." He spoke without a hint of sarcasm or anger. He enjoyed playing the placid clown.

I groaned again and rose angrily to my feet. "I'm going out," I said, ripping my coat from the hook.

"In the rain?" Mom asked.

"Beats lying around this hellhole all day."

"Goodbye, have fun," Dad called merrily as I slammed the wafer-thin door and bounced into the rain-drenched afternoon.

In the park, I was reunited with the equipment that was a permanent fixture of my childhood vacations. Some of the apparatus had fallen beyond repair and was unusable, but the swings were still in working order.

I brushed a pool of water from the seat of one and sat down. Instantly I felt the remaining slithers soak into my pants. I gripped the dripping metal chains, stared out into the bleak distance, and rocked.

The silence contained a certain ambiance, with only the sound of the rain and a horizon of glumness to keep me company. It gave me time to think, although I had very little to think about.

After half an hour or so, the sun began to break through the clouds in the distance, and before long it had penetrated the grayness and illuminated the world. The rain had stopped and was quickly drying underneath the intense heat of the sun's rays.

Now I had something to think about. *Where to go, what to do?*

I decided I was going to hit the arcades. Gun games, penny-slot machines, and kids the same age as me. I would need a lift from my parents—the promenade was a short drive from the park, but they would probably be happy to join me. They could do some shopping.

I hopped off the swing and turned, ready to sprint back to the camper.

I stopped. Someone was blocking my way.

"Hello," she said.

She was young, no older than me. She had blonde hair and blue eyes; a dazzling curiosity on her lips and an intense intelligence in her eyes.

I recognized her.

"Hey," I replied.

She smiled at me, then walked past me and sat down on the furthest swing. Grasping the chains, she turned to look at me expectantly. My own discarded swing was still rocking.

I looked at her, unable to speak.

I knew it was Lizzie. It had to be. She was sitting on the same swing, holding the chains and rocking in the same gentle manner. It had taken me a year before I had forced myself to forget her, and that year was three years ago, but now it all came flooding back.

I cautiously moved back to my swing and climbed on. I exchanged a smile with her and began to rock back and forth.

She caught me looking at her after a few minutes. She giggled. We both turned away.

It was her, definitely, but did she know who I was? Did she remember me?

I shook my head and turned to the quickly sunning horizon.

Of course she didn't recognize me. She had disappeared after that day. She had gone home, happy in her ignorance. Leaving me to stew over the memory of her and what could have been.

She spoke, softly, friendly: "Kieran, right?"

I snapped my head back to her. "Yes," I said, practically screaming.

She smiled, looked down and then turned away, back to the horizon. "Beautiful day, isn't it?"

"Yes," I agreed.

I wanted to talk to her; I rued the fact that I hadn't done so last time. I had felt so comfortable then, so at ease, and I felt that now. I didn't feel awkward. I didn't feel the need to fill such a beautiful silence just for the sake of filling it, but I didn't want to let this moment slip away.

"So, Lizzie," I began, being sure to slip her name in, letting her know I remembered. "Do you want to go to the arcade with me?"

She had reacted to her name as I had reacted to mine, and she was smiling broadly. She halted her swinging by placing a foot on the ground. "Yes," she said. "I would love to."

I was forced to let my parents meet Lizzie—it was as awkward as anticipated, but it was worth it.

We rode together in the back seat of my dad's car while he played love songs on the radio and exchanged jokes with my mother in the passenger seat.

"I don't think Kieran's had a *female* friend before," Dad said after a short while, his eyes glistening in the rear-view mirror. "There's Max, he's very feminine, but he's a boy. Olly and Peter are boys as well, yep," he nodded to himself. "All *boy* friends. I guess that makes you his first *girl* friend, eh Lizzie?"

I released a long groan and dropped my head into my hands.

"I guess," Lizzie replied softly.

I hadn't been expecting that. I lifted my head and looked at her, overcome with an internal joy that threatened to explode me. She was staring at me, smiling her sweet smile.

I felt a warmth rush through my body and at that point I was sure I was in love.

"Have you had many *boy* friends, Lizzie?"

"Drop it, Dad!"

We parked in a hotel lot and were soon walking down the promenade. The brisk sea air spiked goosebumps on my bare arms, which warmed underneath tepid rays from the sun.

The sounds of the arcade—the beeping-whirring calls of artificial thrills, the jingle-jangle rings of boisterous bandits—whistled to my ears long before we reached its neon facade.

With hasty footsteps, Lizzie and I were already a few paces ahead of my parents, but when we were just a dozen feet short of the noisy, luminous building, Lizzie grabbed my hand and pulled, skipping to the entrance with me in tow.

I thought my face would flush with embarrassment or sheer joy, but it didn't, and I held onto her hand even when we were inside the arcade, standing in front of the array of whirring machines.

"I love these places!" Lizzie said, disappointing me by letting go of my hand. "It reminds me of my childhood." She turned to me, her eyes a vision of intoxicated joy. "Come on, I'll play you on *Time Crisis!*"

She rushed off, leaving me smiling in her merry wake.

"You and your *girlfriend* be quick." My dad had caught up; he and my mother were just passing the arcade, the sun beating down onto his sardonic eyes as my mother ducked out of its rays. "Be nice to your *girlfriend*, if your *girlfriend* wants to go somewhere else, let your *girlfriend* go—"

"Dad!"

He beamed and continued walking. "We'll be in the tooth mausoleum if you need us."

That was what he called the sweet shop. He thought he was hilarious.

"Tell your *girlfriend*—"

I didn't hear the rest; I was already weaving through the machines, searching for Lizzie.

I found her holding a plastic gun and pumping coins into a machine. She beckoned me to join her.

"We didn't have any of this when I was a kid," she said, like her childhood was a lifetime ago. "I've always wanted to come back, thought it sounded a bit childish so I didn't." She handed me a bright yellow gun. "I'm glad you invited me," she added, as if my childish personality had been the ticket she had been waiting for.

I took the gun, took up a stance beside Lizzie, and waited for the countdown to finish on the screen, my finger on the trigger as pixelated enemies readied to shoot.

"So, is this, are we . . ." I trailed off, looking at her. "You know what my dad says . . ."

"Your dad is funny."

I laughed abruptly, but Lizzie had an earnest look on her face. "Oh, you're being serious."

"I like him."

I shrugged and turned hastily to the screen when inept bank robbers shot at me. I took a few out and watched as Lizzie annihilated entire fleets of them. Then I caught a staccato of fire from a balaclava-clad beast. The screen flashed up huge red letters, declaring game over and asking me to pay more to jump back in.

Lizzie continued on her own, her arms up in military fashion, the tip of her tongue poking out of her mouth in a concentrated effort. Eventually she finished, and the game sighed its death knell.

"Beaten by the boss," she said.

"He was a big guy; don't be so hard on yourself."

She giggled and replaced the gun in its plastic holster by the side of the machine. "So, what were you saying about your dad?" she asked.

It was harder to ask her when she was staring directly at me. "Nothing," I said. "It's not important. Come on, there's a racing game over there."

I tried to pull her away; she remained, staring fixedly at me.

She grabbed my hand, her fingers clasping the ends of mine. She leaned in close and kissed me gently on the lips, then she pulled away, a smile spreading across her face. "A racing game it is then," she said with glee. "Come on."

For two hours, we played together and laughed together. We blew pocketfuls of change on slot machines, racing games, and dancing games. I beat her at *Sensible Soccer*; she beat me at just about every other game we played.

Afterward she threw her arms around my neck and grinned at me. I thought she was preparing for a long, passionate kiss, but instead she popped another quick peck on my lips and then released me.

When we left the dizzying lights of the arcade, the natural sunlight burned. The clean air and the bright glare took a few minutes to adjust to.

She wrapped her arm in mine and we moved down the street. After a few steps in silence, her face took on a more forlorn persona.

"I'm leaving tomorrow," she told me somberly.

I stopped in my tracks, my arm slipped from hers. "Wh—what do you mean?"

"Me and my parents, we're going home," she explained.

"You can't!" I was crestfallen.

She laughed softly. "We have to eventually."

"Bu—but not now!"

"No, not now. Tomorrow."

"Bu—bu—bu—"

"Don't worry," she said calmly, "I'll give you my number. You can call me whenever you want. We can see each other during summer vacation."

"You live like, what—three, four hours away?"

She shrugged, "More like two."

"It's still a lot," I pouted and lowered my head.

"Don't be so glum," she planted a hand on my chin, pried it up with her forefinger.

"But I thought we—" I allowed my sentence to trail off. "I like you," I clarified. "I like you a lot."

"I like you a lot too." With her finger still pressed to my chin, she leaned in for another kiss. This time it was more than just a quick peck.

When she released me from her puckered lips, she rested her forehead against mine and looked into my eyes. "Don't worry," she said assuredly. "We'll always be together."

I smiled, content. She pulled away.

"If you want me to stay, I guess one day you'll have to ask me to marry you," she said.

I nodded, determined to do just that, then I took her hand in mine and we set off to find my parents.

Lizzie wrote her number on a small slip of cardboard, torn from a box of chocolate raisins. I placed the torn slip in the thin watch-pocket on my jeans, wedging it between the denim so it wouldn't fall out.

I spent the afternoon and evening with Lizzie. On the beach, we walked hand-in-hand over the lapping shore and tossed pebbles into the rushing waves. On the pier, we watched the sea and ate fish-n-chips from polystyrene containers while my father entertained Lizzie with the worst dad jokes he could muster. At the campgrounds, when the light was fading and night was setting, we swung side by side on the swings, talking of anything that came to mind, but mostly just happy to sit, swing, smile, and admire.

The following day I reluctantly agreed to accompany my parents to the rocky shores of a cave-infested beach we often frequented. It took half an hour or so in moderately congested traffic to get there, all the while my hand rested on my pocket, making sure the card didn't climb out and fly away.

After parking the car, we trekked down a gravely slope and marched across a path of thick, wet grass. A ground cobbled with uneven natural sediment lay before an expanse of rocks and sea. In the distance I could see cave entrances; the blackened openings looked ominous in the gloom.

My dad pointed to a large cave in the distance, beyond what looked like miles of algae-covered rocks. "Let's head to that one," he declared.

"Long way," I noted, not wanting to stay out too long.

"So?" he said nonchalantly. "We've got all day,"

I glared at him. He smiled back.

"Only joking," he conceded. "We'll be quick."

Lizzie was leaving in the evening. I wanted to get back to see her before she left. I had arranged to meet her on the swings at three so we could spend a couple of hours together; we arrived at the beach at ten. I had plenty of time.

After a while, the sediment gave way to a shore of rocks and boulders, with pools of murky sea water lurking inside, washed there from the previous tide and waiting to be refreshed by another.

We could see the cave up ahead, its great yawning mouth inviting us in. We stopped on the same ledge, looking down into a stagnant tide pool a foot in diameter. It was no more than a few inches deep, but the water was thick and slimy. I couldn't see the bottom.

"We should go back," Mom offered, looking out at the expanse of rocks intersecting the varying sizes of putrid pools.

"I agree," I said, eager to get to Lizzie.

My dad made chicken noises, looking skyward nonchalantly as if he didn't know the squawking sounds were coming from his lips.

"That's not going to work," I told him.

He made louder noises and flapped his arms.

"Grow up."

He stopped and shrugged. "Fair enough. Long way back though."

We all turned around. He was right. The cave had looked distant at the start of the walk; now the entrance, and the parking lot beyond, was a smudge on the horizon.

"Seems a shame to just turn around," Mom said. "Let's push on."

"What if you fall?" I said, gesturing toward the pools. "The rocks are slippery."

She shrugged. "I'll be fine."

I groaned.

"Nice try, kid," Dad said merrily. He brushed past me and hopped the first pool, turning around to make sure my mother successfully followed. She did so with a sense of adventure in her eyes.

"Oh, this could be fun," she said, venturing off toward the next pool.

I grumbled and followed, placidly hopping from rock to rock, the soles of my shoes gently slipping and sliding on the greased rocks.

I didn't lift my head to watch, but I could hear my parents ahead of me, and they were having a lot of fun.

"Oh, that was a big one!"

"You go, girl!"

I couldn't help but think I could be spending time with Lizzie. We had planned to see each other before the end of the summer vacation, but that was a couple of weeks away, and after that we might not see each other for months.

"Kieran," my dad called back. "Big one there, you'll have to go around."

I looked up to see him slightly out of breath. He was pointing to a large pool behind him; a series of rocks worked their way around its circumference.

I shrugged, not in a patient mood. I quickly weighed the option of jumping straight over the gap, and then sprang forward without much planning. I made it across, I felt the front of my feet touch onto solid rock, but the soles slipped on the algae that formed on the edges. There was a brief moment of terror when I realized I was going to fall, a split second where my face turned from pure placidity into sheer horror.

I felt my legs shoot out behind as my body flopped forward. The green-stained rock came to greet me with ominous rapidity. My hands and elbows clattered into the rock, and I could feel the cold sting of its surface against my skin.

My legs dipped into the water behind me. The cold, shocking sensation of them dangling into the slimy liquid hit me when the sting in my palms faded to a throb.

Dad stepped forward and took my arm. He guided me out of the water and then stepped back. He looked me up and down, a smile slowly breaking on his face as I stood in front of him, dripping wet from the waist down with a scowl of pale disgust on my face.

"Told you to go around," he said calmly.

My mother rushed up to me, her hands on my face. "Are you okay, sweetie? Are you okay? Let me have a look at you."

"I'm fine," I spat, shivery. "Leave me."

She reluctantly backed away, trailing a sympathetic hand on my shoulder.

"He'll be fine," Dad turned around, ready to move on.

"He'll catch a cold!" Mom argued, distraught.

"A cold never killed anyone."

"But *pneumonia* did," she replied, venomously. She turned to me. "Take them off," she said, pointing to my pants.

"You must be joking."

"Pneumonia is no joke, Kieran."

I turned around, exaggeratedly gesturing to the world around me. "I'm not getting naked here!"

"Stop being so vain," she said genuinely.

My dad laughed, clearly enjoying the absurdity of her suggestion. He quickly silenced his laughter when she scowled menacingly at him.

"I'll be fine," I said. "It hasn't even soaked through," I lied.

She glared at me for a moment, seeing if I would crack. Then she settled down, seeming to believe me.

"Let's press on," Dad said. "He can dry out in the cave."

It didn't seem worthwhile to avoid the pools of water for the rest of the way, but I did, dragging my soppy self over every rock and every pool.

The floor of the cave was drier than the immediate land outside, but it reeked with the scent of moisture and seemed to ooze sea air out of every pore. Most of the room inside was in inaccessibly tight spaces but there was a small area in which to sit and dry out.

I took off the pants, wrung them out, and placed them flat out on a nearby rock. My boxer shorts underneath were also soaked. I tried to hide the sodden underwear from my mother but a mother sees all; she forced me to strip naked. The soaked boxers rested next to the jeans, imprinting soggy outlines onto the rocks.

My dad still mocked me so my mother insisted he let me use his jacket to wipe the moisture from my lower body. I took my time and enjoyed every second, standing in front of him as I did so. I watched his face twist in disgust when I reached my nether regions. I reveled in his pain, taking my time to thoroughly dry the area, front and back. I gave him the jacket back with dry legs and a smug smile. If not for my mother, the jacket would have been in the sea, with me following close behind.

My boxer shorts and jeans were still damp by the time we decided to leave, but they had dried out considerably. I wrung them again and slipped them on. The denim clung to my legs like hair to soap, but it felt better than walking around half naked.

It was close to one when we left the cave and began the long walk back. I wasn't happy with the wasted time but conceded that it was probably my fault, although I only told myself that. I told my parents it was *their* fault.

They dallied on the rocks somewhat, insisting on taking in the scenery and walking slowly so they weren't dealt the same fate as me. We arrived back at the car before two.

"Come on, I'll be late," I said in the backseat, kicking my legs, trying to peddle the car like in *The Flintstones*.

"Calm down," my mother insisted.

"I'm hungry," Dad said, starting up the car. "Are you hungry, sweetheart?" he asked my mother.

"Not really."

"I am. Maybe we should stop for something to eat."

"You're joking me!" I interjected.

I thought he *was* joking—it seemed like the sort of thing he would do—but as it turned out, he wasn't. He persuaded my mother to join him for a fish lunch on the deck of a large seaside restaurant. All the while I glared at him and glanced brazenly at my watch.

"You're doing this on purpose, aren't you?" I asked him as he nibbled on a large chip like it was the last crisp in the bag.

He grinned. "Just a bit, yes,"

I groaned and threw up my hands. "This is so unfair!"

"Life is unfair, kiddo," he stated.

"But you don't have to try to make it worse," I noted.

He shrugged and checked his watch. "I'm just playing with you, son, there's plenty of time. A couple extra minutes won't hurt, will they?"

He was wrong. It did matter. Every second that wasn't spent with Lizzie was agonizing, and seemed like a waste.

"You've finished now," I said, looking at his empty plate. "Let's go."

He leaned back in his chair. He sighed deeply, rubbed his stomach, and then stood. I stood alongside him, eager and twitchy. He looked at his watch again, opened his mouth laboriously to speak, and then stated: "I'm going to the toilet."

I threw myself down, frustrated, flustered.

"Your dad is just playing with you," my mother said softly, her husband now strolling sedately through the restaurant to find the bathroom. "He's only being like this because it's affecting you," she pondered for a moment. "And I think he wants revenge for what you did to his jacket."

Another hour drifted by before we were back on the road. I was still angry with my father and he was still mocking me from the driver's seat, but I also noticed he seemed to be going above the speed limit and getting frustrated whenever someone slowed him down. Consciously or not, he was hurrying for me.

We were on the road a mere fifteen minutes, less than a third of the way to the campground, when we hit heavy traffic. Lines of cars, vans, and trucks sat end to end up to the fog-infested horizon, revving impatiently in their own allotted slice of motorway.

"No," I said nervously, peering through the middle of my parents and out through the windshield. "You've got to be kidding me."

Dad groaned. "Looks like there has been an accident," he said casually.

"Just my luck!" I spat.

They both turned to look at me.

"What?" I snapped back. They shrugged and turned away.

"What now?" I wondered.

"Now, we wait," Dad said. He leaned back on his chair, turned up the radio slightly, and settled in for the long wait.

"But I need to get back."

"Sorry, son," he said.

"This is your fault," I told him, annoyed. "If we'd have left earlier we'd have missed it."

"You're probably right," he said. He turned around to look at me over his shoulder. "Sorry, kiddo."

I felt a cauldron of frustrated anger boiling up inside of me. I felt a strong urge to unleash it on him, but the sincerity in his eyes turned that boiling rage down to a simmer. I slumped back in my seat and groaned heavily.

It was after five when we arrived back at the campground. I rushed to the park, holding onto the slithered possibility that her parents had withheld their journey and Lizzie would be waiting for me.

She wasn't.

I waited in the park until the light had been sucked completely out of the day, then I trudged back to the camper.

"She left," I told my parents.

"I'm sorry, son." My mother put a sympathetic hand around my shoulder, but I shrugged it off.

"It's okay," Dad said merrily. "You can see her again in a week or two. You have her number right?"

I perked up somewhat—he was right. I had been so caught up with my desire to see her one last time that I had forgotten about the number. She was my girlfriend now. I had her number. I could call her anytime I liked, talk to her about anything I wanted to. It wasn't like when we had first met and she had promptly disappeared out of my life. This time I could get her back. She was just a phone call away.

I stuffed my hand into my pocket. The smile that had barely been on my face for a second or two was already slipping away. Where I should have felt cardboard, I felt only mush.

The card had absorbed the water from the tide pool and had practically dissolved. I pulled it out of my pocket in bits, some soggy slips fell to the floor, others stuck to my fingers and my palm.

I looked at the mess on my hand in disbelief. In the background, Dad groaned sympathetically. I felt my mother's hand on my shoulder again, and this time I didn't brush it away.

The number was unreadable; it wasn't even clear that a number had ever been there. My hopes of seeing or hearing from Lizzie again had vanished into a mushy mess of soggy cardboard.

8

Love in the Work Place
Part One: Silence

After high school, my life stagnated somewhat. As planned, I stayed on for a sixth form education but I had no desire to move on to college or university.

I took a job packing shelves at the local supermarket at seventeen, and although I despised every minute of the job, I was helped through the tedium by two new relationships.

The first was a friendship with a guy named Matthew. He was a couple years older than me and had been at the store for the last few months. It was his job to show me around during the first week.

"Been there, done that, would advise against."

It was my first day; twenty minutes in, I had been introduced to Matthew and advised to follow him. He was slouching at the back of the store, gesturing to the female staff who drifted by.

He pointed out a scruffy girl of around nineteen unenthusiastically helping an old lady with her shopping.

"I chatted her up on my first day," he explained. "I figured she was the best looking member of staff here, give or take a cougar or two." He winked at me. I wasn't entirely sure why but I smiled back. He intrigued me and I wanted to make a good impression. "You like 'em hairy?" he asked.

"Hairy?" I wondered.

Matthew pointed toward his groin, "Down below."

"Not really," I said slowly.

"Me neither," he said with a distasteful shake of his head, his eyes back on the young girl who had walked away from the old woman and was cursing under her breath at the experience. "Best to stay away from Chewbacca over there then. Never seen anything like it; she could have tied Pigtails on her stomach."

The girl came to within a few feet of us. The look of ugly apathy fell from her face and was replaced with a shy smile, her eyes catching Matthew.

"Morning, Matty," she said happily.

Matthew held up a hand in acknowledgment and she disappeared around the corner and into another aisle, out of sight.

Matthew shuddered.

He wasn't a particularly striking man, but he possessed a certain charm. He was confident, charismatic, and funny. He had the slightest suggestion of dimples which opened up either side of his cheeks when he flashed his cheeky smile.

Matthew thrust himself away from the wall and labored forward, gesturing for me to follow as he cut across the top of the supermarket and glanced down the passing aisles.

The supermarket had been the first job I applied for after leaving school. It hadn't been my decision. My mother had insisted I continue my studies; my father wanted me to learn a trade. I wanted to do nothing for a couple years and enjoy my youth. Applying for a menial job seemed to be the best solution; that way we were all disappointed.

My friends seemed to be having a better time of it. Peter had moved on to college and was studying for degrees in philosophy and psychology, with a view to a career as a psychologist or psychiatrist. An academic path was surprising considering he hadn't been the brightest kid in the class, but it was no surprise he picked one that involved sitting down all day and letting others do the talking.

Olly had initially taken a job at a fast food restaurant, but had been sacked on the first day after refusing an order on the basis that the customer was fat enough and a hamburger was the last thing she needed. On recommendation from the guidance counselor, he moved to a training placement on a building site. He didn't possess any of the qualities needed, but the counselor decided that even Olly would struggle to find people to insult there.

Max had tried and failed to get into college, in what was perhaps the only placement to ever be refused in the history of a college whose doors were open to everybody. No one understood why, but he *had* filled out his name and age incorrectly on the application form. Deciding the responsibility was his, Max's dad had then taken him into the family business. For eight hours a day, it was now the job of everyone else in the printing firm to make sure that Max didn't touch anything.

"You see Michelle over there," Matthew gestured down to the end of the frozen food aisle. A bubbly woman in her mid-twenties was chatting loudly to a male employee anxiously playing with his hands and looking around for the exit.

"Her as well?" I asked.

"Yep, I'm afraid to admit it."

I doubted he was afraid to admit it. He pointed her out, after all. I was confident that if Matthew had drunken sex with a horse, he would still brag about it.

"She looks okay," I said genuinely. The girl was curvy, had a suffocating pair of breasts, and short shiny hair. She looked the sort who had conversations *at* people rather than with them, but she seemed pleasant.

"That's what *I* thought," Matthew said. He nodded slowly at me, as if recalling the death of a loved one. "But she's fucking nuts. You ever heard of a fetish where the girl squeezes the guy's balls until he passes out?"

I recoiled. "God no. Do people really do that?"

Matthew shook his head solemnly. "I don't know—if not, then she tried to start a trend. Don't get me wrong, I like 'em kinky, but there's a line. She picked up that line and crushed the fucking life outta it."

"Ouch," I said through gritted teeth.

"Took me a fortnight before I could come without screaming."

We both looked quietly down the aisle at Michelle. The target of her talking had managed to worm his way out of the conversation and was backtracking down the next aisle, prepared to run if she followed. Michelle waved him away pleasantly and then turned down the aisle, toward us. We scuppered quickly out of view, a blur of color in her eyes.

The next female employee we saw was the assistant manager. She was in her fifties. She was well dressed and well presented, but she looked her age. Her face was lined with stress and fatigue, her skin leathery from years of beach vacations and hard living.

I was not surprised to hear that Matthew had had sex with her as well. Apparently on the assumption that she was the senior manager, but also because she was available and he was horny.

If anyone else had professed such sexual conquests, I would have doubted them, but Matthew was charming and he wasn't choosy.

After an hour of loitering and avoiding work, I began to earn my pay. Matthew showed me into a large storeroom that housed the stock for the supermarket. He told me to stack DVDs, games, and CDs while he headed back into the store to clear outdated perishables.

The storeroom was dark and resembled a bleak warehouse. Everything the supermarket stocked was in there in its packaged form, stacked on massive shelving units that stretched to twice my height and ran in intersecting lines over the black linoleum floor. Fluorescent lights had been fitted in the ceiling above the shelves, lighting the stock but providing a dim gloom for the alleyways in between.

It was dark and musty. The only sounds were the intermittent creaking of plastic and cardboard as the products shivered in the darkness.

I found the multimedia section after a few minutes and set to work pulling games from a bottom shelf and checking them against a list Matthew had given me. A sound from over my crouched shoulder interrupted me and nearly gave me a heart attack.

I turned to see a petite blonde standing over me, her hands clasped together behind her back. She peered down at me with amusement in her eyes.

"You scared me half to death," I said, holding my chest as I clambered warily to my feet.

The smile remained on her face; she didn't say anything.

I held out my hand. "Kieran McCall," I said proudly.

She looked at the extended appendage but didn't grasp it.

"And *you* are?" I wondered. She hadn't been in the store when Matthew had been running through his little black book.

She lifted her eyes to mine again. My hand was still outstretched.

"Are you okay?" I asked in lieu of anything else.

She pulled her right hand from behind her back, but instead of shaking my hand, she grasped my wrist and tugged it to her chest. Then she thrust my hand onto her breast.

She lowered her hand. I kept mine where it was. It felt right.

The smile was still wide on her face.

"Very nice," I said, nodding. "Do you have a name at all? I mean, this feels a little we—"

She dove forward and clasped her lips onto mine. As her tongue worked its way over my teeth, she thrust her pelvis forward, connecting with my groin. Then she took my hand again and moved it around her back, allowing me to grip her backside, firm and teasing underneath her trousers.

At that point I was still a virgin. If she had thrust any closer or for any longer then I would have had to read up on the technicalities of my virginity while I walked ashamedly away and tried to never look her, whoever she was, in the eye again.

I had prepared myself mentally for the first moment I had sex. I reasoned I would be anxious and scared, but knew I would have to take control, to act like a man who knew what he was doing and not to make an idiot of myself. It never occurred to me that my first encounter would be with someone who guided me every step of the way.

She took control of everything and used me like an anatomically correct puppet with lock-in appendages. She stripped me naked and then took her own clothes off. I forced myself to think about something unsexy while I watched her tease her way out of her uniform and expose her tanned flesh inch by inch.

I waited for her and she guided me to the floor. The linoleum was cold against my bare buttocks, and the bottom of my spine clicked and cracked on first compression against the solid floor. I ignored the discomfort and concentrated on her, on us.

She stayed on top. She didn't look at me much during, but I couldn't take my eyes off her. Not because of her evident beauty, but because I wanted to make sure she was enjoying herself. She seemed to be.

She seemed to be lost in her own euphoric world. She grabbed her own hair, closed her eyes and rocked her head back and forth, using my body like a fairground ride.

I finished almost as soon as we started. I gritted my teeth and tried to think sexy thoughts—the thought never occurred to me to look at the naked body writhing on top of me—until she finished. She did so with a gasp and a shudder, then she let her hair down and rolled off without looking at me.

She dressed with me still on the floor. I waited for her to say something ("thank you" would have been nice) but she departed without a word, leaving just a smile.

I dressed with a grin and then looked around excitedly. I thought about running into the supermarket and telling everyone that I had just had sex, but I composed myself, finished my job—hurriedly— and went to tell Matthew.

"You must know her," I pleaded. "Blonde. Short. Tight body."

Matthew shook his head and looked at me as if I was mad. "Doesn't ring a bell."

I hadn't received the reception I had hoped. I thought Matthew would join in with my revelry, even congratulate me, but he didn't seem to know who I was talking about.

"About seventeen. Eighteen." I put a hand on my hip and kicked it out. "Walks with a little bit of a swagger, showing off her ass."

Matthew shook his head.

"Maybe she just started. Like me."

"You're the only starter this week, mate."

"Maybe you just haven't met her yet," I pushed.

"I've met everyone," Matthew said confidently. "Shagged most of them," he added with a wry smile.

"No one could have escaped your notice?"

Matthew sighed, annoyed with the route of questioning. He lowered his head in thought. "Let me see," he said, a finger on his chin. "Nope."

I visibly deflated.

"There was one I never shagged," Matthew said, brightening up.

"Really?"

"Not sure what her name was, cute though. Little minx as well," Matthew looked into the middle distance, reflectively.

"Go on . . ."

"Little sexy blonde thing she was. Very nice body. Tanned. Bit on the short side."

"That sounds like her."

He looked shocked. "Can't be, mate. She topped herself."

"What?"

"Yeah, that's why I never got a shot at her. She had issues, she was shagging the manager and he finished with her. They reckoned it was enough to send her over the edge. She killed herself in the storeroom."

His words sunk in and I felt the life drain out of me. It all made sense.

"She didn't speak," I said distantly. "I thought she was shy, but I mean, well, I—" I paused to look at Matthew; he seemed to be having trouble expressing something. "How did she do it?"

"OD'd on Rampant Rabbits."

"Is that like a rave drug?" I wondered earnestly.

"Dildos, mate. They found her naked on the floor, every orifice plugged. They vibrated the fucking life outta her."

"Really?"

Matthew burst out laughing and shoved me lightly on the shoulder. "You're fucking gullible, mate," he said merrily.

I felt my face redden with embarrassment, although a big part of me was delighted I hadn't lost my virginity to a horny ghost.

"I'm gonna have so much fun with you," he said after a while, sucking in deep mouthfuls of air to catch his breath, wiping a tear from his eye. "Fucking classic mate, love it."

"Hilarious," I said, feeling a reluctant smile creep onto my face.

"Nah, that's Louisa," he said eventually. "She's been here a few weeks. Strange girl, nice body though."

"Have you and her . . ."

"Nope. I tried, but, well," he shook his head regrettably, "she wasn't having any of it."

I was pleased Matthew hadn't been with her and I felt honored that she had chosen me, even if she had done so without giving herself much time to think about it.

"Good for you, mate," Matthew said, tapping my shoulder and bringing a proud smile to my face.

"Thanks. She didn't speak to me though."

"Perfect."

"No, I mean, *at all*. Not before, not after. I'm not even sure she looked at me afterward," I lied. I *was* sure, she hadn't looked at me. There had been a smile on her face but it wasn't directed at anyone.

Matthew shrugged placidly. "She never talks, but who cares? You got yours. Consider it a plus."

I took Matthew's advice and thought of it as just that. Over the next couple days, I thought of little else but Louisa and the episode in the storeroom. I created a whole world of scenarios for her and her reluctance to talk. In my favorite one she had been struck down by nerves after falling head over heels in love with me. It didn't explain why she didn't talk to others, but I didn't let that bother me.

I looked for Louisa during the rest of the shift and on the following day. I couldn't find her. I wondered if I would ever see her again, let alone get the chance to repeat the sexual encounter. Then she pounced on me again in the storeroom.

This time we had sex in front of the vegetables. I had the smell of earth and pesticide in my nostrils as I gave her the best three minutes and twenty-two seconds of her life. I know that because I counted. She hadn't been looking at me again so I checked my progress on a large wall clock over her shoulder.

She finished without looking at me and dressed quickly.

Lying naked, cold, and smiling on the floor, I watched her leave without saying a word.

We repeated the rendezvous three hours later when I went into the storeroom to pick up some boxes of cereal, and then twice the following day. I began to get horny just walking into the storeroom, and even the sight of stock turned me on.

The storeroom became my second home. Fellow employees knew that if they couldn't find me, I would be stalking those darkened corridors with a sinister lust in my eyes. They thought I was weird. Matthew thought I was a god. Louisa didn't seem to think anything of me.

I decided I needed to speak to her. I wanted to have a relationship with her that didn't revolve around sordid—and enjoyable—meetings in darkened rooms. I also reasoned that she didn't know my name, and if it hadn't been for a proxy, I wouldn't know hers.

I took my opportunity during our thirteenth session—not only had I been counting but I had kept a timesheet of each. The longest we had managed was four minutes, five seconds. The longest I personally had managed was eight thrusts; it just wasn't worth timing. I rolled her over and clambered on top. She resisted, and in doing so she made eye contact with me for the first time during intercourse.

On top of her, I stared down into her eyes, thrusting gently to keep her entertained. Complimentary, if anything. I had finished during the struggle. She turned away, her cheek on the cold floor, her eyes staring into a bottle of dish soap.

"I need to speak to you," I said, realizing it wasn't the best opening line for the situation, but struck dumb in the moment.

I heard a soft moan escape her lips and her head scraped up and down on the floor, but she didn't reply, she didn't even look at me.

"Please," I begged, realizing this was exactly how I thought I'd lose my virginity: naked and pleading.

She groaned again in reply, a little quicker this time. I felt some resistance as she thrust her pelvis upward, lifting me an inch off the floor, forcing me deeper. She was in a hurry to finish.

I stopped moving. I remained still.

She thrust against me, telling me she didn't need me to move.

I pulled back, far enough to leave her thrusts fleshless.

"Talk to me," I begged again.

She turned her head. I smiled as I waited for her eyes to meet mine.

I lowered myself into her in anticipation. She was going to speak. She looked over my face: my eyes, my nose, my lips.

"Just hurry up and fuck me, would you?" she snapped.

I had expected a voice that could lull angels to sleep. What I got was the bitter tone of a psychopath.

"But—"

"Fuck me and then *fuck off*," she spat. "I don't need this. I'll go and find someone else. Just hurry up." She turned her head to the side again, her eyes back on the soap.

I was hurt and insulted. I felt dirty. I wanted to pull out and leave—already I could feel my erection growing flaccid in shame—but I didn't want to incur her wrath.

I soldiered on. Treating it like a shameful workout.

We broke our record that afternoon. She lasted for a full ten minutes. I thought she would never finish.

For the last time, Louisa dressed without saying a word, but for the first time I was dressed before her. I tried to catch her eye as I waited for her to leave, but she never looked at me. I never saw her innocent smile or heard her venomous words ever again.

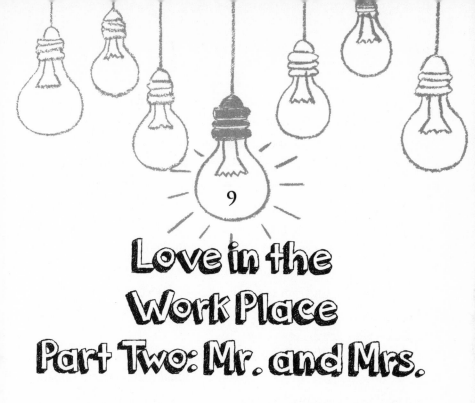

Love in the Work Place Part Two: Mr. and Mrs.

At the supermarket I stacked shelves, avoided a psychopath, counted stock, and took abuse from a pudgy, irritating floor manager for another two years.

I hated every minute of it, but Matthew helped me through the tedium. He became a good friend, and the only one I saw outside of work as I lost touch with my other friends.

I didn't have many aspirations in life, but I did want to quit my job at the supermarket for something that didn't drain my soul. Something in an office. Somewhere I could wear a tie and sit down.

I applied for half a dozen jobs a week, and eventually I landed myself a position with a company that made paper and office stationery. I was going to be stuck in a cubicle all day making and receiving telephone calls. It was nothing exciting, but it was what I wanted.

I got my office, and more importantly, I got my tie.

"It's *The Pink Panther*," I exclaimed, proudly holding up the tie.

"What the hell is *The Pink Panther?*"

My mouth dropped open. The material emblazoned with the comical creation fell back to my neatly pressed blue shirt.

It was my first day. I had started with a smile and that smile hadn't faded when I met a manager who danced on the borderline between grumpy irritant and chronic depressive. It hadn't faded during my first half hour, which I had spent trying to sell paper to an old woman who only wanted to talk about her grandson.

Now, standing in front of a coworker—a short, slim, mild-mannered brunette with shy eyes and thin lips—it dripped from my face like warm ice cream.

"You don't know what *The Pink Panther* is?"

Her eyes lowered to the floor. She twiddled with a strand of hair that sprang from behind her ear. "No," she said faintly.

"How old are you?"

She made eye contact again. "Eighteen."

I shrugged. "Fair enough."

"But you're not much older," she noted. She had released the lock and was now tampering with the plastic casing from a readymade sandwich.

"My dad liked *The Pink Panther* films. I grew up on them, I guess. *Monty Python* as well; he loved *Monty Python*."

"Who?"

I raised a questionable eyebrow.

She laughed. "Only joking."

Her name was Melissa, and I liked her. I had seen her when I first entered the building and was shown around by the manager. He paraded around with the enthusiasm of a dying sloth, but I was heavy on his heels, eyeing up my new surroundings and my new colleagues.

Melissa's desk was on the other side of the room from mine. I had spied her tangled brunette mane as I talked to my first few customers. I caught up with her at lunchtime and had just finished eating my packed lunch with her.

She was shy, but I liked that. She had a certain childish innocence about her that told me she would be a good friend, a good partner. One who wouldn't rape me on the storeroom floor and refuse to look at me.

"Well, I better get back to work," Melissa stood up. She wore a tartan knee-length skirt over black tights; she dusted it clear of crumbs and pulled taut a crease. "I've got to make a personal call first."

"Okay."

"Nice to meet you, Kieran."

I took her extended hand. She had warm, moist hands and a delicate handshake. "You too."

She departed and left me alone in the small kitchen. In the silence, I could hear the sales patter from the main room as employees sacrificed their breaks to increase their commission.

I was enjoying the final ten minutes of my break, thinking about Melissa, when someone else joined me in the kitchen.

She smiled at me as she crossed the threshold. Dark features, glaring eyes.

"Hey," I said meekly.

She didn't reply. She went straight to the fridge, opened it and ducked down to peer inside, her tight buttocks thrust outwardly as she did so.

"I'm Kieran," I said anxiously. The perky cheeks were less than a foot away from me, wiggling and gyrating. "And—and, you are?"

She's flirting, I thought to myself. *Bums don't move like that. It's not natural.*

Like Melissa, she was wearing a knee-length skirt, but unlike Melissa, her legs weren't wrapped in opaque tights. They were bare and exposed.

"Do you like what you see?" she said, without turning around.

Is she talking to the fridge?

"I guess."

She turned, closed the fridge, and sat down opposite me. She had taken out a yogurt and, after peeling back the lid, she licked the creamy substance off its underside, watching me as she did so.

I felt awkward and didn't know where to look. I licked specks of excess mayonnaise from my fingers and quickly stopped, pretending to inspect my nails instead. I didn't want her to think I was reciprocating.

She was attractive—her solid body and raven beauty displayed a woman of no more than thirty-five, the superfluous skin around her neck and the spiderweb wrinkles in the corners of her eyes giving away her true age—but she radiated a devilish aura that suggested she would chew me up and spit me out.

I looked into her eyes again. She had finished with the lid of the yogurt and was now working the tip of her tongue around the lip.

"Do you want a spoon?" I asked.

She quickly cleaned the lip and put the yogurt down on the table. She rested her elbows on the sleek surface and leaned across—close enough for me to smell the strawberry flavors curdling in her mouth.

"I've been watching you, Kieran," she spoke softly. I could feel the words on my face. "I've been admiring you."

I hadn't seen her until she walked into the kitchen. There were a dozen or so employees in the main room. I had met with a few—including Melissa—and exchanged friendly smiles or nods with a few more. This sultry cougar hadn't been one of them.

"Do you want me to show you a good time?" She spoke in even softer tones, a euphoric, almost orgasmic edge to the words. So much so that I had to check to see what she was doing with her hands.

"Sure," I said. I still felt awkward under her promiscuous gaze, but she was attractive and I hadn't had sex with anyone since the storeroom succubus.

I liked Melissa, but I was still too awkward when it came to sex and relationships. Melissa was innocent, shy; I would have to make all the moves with her. But the glint in the eyes of the cougar suggested that I would barely need to move. It said *I have some things to teach you*, and I was desperate to learn.

The tip of her tongue popped out of her mouth again. She used it to gently lick her lips before leaning forward and flicking it against mine.

I thought she was going in for a kiss; I opened my mouth, moved forward. She pulled back an inch. I felt like an idiot. I instinctively tried to hide my embarrassment with a cough and fired spittle over her face.

She didn't react. "In the stationery cupboard," she said softly, ignoring a droplet of saliva on her forehead. "Ten minutes." She sunk forward, teased my lips open with her tongue, kissed my teeth, licked the tip of my nose, and then pulled back. She left the room before I had time to wonder just how crazy she was.

The next ten minutes were even more awkward than the previous ten. I couldn't find the stationery cupboard and had an erect and increasingly agitated penis to deal with. I swept through the building like James Bond, keen for the bulge in my pants not to be seen as I checked door after door, looking but failing to find any marked stationery.

I hoped the erection would die, and indeed I pleaded with it to do just that. But my penis seemed to thrive on anxiety, and the more nervous I grew, the more *it* grew. It was also hard to ignore a little voice inside me screaming *I'm gonna have sex, I'm gonna have sex!*

The majority of the rooms in the building were empty. The company was a fairly recent start-up and had seemingly inherited a mansion to help it grow.

Annoyed, frustrated, and finally growing limp, I ducked out of the shadows after twenty minutes of searching. That's when I heard a noise: a hushed squeak, like the warning call of a dying rodent.

The door ahead of me was open a touch; I could see a thin strip of blackness where the tanned wood met the magnolia doorframe.

There was movement in the darkness, illuminated slightly by the fluorescent lights in the corridor. A gray shuffling. Something living, something big.

I heard the noise again. Louder this time. More urgent.

I remained standing, delighted that my erection had dampened back to flaccidity now that I was apparently being watched by a giant fucking rat.

The door opened without warning, swinging wide and proud on its axis. I made an instinctual jump backward.

Standing in the doorway, illuminated in a jaundiced glow by the fluorescent light from the corridor, was the cougar. She was stark naked.

My blood rushed south again. I remained still, caught in a trance.

In the sickly glow, her pale flesh looked orange. As with her tight features and outwardly visible figure, the naked body before me professed to be a lot younger than it was. Her breasts—no doubt fake, but impressive nonetheless—stood firm above a streamlined stomach, from which only a thin slither of extra flesh hung, descending southward toward a clean-shaven pubic area.

I dove into the room, brushing past her warm body. She smelled of lilies, desire, and shame. The scent of a cougar.

She snapped on the light and told me to get undressed.

"Sorry I'm late," I said, unbuttoning my pants and letting them fall to my ankles. "You know how it is."

I kicked off my shoes and then my trousers. "So, stationery cupboard, eh? Good thing it's not an actual cupboard, we'd never get moved. I'm not even sure you'd fit." I paused before pulling off my sweatshirt. "Not that you're fat or anything. *I* wouldn't fit either." She didn't seem to hear; her eyes were on my boxer shorts, waiting for them to disappear.

"Lot of cupboards in this place," I continued. "You'd think they'd all be stationery cupboards, wouldn't you?" My fingers fumbled nervously on the elastic of my boxers. She was still staring in anticipation, it made me anxious.

"What?" she said, snapping out of her trance. She lifted her eyes to my face, giving me the perfect opportunity to slide out of my underwear.

"Well, you know. It's a stationery company, isn't it? I mean—"

"Shut up and fuck me." She moved forward and grabbed me.

"What about protection?" I asked timidly.

"It doesn't matter." She grabbed my penis roughly, and I yelped and moved back. "I'm on the pill." She moved onto me again, grabbing with more ferocity this time. I closed my eyes and let her.

"I was thinking more about me," I said.

I hadn't bothered about protection with Louisa; it hadn't even crossed my mind. A few months ago, I had seen an advertisement about sexually transmitted infections. After that, a day rarely went by when I didn't imagine that my urine was off-color; my semen hadn't always looked like that; and that pimple was really a small, infectious wart. The paranoia dissipated a few weeks ago, but it was still fairly fresh in my mind.

"You'll be fine," she insisted.

"Really?" I practically squealed. She had a hold of my balls now, and it felt like she had something against them. "But I don't know where you've been."

She stopped, released my testicles from her grip, and took a step back.

"I didn't mean it like that. That sounded bad," I backtracked. "What I meant was—"

You're a slut and are probably diseased, I said to myself.

"—You can never be too sure."

That was the slogan of the advertisement. It was the only thing I could think of; it was hard to think with an erection and aching balls.

"I don't have a condom." She leaned back against the shelving unit, placed her palm on her stomach, and slowly moved it downward with splayed fingers. "Do you want to get dressed and walk away? Or do you want to fuck me?"

I thought about walking away, but not for long.

We did it up against the shelves. She was flexible and nimble for her age. I wondered if she was in her thirties after all and just had really poor skin.

I came instantly. I had experience with Louisa, and I hoped it would turn me into a sex machine, but it didn't. I pushed on regardless, wondering just what damage I had subjected my testicles to over the last few minutes and if they would survive the final push.

She was a screamer and I worried that someone would hear us. I had images of walking back into the call-room to catcalls and jeers. I imagined a look on Melissa's face, one of disappointment, of shame. It said: *I thought you were better than that, I thought you liked me. I had such high hopes for you.* I clamped my mouth onto hers at every opportunity, silencing her by sticking my tongue into her mouth. She resisted initially, shaking her head from side to side as she tried to enjoy her own ride without me interrupting it, but eventually she yielded and her screams died in my mouth.

"You have stamina," she said afterward. She was breathless, her face flushed, her hair all over the place. She looked like someone who had just had sex, but, like my dad used to say, whenever a woman was ill or acting strange, *it's probably the menopause.* I was sure my fellow employees would jump to that conclusion as well.

"Thank you," I said proudly.

"And you like to kiss, don't you?"

I smiled shyly.

I climbed back into my clothes and watched as she did the same. "So, back to work," I said, wondering if I should kiss her affectionately or thank her. I didn't know how it worked when the other person didn't swear or walk away. "Which cubicle is yours?" I asked.

"I don't work here," she said placidly.

"Oh."

"Do you really think I would work in a hole like this?" she wondered in tones of disgust.

"I guess not," I said, confused slightly. "So, what are you doing here?"

"Helping out, killing time," she shrugged impassively. "Whatever. I'm just here because my husband runs the place."

"Husband?"

She didn't reply; she just smiled and planted a kiss on my bemused cheek. Then she was gone, leaving me in a small room wondering how I had missed the signs and contemplating how long I had before the grumpy manager killed or fired me.

On the walk back to my desk, I felt like I was a criminal being paraded through the streets. I was sure all eyes were on me, judging me, waiting to pelt rotten fruit at my head.

I made it to the cubicle next to mine before someone spoke.

"Where you been?"

His name was Jack, or John. It might have been Jason. I had met him earlier in the day. He had introduced himself along with two others and was an unremarkable man.

"I got lost," I said flatly.

"Lost?" He didn't seem to believe me. "The building's not that big."

"Lot of doors," I said, as if that cleared me.

"But this is the only main room. It's *the* main room, it's mass—"

"That's beside the point," I said, feeling flushed under his accusing glare.

He stalled, as though waiting for an explanation, and when one didn't come he shrugged it off and changed topic. "You see Mrs. Mann come through?"

I looked at him with raised eyebrows.

"The boss's wife," he explained.

I shook my head and turned a deeper shade of red.

"She just passed," he said in a friendly tone. "She looked like she'd been on a rollercoaster, wonder what got into her."

"*Nothing*, I don't think *anything* got into her," I coughed and ducked behind the cubicle wall, hiding a face on fire. "I'm sure. I mean, it was probably the menopause," I finished with a laugh, immediately regretting it. Too high, too abrupt, too fake.

I waited for a prompt reply. It didn't come. I lifted my head up ever so slightly, peering above the partition wall. I was half expecting him to be taking notes or phoning the manager to tell him I had slept with his wife.

He wasn't on the phone, nor was he writing on a notepad. He was looking straight at me, his eyes waiting to meet mine as they popped up.

I laughed again and awkwardly pretended to be playing a childish game with him. I cleared my throat and then moved my attention to my call list and my work. Eventually he stopped staring at me.

"Jack is a dick," I told Melissa the following day.

"Who?"

We were in the kitchen again. She was biting into another packaged sandwich; I had already hungrily munched my way through mine.

"Jack," I said. "Maybe John."

She shook her head.

"Jason? The guy who sits next to me."

"Andrew," she said with a nod and a smile.

"Yes, *him*," I shrugged. "He's a dick."

She giggled. I liked her giggle; it was soft, endearing. "What makes you say that?"

I shrugged. "It's complicated. Just, I don't know, watch out for him."

She looked at me silently for a moment, deep in thought. She picked at her egg salad sandwich, grabbing small chunks of it and popping them into her mouth, taking her time to chew them thoroughly.

"Okay," she said eventually.

"He hasn't said anything to you yet, has he?" I asked, trying not to come across as suspicious or crazy but sounding like I was about to murder her and stuff her body into the fridge.

She shook her head, teasing a small chunk of bread onto her tongue and pulling it into her mouth.

"Good, just be—"

Movement from the doorway behind Melissa interrupted me. I swallowed my words and my confidence as the manager's wife walked in.

"Good afternoon," she said, winking at me over Melissa's shoulder.

Melissa turned and replied, just missing the wink. I stayed silent. She drifted into the kitchen with the grace and confidence of a supermodel. I sat rigid with the awkwardness of a teenager *watching* a supermodel.

Melissa flashed me a warning glance. She tried to tell me something with her eyes, probably that the horny middle-aged woman behind her was the manager's wife and wasn't picky about where she had sex, or who with. But I already knew that.

"I better get going," Melissa said, after a cursory glance at her watch.

I watched her leave, feeling a wave of relief wash over me.

"Hello, Kieran." The cougar sat down opposite. She didn't have a yogurt this time, but her tongue was toying with her lips again.

I glanced around, making sure no one was nearby. "Listen," I said, leaning in, "what happened yesterday was a mistake, I don't—"

"A mistake?" she fluttered her eyes like a cartoon character. "Oh, you do say some cruel things," she said, exaggerating offense.

"It's true; it was a mistake, we—"

"So you don't want to do it again then?" she said, perking up.

"What? No, who—"

"Me. You. Now. Storeroom?"

She leaned back, exposing her breasts, which were tightly pressed into a low hanging blouse. A frilly black bra strap had slipped out from under the blouse and ran a tempting line over slender shoulders.

"I don't—"

She plucked at the strap, peeling it away. Then she lowered the blouse, exposing the flesh beneath.

"Just this once," I warned, pointing my finger at her.

"Just this once," she agreed.

We had sex in that storeroom every day for the next two weeks. I found out her name was Charlotte, but she preferred I called her Mrs. Mann. She said it made her feel dirtier. She liked to feel dirty.

The sex started out simple. We met in the storeroom every day during lunch and had sex up against the shelving unit, keeping an ear out for anyone who might pass by outside. But Mrs. Mann grew louder with every session and avoided any attempts I made to silence her. It was almost like she wanted to be caught.

On the fifth day, she told me the storeroom was off bounds and insisted we have sex in the kitchen. I refused, but she undressed and after that it was all an anxious and sexy blur.

I vowed never to have sex in such a risky place again—and told myself never to eat off the kitchen table again—but that was just the beginning. During the second week, she came to my cubicle under the guise of handing out instruction pamphlets, and when no one was looking, she dipped under the desk and gave me a blow-job. I saw Jack looking over at me a few times, wondering why I was smiling and where Mrs. Mann had suddenly disappeared to. He looked like an idiot, but he couldn't be that stupid.

It all came to a head on the third week. I had secured a weekend cinema date with Melissa and was about to face my fears and blow it off with Mrs. Mann. Things were looking up. I was confident I could do it. Then, minutes before the lunch break, the manager burst into the call room.

I had never seen him animated in the few weeks I had been working there. He was grumpy and generally miserable, but here he was slamming his fists onto the empty cubicle desks, throwing pencils, staples, and stacks of paper.

Everyone stopped what they were doing to look at him. A couple of employees had to duck out of the way of flying objects.

"Bitch!" he was repeating over and over. He was practically growling it; the sound seemed to come from a dark place deep inside of him. "Fucking, fucking bitch!" he screamed, just for variety.

I felt my heart skip so many beats I was technically dead. I had worried this moment would come, but I had hoped it wouldn't. I tried to avoid eye contact and told myself that he didn't know I was sleeping with his wife.

"The fucking slag!" he spat, his voice filling the office and the street outside.

Okay, he probably knew.

Tears were pouring from his eyes. His hands were still working aggressively on a nearby empty desk, but he was now slipping to his knees. Everyone was still watching, unsure what to do.

"Are you okay, sir?" one employee said from a distance.

That seemed to awaken Mr. Mann. He jumped back to his feet and pointed at the sympathetic talker. "You! You!" he screamed. "*All of you,*" he waved his hand around the room, looking at each of us in turn but failing to make eye contact with me. "*One* of you!"

Make your mind up.

"What's wrong?" This time it was Melissa who spoke. I felt a sting of empathy for her and was ready to launch into an attack should the angry man pick on her. He didn't.

"Someone has been fucking my wife!" he spat, throwing his arms around maniacally. "In my office! On my fucking desk!"

I gulped. The office had been her idea. The kitchen didn't seem appropriate anymore.

Mr. Mann continued his tirade for ten minutes before flopping to the floor, exhausted. An awkward pause followed where everyone exchanged glances and silently asked *should we go to lunch now?* And when the first person did, they all followed. Leaving Mr. Mann in a sobbing heap.

A handful of employees disappeared outside for a smoke, hoping to relax and exchange gossip after the spectacle. Together with Melissa, another female employee, and a man named Paul, I ducked into the kitchen for a sandwich and some gossip.

"I think it's Jack," I said, fairly quickly.

They all looked at me. Paul spoke first, "Who?"

I waved my arms about as if to pluck his name from mid-air.

"I think he means Andrew," Melissa clarified with a giggle, the innocence of which had been affected by the scene in the call-room.

"Could be," Paul said.

"He seems the sort," the woman agreed. "I've seen Mrs. Mann near his cubicle a lot."

I nodded exasperatedly. "Me too," I agreed. "I'm right next to him. I see her all the time." I felt bad for lying, so it felt good to tell the truth.

"He kept talking about how she looked the other day as well," Paul added, "That she was flustered a lot, that she had a glow. Looked like she had sex a lot, he said."

"Seems an odd thing to say," Melissa remarked.

"Very odd," the woman agreed.

"Indeed," I added, feeling as if I should get involved.

"And he *is* a very shifty character," Paul added.

The rumor mill had started turning already. I had blurted out his name on a whim, keen to keep my job and not to lose Melissa. But as the belief spread, I began to feel bad for Andrew. I didn't like the guy—there was something so innately dull and mediocre about him—but it still wasn't right to let him go down for something he didn't do.

Paul began to say something else but was cut short by the sound of restless sobs. We all turned toward the door to see our despondent manager trudge through, his head held low as the remnants of despair trickled out of his mouth.

I felt terrible seeing him in that state, even if it was a refreshing change from his usual facade of Dickensian cantankerousness. I wanted to stand and own up, but I restrained. My honesty wouldn't make him feel any better and it would make me feel a hell of a lot worse.

"Derek, sit down," Melissa said reassuringly, the deepest grain of sympathy etched in her soft tone.

He flopped down on an empty chair. I immediately felt uncomfortable in my own skin and wanted to jump right out of it. Preferably into a large hole.

Melissa rested a hand gently on his slumped shoulders. I wished she would do the same to me. I needed reassuring as well. I was shitting myself. "Talk to us," Melissa said to Mr. Mann. "You can tell us anything."

"We'll help you find out who did it," Paul said.

I looked at my fellow employee, staring daggers into the side of his face.

What a stupid thing to say, I thought. *I should have blamed him instead.*

Mr. Mann shrugged; he was in a world of his own. "I don't know who did it, but I know her type," he explained slowly, lifting his head up to meet the gazes of his expectant employees. "She likes them young, dumb, and innocent."

I was looking at the floor but I was sure he was staring at me at that point. I could feel his eyes burning into my guilty head.

"She senses their fear and stupidity like a shark sensing blood," he continued as everyone hung on his words.

If I had gained anything positive out of this situation, it was to be that at least an attractive woman had liked me without even getting to know me. Now I was beginning to doubt whether she had at all. Maybe she just thought I was stupid and naive. Maybe I *was* her type.

"I'll find him," he finished, determined.

I looked up slowly, expecting to see him glaring at me. He wasn't.

"Like Paul said," I explained. "We'll help."

He looked at me and smiled softly. "She's a bitch," he said after a short pause. "She's done it before, more than once. I thought she had finished, I thought we were okay now."

"How did you find out?" Paul wondered.

Both women had arms around the manager now. His sobbing had ceased but the melancholia lingered on his breath like a stale mint.

"My desk had been cleared. My files, everything, just shoved aside or to the floor."

I cursed to myself. She had promised she would clean up.

He continued: "I found her knickers as well. She left them there on purpose; she did this to hurt me. I just—" he broke down again, catching his head with outstretched palms and sobbing loudly into them. "I don't know why she does it!"

"She doesn't deserve you," Melissa said comfortingly. "You're a sweet, sweet man."

"And she's a bitch," I added, maybe a bit too personally.

Melissa stared at me. I stared right back. "Well, she is, isn't she?" I insisted.

"You can't say that—"

"He's right," Mr. Mann said, rising to meet the room again. "She *is* a bitch. I should have never married her. I should have never forgiven her."

An unsure silence descended. No one knew how to follow that remark.

We all contemplated the silence for a moment. Derek wiped tears from his eyes. His breathing slowed. He seemed to soften again, but he was exhausted, beaten by the tears.

Eventually he broke the silence. "She likes to take their virginity and rub my face in it."

"Sounds messy," I said quickly.

Everyone around the table looked at me and I immediately regretted speaking. I hadn't wanted the awkward silence to coat the room again so I had said the first thing that came to my mind.

I slapped a hand to my mouth. "I'm so sorry," I said through the gaps in my fingers, "Sometimes I try to make jokes when I'm uncomfortable."

"Am I making you uncomfortable?" Derek responded without missing a beat.

"No. No. Not in the least," I hesitated, hoping someone would cut in and save me. They didn't. "I mean *yeah*, a little bit. But you have every right, considering."

I ran that over in my head quickly. Did it sound like I said he had the right to make me uncomfortable because *I* was the guilty party? *Shit.*

"Because of your wife," I reiterated. "Being a slut and everything," I finished with relief. Everyone was staring at me, wide-eyed disbelief on their faces. I didn't mind, I could have said a lot worse. I almost had.

I sat defiantly next to Mrs. Mann. She had collared me outside the building and lured me to her car. She had adjusted her seat all the way back and slipped out of her knickers before I had even looked at her.

"Come on," she pleaded alluringly, waiting for me to climb on top of her.

The car was parked right outside the building. Anyone entering or exiting would see us together. This was what she wanted. Derek and I were right; she *was* a bitch.

"I refuse to have sex with you until you tell your husband I never had sex with you," I demanded.

She sat upright again, a sterner look on her face. "He knows?"

I turned rapidly in the small confines of the passenger seat. I could feel the faux leather cover squeak against my jacket. "You didn't know?"

"Well, he hasn't been home for a few days," she said softly, trailing off.

"He's been sleeping in his office," I said matter-of-factly. Turning back to face the building, pulling the trails of my jacket with me.

"I didn't know."

"Well, you do now."

I looked at her out of the corner of my eye. She seemed hurt, and she looked introspective. All along I had assumed she was some form of life-sucking sex demon, but now I realized she might actually have feelings.

"And he thinks it's you?" she asked.

I shook my head. "I don't want him to either," I said. "I have a *thing*—a potential thing anyway—with a woman. I like her. I don't want her to know."

Mrs. Mann nodded. She was staring out of the window, toward the building, her eyes caught in contemplation of the middle distance.

"I thought you wanted him to know," I said, feeling slightly befuddled about her intentions.

"I didn't. I *did*," she shook cobwebs out of her head. "I don't know. I *thought* I did. I enjoyed the rush of him finding out, and, I guess, maybe I wanted to hurt him, to pay him back—"

"For what?"

"He doesn't fuck me anymore."

"So you get revenge by fucking everyone else?"

She nodded.

"Okay," I couldn't help but smile at the madness of it. I felt a sudden need to leave; being with her was corrupting my sanity. "I have to go," I said, gripping the door handle. "Just don't tell him, okay?"

Her head was hung in thought.

"I won't."

I climbed out of the car when a thought struck me and forced me to dip my head back in. "Oh," I said, waiting for her to look at me, catching her eyes in a smile. "If it helps, tell him you were fucking a guy named Alan."

"Alan? What did he do?"

"I don't know, but he's a dick, he probably did something to deserve it."

Mr. and Mrs. Mann made up the same day. Their argument could be heard all over the building and it culminated in some very aggressive sex, which could be heard all the way to the parking lot.

Afterward Mr. Mann came out of his office with his fly unbuttoned, his shirt astray, and a large smile on his face. He sacked Alan without explanation and then went back in his office for another ear-busting session with his wife.

As luck would have it, there *was* an Alan who worked at the company. Obviously he wasn't the guy I was thinking of, but it was far too late by the time I realized.

A few weeks later, Mrs. Mann grabbed me in the hallway and bundled me into the storeroom. She kissed me deeply—without tongue—and then pulled back. I was protecting my groin and about to plead with her not to have sex with me when she pressed a finger to my lips, whispered *thank you* into my ear, and then backed out and left me alone with one of the most awkward erections I have ever had.

Through no intentions of my own, I had sparked the sexual relationship that she had always wanted with her husband. I had also started a relationship with Melissa outside of work. We had been on our first date, and although we had only exchanged a brief kiss at the end of that date, I felt better about that moment than I did about the whole sordid affair with Mrs. Mann. It felt real, natural. It felt like I was on to something good.

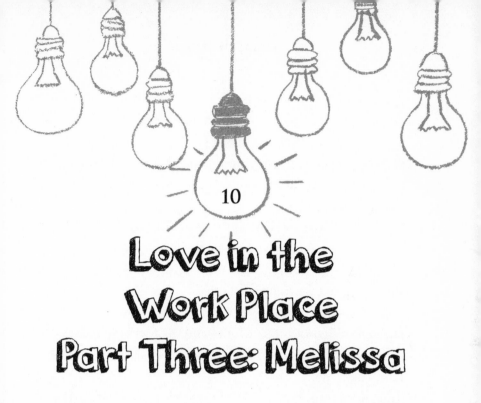

10

Love in the Work Place Part Three: Melissa

After a fairly productive first date at the movies (no embarrassing moments, one memorable kiss), Melissa and I arranged to see each other the following weekend. She gave me her phone number and asked me to call, even though we would see each other at work throughout the week.

On the first date, I had suggested the movies after she mentioned a film she wanted to see. For the second date, she didn't drop any hints and I was left to my own devices. Sensing that would lead to trouble, I consulted Matthew.

"Blow her mind," Matthew told me over a beer and a game of pool. "Take her somewhere she'll remember."

"Like?" I asked, leaning lazily on my cue as I watched him line up a long shot on the yellow.

"I don't know," he said distantly, sinking the shot. "That's up to you." He stood up, looked me in the eyes. "But it has to be fucking good. Be impressive, be different. Give her something to remember you by. Something to tell all of her little friends."

"Remember me by? I'm not dying."

He took a long drink and grinned at me over the rim of the glass. "Listen, she'll be expecting dinner, don't matter if you're broke or not."

"I am," I nodded. I really was.

"Well, seein' as you're taking this route, a dinner is the done thing. And you don't wanna do the done thing."

"*This route?*"

"Asking her out for a date an' all that."

"I like her, what else am I supposed to do?"

"Leave that shit for the romantics and the films. Nowadays, you like a girl, you take her out, get her pissed, and fuck her."

"How charming."

"Way of the world, mate." He finished his drink, still grinning proudly, forever endowed with a sense of hilarity. "Anyway, what was I saying?" he frowned, pondered, "Something special!" he said, his eyebrows raised in glee. "Surprise her, delight her. Blow her fucking mind and then maybe she'll blow yours."

"We could just go to KFC; she said she liked fast food."

"You ever feel horny after you've eaten?" he asked plainly.

"I don't think so."

"Exactly!" he raised a hand and an outstretched finger like he'd had a Eureka moment. "Neither will she. Look," he put down the cue and laid his hands on both my shoulders. "Listen to your Uncle Matthew. Take her somewhere different. Surprise her. Romanticize her. Ply her with drink. She'll be grateful. She'll probably let you fuck her up the arse."

"Are you drunk?"

"Very much so."

Despite Matthew's questionable toxicity, I followed his advice. Melissa was my first real girlfriend, and I wanted a date that matched the uniqueness of the relationship.

I arranged everything for a perfect Saturday afternoon. A drive to the seaside. A stroll on the dunes. A picnic on the beach, and an evening in my flat, under the glow of candles, where we could get to know each other with a few glasses of wine.

I spent all week planning it.

My flat alone took two days of clearing and cleaning. I had only been living in it for a couple months but in that time it had accumulated all the detritus of a bachelor's life. Magazines, papers, clothes, dirty dishes, pizza boxes, and empty pop cans lay strewn about like paint flecks on a Jackson Pollock canvas.

I picked Melissa up around noon and headed for the seaside. I didn't know where we were going, but I was confident I could find my way to the coast.

Melissa was excited. She had an inkling I was planning something when I asked if she was free during the day, but as the car coasted along in the general direction of the sea, she was practically bubbling with childish glee.

"Roller rink?" she asked.

"No."

"Ten-pin Bowling?"

"No."

"The circus?"

"No."

"The beach?"

I hesitated. "No." She didn't seem to notice.

"You're not taking me abroad, are you?"

"To France?"

She nodded.

"No."

"Hm," she put a finger inquisitively on her chin. "Are you taking me to the woods to murder me?"

"Damn. You've guessed it."

"Oh joy!" she exclaimed with a grin.

"Act surprised though, won't you?"

"Of course," she nodded. "I'm sure I will be."

I stopped following the road signs when I saw the sea on the horizon, then I just followed the blue and pretended I knew where I was going.

"The beach!" Melissa exclaimed. "So you're not going to brutally murder me after all."

I pulled the car into a small parking lot. Gravel chips crunched underneath the tires as I maneuvered into a free space. The lot was full, at least a dozen cars were crammed into the small space, but I couldn't see anyone around.

The gravel foundation stopped at a ridge of thick, wild grass, which stretched long and ascendantly into the distance. I could just make out the sea at the point it converged with the pale blue sky.

A wind kicked across the grassy dunes and cut through the lot and my short-sleeved shirt, raising the hairs on my arms and my partially exposed chest.

I took my coat from the backseat and slipped it on before handing Melissa hers. She wrapped the padded arms around her body and tucked her neck into the plush lining, peering at me above a spiked collar.

"It'll be warmer on the beach," I assured her.

She smiled to tell me that she didn't mind.

"Come on." I wrapped my arm around her and pulled her close, stealing her heat.

I set off across the dunes with Melissa under one arm and a picnic basket cradled in the other. We walked along a sandy path that cut through the thick grass and wove between hardy flowers, mounds of dirt, carelessly dropped litter, pebbles, rocks, and curious insects.

"I'm not scared of bugs," I assured Melissa after a slightly feminine attempt to avoid a swaying moth. "I just think the world would be a better place without them." I waved a hand around my head to make sure the brightly colored insect had disappeared.

"I don't think the world can function without them."

"I'm sure we'd manage," I said, picking up the dropped basket and wrapping my arm back around Melissa.

She tilted her head and frowned at me. She was about to call me a sissy when I interrupted her.

"Look, other people," I said, nodding ahead and smiling victoriously when Melissa followed my gaze.

We had been walking along the path for ten minutes, taking the scenic route around the wildlife-encrusted edges. The beach was ahead of us now; we could just make out a few blobs of the human variety resting on its surface.

At Melissa's insistence, and to my delight, we walked until we found an empty section of the beach. While there, I took out a knitted blanket from the basket and stretched it across the cleanest square of sand I could find.

A heavy sigh escaped Melissa's mouth and she flopped down onto the blanket, stretching out as I watched her admiringly.

Further down the beach, I could see a small group of people enjoying the mild sunshine and the sounds of the waves lapping at the shore. A few of them were strewn out on the sand, in deck chairs or on blankets similar to the one Melissa writhed on. I noticed a lot of pink amongst them, and small dark patches indicative of Speedos or trunks around their groins.

It had occurred to me to wear a pair of trunks and see if Melissa fancied a dip in the ocean, but it was cold, I hated wearing trunks, and we weren't kids. A picnic was fine.

"They must be swingers or something," Melissa sat up and followed my gaze. "Or a tour bus of oldies. My parents do it all the time. Old people, kids, and dogs. They all love to gather on the beach."

I nodded and took out the prepared food. We had a few hours before we went back to my flat, but I prepared a light meal anyway, just in case the picnic on the beach led to something that a full stomach wouldn't appreciate.

I laid everything out and sat down next to Melissa, facing the ocean.

"I never knew you were such a romantic," she said softly, turning to smile at me.

"Me neither."

I kissed her, tasting the salty moisture of the sea air on her lips.

When I pulled back, I noticed the pink blobs in the distance had stopped frolicking in the sea and seemed to be looking our way. I was sure that even the seated oldies had perked up to peer at us. I shrugged it off as paranoia and took a bite of a tuna sandwich.

"You make these?" Melissa wondered.

"My mother did," I replied, rather embarrassed.

Melissa smiled cheekily above a bitten triangle of sandwich.

Further down the beach, a couple of blobs had broken away from the group and seemed to be coming our way. I pointed them out to Melissa; she turned, shrugged, and then looked back at the sea.

"Probably swingers," she said again. "Come to ask us if we want to join in."

"How do they know we're a couple?" I wondered.

"Are we?" Melissa asked.

I hesitated, dislodging a chunk of bread from my throat. "I meant a couple as in a man and a woman. Two people, not, you know."

Melissa stared at me for a fleeting moment, studying my face, then she shrugged it off. "They probably don't care. Two dicks, two vaginas, one of each. I don't think they mind. More the merrier for them. Just ignore them and they'll leave us alone."

I did as Melissa instructed and turned my attention to the sea instead, staying close to her and enjoying her warmth; listening to the soft sounds of her eating as her jaw worked through my mother's sandwiches.

"This is nice," she said after a while.

She turned to me with a broad smile. I pulled away to look at her, and only then did I see that the approaching blobs had moved to within fifteen feet of the blanket. Three of them in total, two men and a woman, and as it turned out the black patches around their groins weren't Speedos. They were pubic hair.

All of them were naked.

"Oh my god," I said softly.

Melissa bolted upright and turned to see what had startled me. I heard a soft sound escape her lips when she saw them; it began as startled horror and faded into amusement.

The two male nudists, their scrotums cradling small penises and swinging with the movement of their pudgy, hairy bodies, looked to be in their sixties. The woman appeared to be a lot younger. Her breasts hung down to her bulbous stomach like saggy pendulums, but her face was wrinkle free.

Melissa turned to face me; her hand was covering her mouth, suppressing a giggle.

"Hello there," one of the men called, waving a hand that seemed to move in step with his wandering ball-sack.

"Hi," I offered in reply, my voice far too soft for them to hear. "Hello!" I tried again, too loudly this time. I cursed myself under my breath and then realized that if anyone here had the right to feel embarrassed, it shouldn't be the guy whose greeting was too loud.

They were upon us now. The woman drifted around the top of the blanket, closer to me. The two men hovered behind Melissa. Now I couldn't even look at her for fear of the flesh-sacks that hovered above and behind her head.

One of the men—the one who hadn't spoken yet—stretched, smiling out to sea as he did so, breathing deep the sea air. *Lovely day, isn't it?* his mannerisms seemed to say, as his twisting, bending torso exposed his hairy crack.

"Do you know where you are?" the woman asked politely.

The Twilight Zone? I thought.

"The beach?" I said aloud, feeling that the pendulum effect of the two scrotums had hypnotized me.

The woman looked from Melissa—now trying to hide her giggles behind a scrunched-up face—to me. "I can't help noticing you're not nude," she said.

"I noticed that too," Melissa replied, looking like she was going to explode.

"But this is a *nude* beach," the woman pushed, elongating the word *nude* and seeming to look at my crotch as she did so, perhaps expecting my penis to pop out at her command.

"We just thought we'd come over and tell you," the non-stretching man said.

"You *have* to be nude to be on this beach," the woman added.

"It took three of you to tell us that?" I wondered, suddenly snapping out of the trance now that things had stopped jiggling.

They all exchanged glances, then the woman added, "We just wanted to make sure you weren't here to . . ." she paused and looked away awkwardly. I found myself momentarily amazed that a woman who walked around naked staring at penises had any sense of shame.

"—to spectate," the stretcher said, his eyes bearing down on me.

"To spectate?" I returned his fierce gaze. I didn't know where else to look. His penis was calling to me like a car wreck.

The woman nodded knowingly. "There are a lot of perverts around here."

Melissa's restraint broke and she exploded into a fit of laughter.

They looked offended. I didn't blame them. But her laugh was contagious; it took a great effort not to join in.

"Please leave the beach," the woman said, maintaining a polite tone.

"We don't want to have to call the police," the stretcher added.

Melissa forced a hand to her mouth. I watched her bright eyes sparkle with amusement above the compressed flesh of her palm.

She raised her free hand to the nudist, held their attention until the laughter was stifled, and then told them: "We just got here, we're not leaving."

"We're not bothering you," I said. "Why don't you go back over there, we'll stay—"

The woman interrupted me: "If you're not nude you can't stay." The politeness had now completely gone from her tone. She looked annoyed and flustered; a visible red color had fused into her cheeks.

I was about to concede defeat when Melissa stopped me in my tracks.

"Fine!" she shouted. She bolted upright, just avoiding stepping on the remaining sandwiches. "Naked it is!" she exclaimed.

She began to strip. I saw the eyes of the two men light up. Even the woman seemed happy with the prospect of Melissa's naked young body.

"Melissa," I began. "You don't have to—"

"It's okay, Kieran." She turned to look at me. I noticed a maddening sense of eccentric adventure on her face. "I don't mind."

After tearing off her jacket and stepping out of her shoes, she peeled off her blouse, exposing a red bra and a flat stomach. She dropped her trousers with one swift movement. I thought she would stop there, leaving her bra and matching underwear exposed to the elements, but she kept going.

Naked, her clothes discarded on the sand, the eyes of four admiring spectators on her, she threw her arms into the air and took in a deep and exhilarating breath.

I had restrained my curiosity when looking at the nudists, but couldn't do so with Melissa—my eyes refused to peel away.

I was staring at her lustfully when I realized everyone was now looking at me in expectation.

"Well?" said the woman with the saggy boobs.

"Now who're the perverts?" Melissa snapped. "I undressed; I gave you what you wanted. Now go back to your area and leave us alone.

Kieran will undress when he is ready. And he'll do so for *me*, for *my* eyes, *not* for yours."

The woman looked humbled. She paused for a moment to work out a reason to object, but eventually she sulked off, dragging her friends with her.

"That was amazing," I told Melissa when the saggy backsides of the three nudists were bouncing away.

Melissa grinned widely. "Thank you," she closed her eyes and stretched. I drank in more of the beauty of her slim, naked body. "I enjoyed it," she said. She noticed me staring and then promptly averting my eyes, but she didn't comment, nor did she hurry to dress.

"Do I have to undress now?" I wondered.

She laughed and shook her head. "I'll put my clothes back on soon. They won't come back," she smiled at me, then looked reflective. "Do you think that was a dumb thing to do?" she wondered.

Sitting down slowly, using her previously discarded jacket to conceal some of her dignity, the exposure seemed to dawn on her.

"Not at all," I said truthfully. "I thought it was amazing."

I leaned in to kiss her. She seemed unsure at first, still feeling vulnerable in her nakedness, but when our lips locked, she softened.

11

Melissa, Jessie, and Everyone Else

I was still with Melissa a few months down the line, and things were going well.

At the end of our unorthodox second date, I had taken her back to my hastily tidied flat where we shared some insightful conversation over a couple bottles of wine and then spent the night together. She stayed over for the rest of the weekend.

The following weekend, we repeated the date, without the cold beach and awkward nudity.

For the first time in my adult life, I had a girlfriend. I took her to meet my parents (who she loved), I brought her along to share a drink with Matthew (who she thought was insane), and I tried to spend as much of my free time with her as I could.

She was beautiful, funny, lovable, generous, and sweet. She was everything I wanted, but after two months she transformed.

It began on the night of our three-month anniversary. I had noted the date on my calendar and had been planning for it all week. A quarter of a year, twelve weeks; it was a big deal.

I cleaned my flat and loaded it with candles and cushions I borrowed from my mother. When I had finished, it looked like a feminine paradise. It was a little on the tacky side—the vibrant cushions juxtaposed against the bleak backdrop of the flat made it look like a schizophrenic had been allowed to redecorate his cell—but I was sure she would like it.

I played some soft classical music in the background; cooked a heavy pasta meal for two; bought a few bottles of wine; and set a table in the center of the flat, away from the corners where I had piled most of the junk that previously covered the flat.

I was riddled with nervous energy, unable to stand still or sit down. But Melissa was distant; from the moment I let her into the flat, she was despondent.

I thought maybe I was imagining things, transferring the stress of a heavy day onto her. So I ignored my paranoia and pushed on with the night.

After sitting her down and offering her a bottle of wine, I gave her some of her presents: a large cuddly toy, a single rose, and a box of chocolates. Then I sat down opposite her and watched as she cradled the objects awkwardly.

"What's all this for?" she wondered.

I assumed she knew about the anniversary—how could she not? But she didn't know I had planned all this in celebration of it. She had been invited around on the rouse of ordering a pizza and watching a film, an event that had become almost daily over the last few weeks.

"It's a big night," I told her, staring deep into her eyes and not breaking contact when she looked away. "I wanted to make it special."

We ate dinner in relative silence. I slopped creamy sauce down my top twice—the first time I disappeared to change my shirt, the second time I didn't bother. I didn't want to let my dinner get cold.

After a dessert of store-bought pastries and cheesecake, I told her I had something special to give her and I disappeared into the bedroom.

I returned with a key to the flat. The main thought behind the meal had been to ask her if she would move in with me, taking advantage of an anniversary to extend our relationship even further. The flat was small and fairly dilapidated, but she still lived with her parents and often complained about them. I had been thinking about asking her to move in for a few weeks; she was around the flat most nights anyway. Tonight was the perfect time to spring the question.

I cupped the key in my palm, walked to her side, and placed a hand on her shoulder. When she looked at me, I saw despondency in her eyes, and I thought I noticed something else: fear, anxiety, distress.

I fell onto my knee by the side of her chair and looked into her curiously ambivalent eyes. She spoke before I had the chance to.

"Oh my god!" She threw her hands up and sprang out of the chair.

I had run the scenario over and over in my head, and on more than one conception, she said those exact words. In my imaginings, they were said with ecstasy, possibly with a small tear bubbling in the corner of her eye, or a look of deep and unbreakable love on her face.

"I don't fucking believe it," she continued. No tears, no ecstasy, no love. She seemed infuriated. "I can't do this." She backed away from the table as she spoke. "This is getting out of hand. You're going too far."

"What do you mean?" I asked, still on one knee, the key still held behind my back.

"First the phone calls and text messages. Then the visits. The *pizza* nights. The *movie* nights. The weekends at your parents, *my* parents, the *restaurants*, the *zoo*." She threw her hands up exasperatedly. "It's all too much, Kieran. And now, what? You're going to ask me to marry you?"

I hesitated, gripped the key tighter. "Well, I—I—" I stuttered.

"You're smothering me, Kieran," She was breathless, beaten. "I can't take it anymore. I'm sorry," she spoke with a touch of sincerity but she looked more exhausted than sorry.

She grabbed her coat from behind the chair, averting her eyes from mine as she threw it over her shoulders.

I stood up, exposed the key in my open hand. "I'm sorry, I didn't mean—"

"Too late, Kieran. Too late," she repeated softly.

"We can make this work," I argued.

She shook her head. "Maybe," she said, hanging her head, almost in shame for the outburst. "We need some time apart. I need a break from you. Time to think."

She offered me a sincere smile and then left. She didn't see the key in my hand and I didn't mention it. It didn't seem relevant.

The following week, Melissa handed in her notice at work. She said she was going to concentrate on her studies and take some time off.

I was confident I could get her back at the end of the proposed break, but Matthew told me otherwise.

"She just said that," he insisted. "I'm sorry to break it to ya, mate, it's over, she doesn't want you back."

He wasn't sorry; he didn't like Melissa, mainly because she saw through his charm and knew he was a sleazy womanizer.

"I told you she was evil," he added. "I told you to never trust the shy ones, they're always fucking crazy."

I was depressed, but I was still confident that Matthew was wrong and Melissa would take me back.

I wanted to stay close to her, to keep up the pretense of a struggling relationship as opposed to one that had ended. I left messages on her answer machine. I emailed her. I texted her. It wasn't as obsessive as it had been, but I didn't let a day slip by without asking how she was or telling her what I had been up to.

She didn't reply to a single message and she never picked up the phone when I called.

I had all but given up hope by the third week and had let a few days pass without getting in touch. Then I let Matthew take advantage of my weakened state and agreed to join him on a double date.

"I picked up this shy girl once," Matthew continued as I stared absently across the dressed table at him. "Barely spoke, giggled a lot, was always smiling. I bought her a few drinks and took her back to my house; she turned into a fucking animal." He raised his eyebrows and took a small sip from his glass of wine. "Spent the next morning drying my asshole and cleaning chocolate outta my pubes."

I twisted my face in disgust, the melancholia momentarily forgotten.

Matthew shrugged, clearly amused. "Just saying, you gotta watch out for the shy ones."

"Melissa wasn't like that," I said softly.

"What about the time at the nudist beach? Not the actions of a shy girl."

I shrugged. "She could be slightly eccentric, I guess."

"And didn't she ask if you wanted to have a foursome with her friend and husband?"

I nodded slowly. I still hadn't understood her motives. I had turned her down at the time; I thought she was joking, or testing me. She wasn't; she had been disappointed.

"She'd had a lot to drink then," I said, unsurely.

Matthew opened his mouth to repeat something banal, and then he noticed his date and her friend enter the restaurant. "Finally," he mumbled, standing up and pasting a smile on his face. "Thought they'd never come."

I rose unsteadily to my feet. I had *hoped* they wouldn't come.

The date was less traumatic than I had expected and I was able to unwind and forget about Melissa. By the time the two of them disappeared to the bathroom, I was visibly elevated, and Matthew noticed.

"Told you this was a good idea," he said, pointing his glass of wine at me, the red liquid sloshing drunkenly around the broad bowl.

I nodded. It had been. I liked her; she was loud, merry, enthusiastic. She was the opposite of the introverted and withdrawn Melissa. I didn't know if I liked her just because of her contrast to Melissa or if I actually valued those traits in a woman, but it didn't matter.

"Why are you with Melanie?" I said, referencing Matthew's date, the skinny, bubbly brunette who had laughed at everything and had no opinions of her own to express. "I thought you didn't like them shy? She seems very shy."

Matthew grinned. "I said they were crazy, I never said I didn't like them that way."

"And the night with the chocolate pubes and anal lube?"

"Best night of my life."

I nodded, understandably.

"You like Jessie then?" he quizzed, picking herb-infused flesh from the remaining bones of his main course.

"She's sweet," I said. "Not as shy as Melanie."

"Unlucky for you, huh?"

The night had been spent as a group, conversing as four people. But when the girls returned from the bathroom they had a different agenda and concentrated solely on their separate dates.

The more I found out about Jessie, the more I liked. She was attractive, her skin the darkened shades of middle-eastern parentage, her eyes a hypnotizing shade of black. She was exciting, passionate about everything she talked about; she was witty, possessed of a boisterous laugh that she threw her head back to fully commit to.

After dessert, we stayed for a few drinks and then went back to the flat that Melanie shared with Jessie. When Melanie disappeared into one of the bedrooms with Matthew, I stayed on the sofa with Jessie.

"Do you want to join me in the other room?" Jessie asked after a patient wait, her eyes twinkling with the promise of sex.

We had been listening to Matthew going at it for twenty minutes or more. Melanie's bed squeaked under their movements, the headboard banged intermittently against the far wall, vibrating noise throughout the small flat.

They had tried to drown out their intercourse by playing rock music, but that had only encouraged Matthew to thrust in time to the songs. It was disconcerting, but Jessie didn't seem to mind.

"I can't," I told her, hanging my head.

"It's okay," Jessie replied understandably. She pulled away, put her glass on the table, and then looked at me earnestly. "Is there a problem *downstairs?*" she wondered.

"With this racket I wouldn't be surprised."

"No," she scratched her forehead. "I mean, you know, *downstairs.*" She nodded toward my groin.

"Oh, oh, God no. I'm fine." I shifted uneasily on my seat, and then opened my legs wide, as if to show that I had the correct equipment hidden underneath my jeans.

She seemed relieved. "What is it then? If you don't mind talking about it."

"I have a girlfriend."

"Oh," the relief vanished in an instant. She deflated like a balloon.

"I think," I added.

"You think?"

"It's complicated."

"Long distance?"

"Very."

"Oh."

"Well, *not really.*"

She looked perplexed.

"Not at all," I clarified. "But it *is* complicated."

"I see."

"I like you though," I was quick to add.

She smiled gratefully. "That's nice."

She picked up her glass of wine, tucked her legs underneath her, and then stared at me deeply. With her somber expression, her slightly tired features, and the halo of light emanating from the lamp behind her, she looked like an Eastern princess. Being alone with her at that moment, with the edge of her exuberance extracted by the night and her beauty intensified by the light, would have been perfect, if not for the fact that Matthew was now humping and grunting to the tune of "We Will Rock You."

"Maybe we can do it another time," I said.

I was entranced by her and knew that I needed to get a definitive answer from Melissa before I did anything with Jessie. As nasty and standoffish as she had been, she was too sweet to cheat on.

"Definitely."

"And I'll sleep with you then," I joked. "I promise."

Jessie laughed. "I'll keep you to your word."

My good mood continued until the following Saturday morning. I had initially planned to mope around the house all day and maybe leave a few more messages on Melissa's machine. Instead I woke with a start, made a hefty breakfast, and then took a call from Jessie.

"You sound jovial this morning," she noted after my energetic greeting.

"Jessie, hey, how are you?" I asked, the phone pressed between my ear and shoulder as I buttered some toast.

"I'm good, a little hung over, but good. Nothing breakfast can't fix."

"Is Matthew still there?" I wondered.

"No, he left in a rush this morning."

Matthew always left in a rush after sex. Melanie was lucky he stayed until morning; usually he was out the door before the sheet stains had time to dry.

"Listen," she said, "I was wondering if you'd be up for a little fun tonight."

"Fun?"

"A little party," she hesitated; she seemed ill at ease. "Melanie and I are throwing one of *our parties*," she said this like I knew what one of their parties entailed. I didn't, but a party was a party.

I switched the phone from my right ear to my left. "Sounds great."

She seemed relieved; I could hear a sigh crackle down the line. "I was going to ask Matthew, but I didn't catch him. Maybe you can invite him?"

I agreed to ask Matthew along and hung up after getting instructions on the address and time.

After a short afternoon nap, I dressed and prepared for the party. I hadn't been able to get in touch with Matthew and didn't mind; I had a feeling the night was going to be about me and Jessie anyway.

I left a message on Melissa's phone, asking her to ring me. I said it was urgent. I intended to tell her it was over and therefore get permission to sleep with Jessie, but she didn't phone back. I left the house less happy than when I had woken that morning, but I was content I was going to see Jessie again, even if I wasn't going to sleep with her.

The address I had been given led me to a detached farmhouse in the middle of nowhere. The building sat on its own at the end of a long country road, which cut a winding path through fields blistered with hay bales and the quickly graying forms of sheep and cattle.

A long stretch of road in front of the house served as the driveway, numerous cars were strewn on its bobbled surface, a vast mechanical cornucopia as far as the darkness allowed me to see. All the cars were in better condition than mine, which could barely be classed as a car.

I parked behind the house, nestled between a thick hedge and the side of a damp sodden barn, so no one would know I was the guy who arrived in the painted wheelbarrow.

I didn't know if I was headed to a formal party, a dinner party, or a drunken rave, so I had dressed to prepare for all occasions. I wore jeans so dark and well ironed they could pass for formal trousers if no one paid too much attention, a plain black shirt buttoned to conceal a casual tee shirt, and a black denim jacket.

The house was lit up from all angles. Three windows at the top and two on the bottom blazed with red, blue, and yellow lights. The stone bricks breathed music.

I heard sounds of exertion as I stepped to the front door. I thought I heard someone scream, nothing blood curdling; something pleasurable. The overexcited calls of a woman enjoying herself perhaps.

I removed my jacket, deciding that I certainly wasn't heading into a dinner party, when the front door flew open and a short man with flabby man-boobs and a frighteningly large penis, burst out into the night.

He brushed past me as though he hadn't seen me. I moved aside, wondering if it was his knee or his dick that had whacked against my thigh.

"I want to dance!" he yelled, throwing his arms into the air. He hopped onto the gravel driveway and sidestepped around a convertible. His bare feet crunched against the coarse stones; he didn't seem to mind. "I want to dance and sing with the fairies!" he continued, disappearing into the blackness.

I removed my jacket, contemplated running back to my car, and then stepped into a halo of fluorescent light that engulfed the hallway ahead of me.

I waited by the door for a moment, my hand on the handle, my eyes on the fields where the fairy-dancer had disappeared. I didn't know whether I should leave it open for him to return or not. I certainly didn't want him to—

"Hello, Kieran."

The voice came from behind me; someone had joined me in the hallway. I recognized the voice instantly; it was the voice I spent all last night listening to, the voice I had driven for an hour to hear.

I turned around with a broad and expectant smile on my face, but that smile faded into something obscure when I saw that Jessie was completely naked.

"Am I early?" I said.

I knew I was late, but I didn't know any other reason for her to be naked. Not that she would walk around the house naked before a party anyway—it wasn't even her bloody house.

"No, no, you're just on time," she said.

She walked toward me with a welcoming smile. I remained standing, my eyes unable to leave her breasts, which were as perfect as her face.

"Let me take your jacket," she said softly.

I took off my jacket and watched with a low jaw as she took it to a nearby walk-in closet and hung it up among a mass of other jackets and items of clothing.

"Don't worry about your clothes," she assured comfortingly, "you can take them off when you're ready."

I hadn't been worrying, but now I was.

"Follow me." She turned around and sauntered off down the hallway, her naked buttocks slipping into a swagger, the tight flesh barely moving as she strode.

She stood in the open doorway to what I assumed was the main room, but it wasn't until I walked by her side did I hear the noises that should have been apparent earlier, if not for their velocity then for their magnitude.

Men talked softly, harshly. They grunted and they groaned. Women huffed and puffed, expressing intermittent calls of pleasure, pain, and ecstasy.

I peered into the room and instantly my heart sank. I realized that as sexy and seductive as Jessie was, I wasn't going to have sex with her. Not tonight, not ever, but there were plenty of people who were.

The room was a writhing mass of flesh. A dozen males and females were caught in the midst of mass intercourse. I hadn't just shown up late to any party, I had shown up late to an orgy, and they had started without me.

The furniture in the room had casually been coated with plastic or draped with sheets and pushed aside. The floor was covered with mattresses and pillows as couples of varying ages fornicated on them.

Just a few feet in front of me, a young man with aggressive stubble and heavily tattooed arms straddled a tall blonde over the protected couch, grasping her hips and asking her who he was with a snarled expression. Apparently he was just as confused as me.

In the center of the room, a middle-aged man lay flat on his back, staring at the ceiling with glassy and distant eyes while two women hovered around him. In the corner of the room, nestled in a groove where I assumed the television usually sat, a guy in his late teens snorted intricate lines of white powder from around the areolae of a small-breasted teen. It seemed like an extravagantly pointless way to get high, but they were both loving it.

In the other corner, a young woman looked at me over the heaving shoulders of a guy that had her pinned up against the wall. She stared with glistening eyes, licking her lips. She nodded when she saw me looking, a gesture that said *come and join in*. I turned away quickly.

"This—this," I stuttered and looked at Jessie. She seemed enthralled by the sex, *"This is an orgy,"* I whispered, as if informing her of something she didn't know.

She looked at me, slightly bemused. "Of course it is," she stated.

"Bu—bu—bu—"

"I thought you knew," Jessie rested a reassuring and apologetic hand on my shoulder.

I shook my head rapidly.

"Oh, I'm so sorry," she backed out of the room, tugging me with her.

"Maybe I should . . ." I trailed off, hooking a thumb over my shoulder toward the door.

"No," she pulled me closer. "I'm so sorry," she said genuinely. "But, please, please." She looked deep into my eyes, forcing me to listen, to believe. "Stay. Just try to have fun."

"It's not for me," I assured her.

"Then don't do anything. Wait for me," she pleaded.

She had puppy dog eyes. I had no intention of sleeping with her—I didn't know where she'd been—but I couldn't say no to her.

"Okay," I conceded.

She grinned, normality restored. "I need to prepare a few things, then I'll get changed, and we can—" she shrugged and looked toward the door. "Go somewhere maybe?"

"Sure."

"Excellent, wait here."

She ambled off down the hallway. I tried to enjoy watching her move again, but when I looked at her firm backside, I imagined what the nipple snorter and his friends had done to it.

I tried to wait for her by the door, but the noises distracted me so I ventured upstairs. It was darker up there, quieter.

I took the steps slowly, keeping an ear out in case anyone was fucking on the stairs or in any of the rooms.

I found myself admiring the house. The floors were coated with thick, dark wood. The wall leading up the stairs hung with lines of calming landscapes and seascapes.

The top of the stairs led onto a plush rug that stretched out onto a large squared hallway, immediately branching onto four closed doors, with a hallway leading down to another.

I ignored the rooms and followed the hallway. The walls upstairs were fitted with portraits of a happy family. I stopped when I recognized Jessie in one of the photos. She was hugging an elderly man and woman, nestled between them, a broad smile on her gorgeous face.

In the next one, she was younger, eleven or twelve maybe, the old couple now a middle-aged pair, watching their daughter frolic on the swings in a park.

Then a picture of a sunny vacation. Jessie as a youngster, no more than seven. Her mesmerizing features yet to form, her long dark hair cut short. Pictures of Jessie in the sea, in the pool, on the beach, in the car.

There was also a framed picture of Jessie with Melanie. It hung near the corner wall, before the hallway turned toward its final stretch and the remaining door.

I paused to take a second look, suddenly realizing that I hadn't seen Melanie downstairs. Jessie had said the party had been thrown by her *and* Melanie. I tried to think if she had been in the living room, maybe I missed her, maybe—

I paused and pulled back. I heard a noise. A voice. A voice I recognized.

I peeked around the corner. The door at its end was open slightly. A soft ambient light streamed through the gap, merging with the stronger hallway fluorescence.

There were no sex sounds through the door, none that I could decipher anyway. No heavy groaning, no—

There it was again. The voice.

It sounded female but it wasn't Jessie. It wasn't Melanie.

I turned the corner and moved a few steps forward.

Soft talking, barely audible. I listened, strained. It was definitely her. It had to be.

I raised my hand to the door; I felt the flat mahogany against my palm, readied to push.

But it couldn't be, could it? I wondered. *Here, now?*

I'm just hearing things.

I pulled away, but the voice called again and was followed by a deeper voice in reply, a male voice.

I shoved open the door and stepped forward.

The room was heavy with smoke. There were two windows inside but both were covered with red sheets, blocking out what remained of the daylight and leaving nowhere for the smoke to escape; it sat heavy in the air, thick from floor to ceiling.

There had been no sex sounds in this room, but there was certainly a lot of sex.

Melanie was on her back, receiving oral sex from an enthusiastic youngster. Her eyes were closed and she seemed dead to the world.

On the couch, mumbling under her breath in a haze of smoke and a torrent of ecstasy, was Melissa.

I wanted to turn and leave; I could scarcely believe what I was seeing.

"Melissa!" I couldn't help myself; the word forced its way out of my mouth.

The guy nibbling gently on her breasts was the first to notice me. He looked up at me with something resembling mild contempt. The man with his fingers between her legs and his tongue in her throat did the same.

I heard her mumble again, upset that the two men had stopped. She slowly sat up, followed their eyes, and saw me.

I expected to see shame or embarrassment, but I only saw anger and pure rage in those drug-filled orbs. She bolted up and strode toward me, her hair matted with sweat and stuck behind her head, her makeup forging her face into the features of an insane jester.

"You're fucking following me now!" she growled. I had never heard that tone from her before, never seen that degree of anger and hatred in her eyes.

I took a step back, away from the smoke-filled room. She bounded after me.

"You're fucking sick!" she spat spittles of hate as she spoke.

She looked unsteady on her feet—she probably hadn't moved for a couple of hours—but she strode on with determination.

"You're perverted! You're disturbed."

I continued to back off; I had already turned the corner and was now heading for one of the unmarked doors. Not willing to enter, God knew what else I would see.

She was inches away; I could smell stale smoke and vodka on her breath.

"You're pathetic," she said, raising a hand and using it to prod an accusing finger into my chest. "You're fucking wrong in the head!"

She continued to poke me. I held up my hands in defense. I dragged some words to my throat, but when I tried to speak them, they crackled out and dissipated.

"How did you get in here?" she demanded to know. "Eh? How!"

My arms were still held up. Her finger was now a permanent fixture on my chest. I could feel it pressing into my sternum.

The memories of the times we had spent together flashed before my eyes and were instantly erased and replaced by this furious, spitting she-beast who stood in front of me.

A couple doors opened behind me. I dodged the emerging spectators, shifted to the top of the stairs; Melissa followed, prodding. A few more naked bodies appeared in the doorways, craning their necks to see over the initial onlookers. All were drunk or drugged, all amused.

Melissa turned to them: "He *used* to be my boyfriend," she said, wickedly. "He came here to spy on us; he's probably had a wank watching some of you already."

I shook my head and stuttered a hastily and incoherent objection.

The faces in the doorway looked appalled; some of them were advancing toward me. I backed up to the edge of the stairs.

Melissa stayed on me. She looked me up and down slowly. "You're a disgrace," she muttered with a twisted face, and then she shoved me.

I remember very little about the next few hours.

I had glimpses of falling, tumbling, hurting. All around me I could hear calls of disgust, triumph, and pleasure. I remember looking up and seeing Melissa's twisted face as she glared down at me, naked. No longer attractive, now the body of a shrunken devil, the face of an evil sociopath.

I saw Jessie. She was fully clothed, she looked concerned. She was screaming at the others, threatening them.

I was reluctantly bungled into the backseat of a car by two naked, sweaty men. Then a car journey, I didn't know how long, aided all the way by Jessie's soft, worried voice.

I woke up in a hospital bed with a very bad headache.

Matthew was sitting by the side of the bed, reading a magazine with little interest in its content.

"Where am I?" I said. I expected a croaked voice, but it came out fine.

Matthew looked at me and then closed the magazine and placed it down. Somewhere in the far reaches of the hospital I heard a loud clatter of dropped equipment. The sound screeched like lightning bolts in my head. I closed my eyes, scrunched my face, and waited for the pain to go away.

"Hospital, dipshit. Where else?" Matthew said casually.

"Where's Jessie?"

I opened my eyes in time to see Matthew shrug. "She brought you here, phoned me and then left. Told me to say she was sorry. She left her number, said to ring her."

I nodded.

Matthew slowly folded his arms across his chest and glared at me. "So," he said slowly. "You went to an orgy and you didn't tell me?"

"I didn't know."

He didn't look too impressed; he sensed he had missed out.

"You should have told me about them," I said. "I got knocked the fuck out because of you."

He held up his hands. "Melissa knocked—"

"Your fault!" I spat. "You should have told me they were like that."

Matthew gave in, slumping. "You're right, my apologies. But I honestly didn't know. I never listened to her—she rarely spoke and when she did we were drinking or fucking, never a good time to try to get me to listen."

I allowed myself to calm down. "Fair enough," I said. "It's over with now, it doesn't matter."

"No," he said, looking shocked. "They didn't tell you, I mean, you don't know?" he said, worried.

"What, what is it?"

He averted his eyes, looked at the bed, and then darted them worriedly around the hospital dorm where five other patients rested. He looked anxious and that made me worry.

"Is something wrong with me?" I said. I tried to sit upright, but the movement sent stabbing pains around my skull.

"I'm sorry to tell you, I mean, I don't—"

"What is it?" I demanded.

"They had to operate," he said simply.

"What?"

"They cut off your dick, said you probably wouldn't be needing it anymore anyway," he said with a smirk.

"You wanker!"

"I'm sorry," he said, pulling back in case I found something to throw at him. "I've been sitting here thinking of that one for a while, fuck all else to do but watch you snore and drool."

I relaxed, content; my heart still racing.

"So, you gonna phone her or not?"

"Jessie?"

"Who else?"

I liked her and the warming images of her concerned expression were still fresh in my mind. But I didn't like her lifestyle and I knew that for every second I was with her, I would see Melissa as she pushed me down the stairs.

"No," I said convincingly. "I've had enough of women for now."

12

Orange and Red

It took me a few months to get over Melissa and the carnage that followed our relationship. After that I was wary, but happy to return to the dating world under the tutelage of my sexually indiscriminate best friend. I wanted to date a few girls, find one I liked, and cautiously step into another, hopefully better, relationship. Matthew told me I should *play the field*, although he didn't say it as succinctly as that.

"You need to get your end away, mate," he told me assuredly.

He hated Melissa. He hated my brief moments of celibacy while my bruised body and ego healed, and now he was in his element.

"Sleep around a bit, stop settling for the first lass who smiles at you. Have some fun. Do what I do."

"I've heard what you do," I told him. "And quite frankly, most of it sickens me."

Matthew merely shrugged, a touch of pride in his eyes. "You don't need to be *that* kinky, but you do need to fuck a few more girls, get some experience."

I tried not to listen to Matthew when it came to the opposite sex, but I had to acknowledge that he had a lot more experience with women than I did. He also rarely entered into relationships, never seeing any girl for more than a week or two at a time, yet he had slept with more women than I had even spoken to. I didn't admit it to him at the time, but I envied the ease with which he cruised through his sexual encounters, and I was prepared to let him teach me to become as sleazy, sex-mad, and uncommitted as he was.

I agreed to go on a pub crawl with him and he treated the following weekend like a military operation. He committed himself to a forty-eight-hour celibacy, insisting that all of his time and efforts were to be taken up with getting me with as many women as possible.

We were only a few hours into the weekend when he spotted the first target: a heavily tanned, almost orange, blonde with a simpleton smile and a giggly nature. She had paraded her slim body past our table a few times during the last half hour, her glittered, fluttering eyes looking down at me seductively as she did so.

"She wants you, she's an easy mark," Matthew said.

"So, what do I do?" I wondered, deciding against questioning him on his terminology. "Should I buy her a drink?"

"That's a good start, but if that's the way you're gonna play it you might want to wait for a bit. It's early and she's still relatively sober. Buy her a drink now and you'll be doing it for the rest of the night. Cost you a fortune, you'd be better off with a hooker."

I looked at the tanned girl; she was standing by the bar surrounded by a circle of friends. She was laughing loudly, her body dancing to the beat of hysterics, but none of her friends were joining in; a couple of them looked embarrassed, the others smiled politely and waited for her to quiet down.

"She looks dumb," I commented.

"Exactly."

"But I don't like them dumb."

"It's just sex," Matthew argued. "She has a nice body, decent face. She'll do."

"What if it becomes more than that?"

Matthew paused in the middle of taking a long drink. He put his glass down on the table firmly and pointed a menacing finger at me. "You're not starting a relationship with her. I'm warning you. We're not here for relationships, so don't get any ideas. If I hear you talking about relationship shit with her I'll drag you outta here by your balls, got it?"

"Fair enough." I took a long, submissive drink, feeling like a child who had just been told off. "So what do we do now?" I wanted to know. "Do we just wait?"

"Let's scout around, see if we can find a better match, just in case the ditzy blonde turns out to be prudish."

Number two was an athletic redhead with a proud stance and a confident gait, and she dripped with self-assurance. Her shoulder-length hair shone in the flickering lights; curled locks of the radiant red hung down either side of deep brown eyes. Her angelic hair and her soft, feminine features, were set into a scowl, which had been infused with just enough masculinity and arrogance to offset her femininity and create neutrality.

She was beautiful, but her hard body was equalled by her hard glare.

"She looks too dominating. If she wanted to start a relationship I wouldn't be able to say no. I might run away, but I would never be able to say no to her."

"That's a good thing," Matthew said, leaning forward in excitement. "It means she'll make you do the crazy shit I'm always telling you to do. She'll teach you a few things, and trust me, it feels good to have a commanding woman treat you like shit."

"You have issues."

"Fuck you," Matthew replied with a smile.

"What if she wants more than sex?"

"She won't."

"But what if she does?"

Matthew shrugged. "Run, I guess."

"But she looks like she could catch me."

"We'll deal with it when it arises; first we need to get her on the hook. Right," he produced a coin from his pocket, flipped it and asked: "heads or tails?"

"Heads."

"Tails. The blonde goes first. Easy enough; she likes you, she wants you, not so sure about the redhead."

Under Matthew's instruction—*get her away from her friends who are no doubt more intelligent*—I caught her eye and beckoned her over. I introduced myself and then let Matthew take over.

Her name was Tiffany and she was a beauty therapist, a subject Matthew suddenly became an expert in. He introduced me as a modest businessman with a line in beauty products and studios, and before I knew it, I had her devoted attention.

"He doesn't like to talk about it," Matthew said, his face a picture of hilarity as he stared over the top of Tiffany's bare shoulder. "But he's a genius, I'm sure he could teach you a thing or two about the business."

"Really?" she said, her career prospects gleaming beyond the dollar signs in her eyes.

I smiled and shrugged, not sure what to say.

"That's so interesting," she shifted over to me, her hand moving onto my thigh.

I tried to reply, but I wasn't sure if I spoke a word or merely mumbled an incoherent noise. I cleared my throat just in case and downed the rest of my pint, watching as a grinning Matthew made his way to the bar to order more.

Within the hour, I drank another three pints and was feeling good, the nerves were gone, and I had also been in Tiffany's company long enough not to be taken aback by her stray hands.

In that time she hadn't said much but she had spoken a lot. She also laughed a lot; the noise made me cringe and I had to dig my nails into the palm of my hand to stop from grimacing.

She finished her third and winked at me, saying: "I think I should go to the bathroom."

She had been winking and staring at me strangely for the last hour. I assumed she had a tic disorder or didn't understand social convention.

"Okay, I'll be waiting for you," I said.

"Maybe you could join me?" she said, almost shyly.

"I don't need to go." I could see Matthew shaking his head as I spoke.

"Maybe we can find something else to do then?" Tiffany persisted.

"In the bathroom?"

She smiled.

"I don't think—" I stopped, feeling a foot slam into my shin. I looked up to see Matthew looking at me with wide eyes. He was twitching his head violently, either telling me to move or having a seizure.

"Oh, okay," I said, still a little unsure. "I'll meet you in there."

Tiffany pulled away from the table with a grin and ambled off toward the toilets, swinging her hips with great exaggeration, knowing I was watching her leave.

"You nearly blew it," Matthew said, when Tiffany had drifted into the wall of noise beyond our table.

"Just so I'm perfectly clear, she does want me to have sex with her in there?" I asked.

Matthew nodded exaggeratedly.

"Don't look at me like that, how am I supposed to know? Why do people insist on euphemisms and riddles? Whose benefit are they for exactly? If she doesn't want you to know, why doesn't she just whisper it in my ear?" I sat back and drained the last of my pint.

"Well, go on then," Matthew pushed.

I shifted uncomfortably in my seat and averted my gaze, "But it's dirty in there."

"Don't be a pussy," Matthew said.

"I don't have any protection on me."

"It's a bathroom. There'll be a condom machine in there, I'm sure."

"I meant like rubber gloves or bleach."

"Get in there and fuck her now," Matthew ordered, thrusting a finger in the direction of the bathroom.

"Fine," I grumbled, standing.

I waded through the crowd and made my way to the back of the pub where a small corridor led down to a back exit flanked by two doors: gents and ladies.

I usually liked the quiet and the solitude of a bedroom, where, with time and comfort, I could enjoy the sex and the closeness. A quickie in the stalls had never made it into my list of fantasies and had never appealed, but Tiffany was very pretty and she had a great body.

The door to the gents was open and Tiffany was standing with her foot in the jamb, her neat orange body resting against a sink and beckoning me.

I ducked inside. I half expected to see the row of urinals in use; a line of men preparing to commentate and criticize my performance, but there was no one else inside.

Tiffany clasped my hand in hers and turned, leading me past the urinals.

"It's quite clean in here," I noted happily.

"What?" she asked over her shoulder.

"Nothing."

She led me to the far stall and shoved me inside. She slammed the door, engaged the lock, and then pounced on me, thrusting her tongue between my lips, her hand clasped around my neck.

I returned the kiss with my eyes on the stall door, fearful that it would open to expose a crowd of onlookers. I thought about pausing to check that she had locked it properly, or asking her to check, but I didn't want to spoil the moment.

"I want you so badly," she said breathlessly. "Fuck me, Mr. McCall, *fuck me*."

I had never been called *mister* during sex before, but I didn't let that worry me. I had other things to concentrate on. Like the bathroom door.

With a heavy, excited groan she turned around and pressed her buttocks up against my groin. She ground momentarily.

"Fuck me, Mr. McCall, fuck me hard."

"Okay."

"Fuck me good, fuck me hard."

I shrugged to myself, unsure how to reply a second time. I wasn't good with dirty talk.

Standing straight again, her back pressed against my chest, she kissed me over her shoulder while working her hand under her skirt, toying with the G-string. She worked the thin material free and then slid it down her legs, letting it fall to her ankles.

Her hands then went to work on me, yanking my trousers and boxer shorts down with great ease. She stroked and caressed my erection, kissed it, and then, producing a condom, she popped the prophylactic in her mouth before cupping her lips over the tip of my penis and working the rubber down with her lips.

At that moment, I heard the door to the bathroom creak open. I heard a man cough and whistle his way inside.

The ecstasy inside me was replaced by fear. I had let excitement take over and had banished the thought of someone stumbling in on us, but with the sound of that click, cough, and whistle, it all came back.

My eyes shot to the stall door. I could hear footsteps echoing their way across the bathroom floor. I moved forward, practically diving for the lock, forgetting about the girl currently fitting me with a condom.

Tiffany stumbled backward under my movement. Her backside rolled over the back of her ankles and her head flew backwards. I heard the sound of surprise escape her lips, I felt the breeze of shock bounce off the rubber and tickle my thigh, and I felt her teeth graze my penis moments before the back of her head clattered against the toilet door.

The door was locked after all, but under the impact of Tiffany's head, the lock buckled, popped. The door flew open.

Tiffany had slipped into unconsciousness on impact, not a sound escaped her lips during the blow. She was silent and limp as she flopped toward the tiled bathroom floor.

She was caught by an unsuspecting man whose whistling promptly stopped when a half-naked orange girl fell against his legs.

Reaching down to stop Tiffany from rolling over or slipping past, the man looked up at me still standing in the stall with my pants around my ankles and a condom half-fitted onto my dying erection.

I said the first thing that came into my head, regretting it immediately: "It wasn't rape, I swear."

Tiffany regained consciousness a few minutes later. The bathroom was packed with interested observers; one of which claimed he was a doctor, but may have just fancied a feel.

The man who had caught Tiffany became her protector. He left me alone with her for a fleeting second when he ran into the club to ask for a doctor and an ambulance, but even then he had remained in the doorway to keep an eye on me and the injured girl. At that point, I had hurriedly removed the condom and pulled up my trousers.

I was tempted to pull up Tiffany's knickers as well; it didn't seem appropriate to leave her exposed under the thin material of the short skirt, but it occurred to me that her rescuer would kill me if I went anywhere near that area.

Tiffany was the one to finally restore her own dignity by pulling up her knickers, although a dozen onlookers had seen their fair share by then.

Groggy, confused, and irritated, she had awoken to softly spoken reassurance and a question: "Did he hit you?"

"No. Not intentionally, I don't think."

I tried to explain myself at that point, but I talked myself into circles under the watchful eyes of many and was saved by the sound of two paramedics barging into the club.

They took Tiffany away for precautionary tests. Under the guidance of the paramedics, she walked out of the club and into the ambulance, her protector hot on her heels.

She shot me one last ambivalent glance before she left. I didn't know what she thought of me, but it was a fair assumption that we would never get to finish what we started.

When Matthew finally stopped laughing, we moved on to another club, but the night had already died for me. The alcohol had worn off in the fear and excitement and I had no desire to speak to another woman, let alone try to pick up one. I called it a night and called a taxi, freeing Matthew from the restraints of responsibility and unleashing him on the women of the city. He picked up a girl before I even arrived home.

"Keep your dick in your pants until you get her home this time. That's a beast; we can't afford to unleash it early." It was Saturday night and Matthew was back on the clock. "No bathroom sex. No hospitals. Right?"

"Right."

Despite my protests, we went back to the same pub as the previous night. I wasn't looking forward to being seen and taunted by legions of witnesses who had already turned the bathroom incident into a folk tale, but I needn't have worried; no one seemed to notice me. Even the bar staff saw too many different faces to distinguish one stranger from another, and most of the bouncers hadn't been there the previous evening.

Number two was there, though. The athletic redhead (*heads* on Matthew's coin) came in just as we were about to head out. Her hair was pinned back this time, caught in a tight ponytail, pulling her soft skin back across her fierce bone structure.

She still wore the same look of masculine arrogance. Her dress— sequined, black, long, figure-hugging—wasn't as seductive or showy, but I was more attracted to her. I craved the dominance I saw in her. After the previous night, I just wanted to lie back and let the woman do the work, that way I couldn't mess it up.

Matthew wormed his way over to her and got her talking. I saw her looking my way a few times and smiled. She smiled back.

"She wasn't here last night," Matthew said when he came back. "During the incident." He couldn't say or think of the *incident*— spoken with air quotes—without smiling. "So that's a start. Her name is Katie, she's an athlete, on some sort of break, an excuse to get wasted I guess. I told her you were shy, took a shot she would like the shy and retiring type, turns out she does. That or she's desperate, either way, she's coming over soon."

Katie was just as instantly affectionate as Tiffany had been, but far more forceful. Within five minutes of meeting her, she stuck her tongue down my throat; I was so surprised I almost choked. Five more minutes passed before she jammed her hand down the front of my trousers.

Matthew didn't have to lie for me; there was no need to create the image of a successful businessman or a driven entrepreneur.

Katie was prepared to go home with the first man who chatted her up, and tonight that was me.

Matthew disappeared when Katie tried unbuttoning my trousers, signaling for me to phone him later to let him know how things went. I wanted to follow him out of the pub, but I stayed in Katie's strong grip, deciding to follow Matthew's advice: *if she's kinky and dominating, just go with it, because she'll crush your balls if you say no.*

"Listen, maybe we should go somewhere," I said breathlessly, pulling away from her tight embrace and quickly buttoning my trousers. One stranger had already seen my erection this weekend, I didn't want to extend that to an entire room full of people.

"My place?" Katie volunteered without hesitation.

"Sure."

She grabbed my hand and practically dragged me out of the pub.

I tried to make small talk with her as we scurried along the busy streets—ducking through an alleyway, weaving through a yard, seemingly taking a path that Katie had dragged many men down before—but she was in a hurry. Her replies were brusque, one or two words usually sufficing.

Katie finally spoke to me when we arrived at her flat.

"I bet you're a dirty boy, aren't you?" she said, slamming the door behind her and leaving me in the darkness of her hallway. I could hear her heavy breathing quicken.

I was so desperate for a conversation that extended beyond a grunted reply, I found myself answering just to please her, in the hope that she wouldn't fall silent again, "Sure, I love all that . . . stuff. I could show you a few things; take you places you've never been before."

I was smiling in the darkness, content that I had played the role well. The smile faded when Katie snapped on the light and exposed her living room.

The walls were covered with paintings of naked men and women. The women were strapped onto racks, some gagged; some blindfolded; some with probes and industrial-looking gadgets inserted into orifices. Men were oiled, whipped, and leather clad, with complex and painful clamps fixed onto their scrotums or nipples.

Everything was graphic and forceful. The images had been sculpted by an artist, but the realism of the pencil strokes and the sheer quantity of pictures made me feel uneasy.

I thought about what I had just told Katie and gulped. I wasn't sure a place existed where she hadn't been before.

"You like?" Katie asked, her eyes turning from me to the walls. "I did them all myself, it's a little hobby of mine."

"They're good." I said genuinely. The paintings were good; it was the content that freaked me out. "You're very talented."

"So, *bad boy*," Katie stepped in front of me and roughly shoved me backward. I was ashamed to hear a soft yelp escape my lips as I tumbled onto a leather sofa, but Katie didn't seem to hear it. "Why don't you show me a few things?"

"Do you mind if I use your bathroom first?" I said, clambering back to my feet and stepping away from her in case she tried to shove me again.

She shrugged her shoulders and pointed to a door at the back of the room. "Through there. Don't keep me waiting," she warned. "I hate to be kept waiting. You better come back here with something good, teach me something *special.*"

I hastily ducked out of her sight and stumbled to the bathroom, out of breath and wondering if I should make for the nearest window and jump.

I found myself in a clean, newly renovated bathroom. The top half of the walls were fitted with sleek black tiles that reflected florescence from the light above, the bottom half gleamed with fresh white paint.

The furnishings shone with the same radiant gleam that glittered from the tiles and the immaculately clean walls. The bath almost sparkled in its bleached perfection.

Shower gels, shampoos, and soaps had been arranged with the finesse of an anal retentive and stacked neatly, side by side, by an obsessive compulsive mind.

No brightly colored loofahs, sponges, or scrubs. Nothing was out of place; nothing was excessive; everything was clean, clinical.

Leaning against the door, I waited for an idea to enter my head as I surveyed the surroundings. I had already checked the window; it was too small to climb through.

My phone buzzed in my pocket and I quickly dug it out, happy for the distraction, partially hoping for a message from God telling me there was a wormhole in the sink.

It was a text message from Matthew: *How's it goin?*

I decided he would have the answer, he would know what to do. I replied to Matthew's message with a phone call, he answered immediately.

"Not too well I take it," he said, disappointed. "You home already?"

"I'm in the bathroom," I whispered back.

"As long as she's not with you."

"I don't know what to do," I said, ignoring his comment. "I need your help."

"Lift the seat, aim, try not to make a—"

"Cut the shit," I spat. "This is serious. She's kinky, *really* kinky."

"Nice one."

"But I'm not."

"I'm sure she'll teach you."

"But I made her think I was kinky, I started talking, I got carried away. Now she says she wants to experiment with me, try something *new*. I don't know anything new. I'm a missionary man. Doggy style is exotic for me."

Matthew laughed. "Okay." He cleared his throat and paused to think for a moment. I could hear the kinky images running through his mind followed by mental hysterics as he pictured me performing them. "Okay," he repeated. "So, if you want to impress her and follow through with this, you need to suggest something a little out-there, but not too out-there; you don't want her thinking you're a perv, just in case she's more normal than you think. You have to find her level first."

"Right," I agreed.

"What about A.T.M?"

"I don't have my card."

Matthew laughed so hard I had to pull the phone away from my ear.

"No, no," he said, the remnants of amusement still in his breath. "It means Ass to Mouth."

"Are you serious?"

"Uh-huh."

"People do that?"

"Sure."

"Why?"

"It's different; it's unusual, it's not normal."

"It's not normal for a reason. No, I can't do that, it's disgusting."

"You could try pegging," Matthew continued. "I'm sure she'll be game for that, if she's kinky she'll probably have the equipment as well."

"Equipment?"

"A strap-on."

"Like a dildo? Okay, I can do that, that's clean enough. How does that work? Won't my dick get in the way? Do I wear it over my clothes?"

"You don't wear it, *she* does," Matthew said.

"I'm going to hang up on you now."

"You said you wanted something kinky!"

"Maybe I should just leave," I said, liking the idea as soon as I voiced it.

"It's up to you; you could be missing a big chance here. Is she hot?"

I pictured Katie in my head. Her flowing red hair, her delicate features, her inviting lips, her radiant green eyes; her athletic body, toned and tight, fine-tuned through years of exercise.

"She's very sexy," I said unsurely. The images of her innocent beauty changed, and the angry, arrogant personality traits took over. I imagined her snarling face above mine, growling at me as she raped me with a strap-on and demanded I call her *daddy*. "I can't do it," I said. "I need to get out of here. I'll phone you later." I ended the call.

Tentatively pushing the handle, trying not to make a sound, I opened the door and peeked through.

I could see the hallway through the gap. The door opposite leading to a bedroom was closed; the door further down the hallway that led into the living room was still wide open, the light striking through and bathing the laminated hallway floor.

I stuck an ear to the gap and listened. I could hear the muffled noises of fabric against fabric, either Katie was getting undressed or she was polishing her whip.

I hadn't seen a back door to the property and there was no chance I could get to the front door with Katie in the way.

Peeling the door away from the jamb, I made for the bedroom, praying it held a window large enough to aid my escape.

The bedroom was as clean and inviting as the bathroom, but the walls were decorated in just as many drawings as the living room. I saw the window on the other side of the room. It was big enough for me to get through.

A picture above the bed caught my eye and I stopped. It was bigger than the others and I had initially assumed it to be another drawing, but this wasn't from Katie's hand, this was Katie herself.

She was naked and snarling at the camera. She lay on her front, her silky body lying flat over a white table. Her breasts pressed tight against her ribcage, her buttocks lifted slightly into the air as she sensually caressed the table top with the tip of a thin strip of pubic hair.

I was impressed. I knew she would be hiding a great body, and even the best body in the world wouldn't have forced me to stay, but I was mesmerized. The photo was professional, sensual. She looked stunning.

I thought about turning back, going into the living room and putting up with whatever Katie had to throw at me, but the thought was fleeting.

I moved over to the window, sidestepping around the bed. My hands were on the frame when Katie walked into the room.

I turned at the sound of creaking floorboards to see her standing in the doorway. She was naked, her form silhouetted by the halo-glow from the hallway light behind her. I was spellbound by the silken curves of her body: her long, toned legs; her flat stomach, defined by gentle curves of muscle; her pert but ample breasts.

"Where do you think you're going?" She didn't sound mad but there was a touch of malevolence in her voice.

"I—I—" I tried to work out an excuse but it didn't come and the longer I waited the more stupid I looked. "I'm sorry," I said simply. I didn't want to turn my back on her, fearful she would pounce, but I knew if I stared any longer I would change my mind.

I turned around, gripped the window and pulled—it didn't budge. The wood creaked in response but the pane didn't move. I tried again, harder, but it still refused to move.

"That window doesn't open," Katie said plainly behind me. She still hadn't moved from the doorway.

"You're shitting me," I mumbled, my face flushing red, partly from exhaustion, mostly through embarrassment.

I turned to face her but couldn't look her in the eye. "I need to leave," I said, staring at the floor. "You mind if I use your door?"

Katie replied by stepping aside, leaving the beckoning light from the hallway to blare through unobscured.

I trudged forward. My heart picked up its pace when I passed her. I half expected her to jump me, but she didn't move. She allowed me to drift into the hallway.

"I'm so sorry," I said, ducking my head back in the bedroom, allowing myself one last glance at her naked form. Now that I knew she wasn't setting herself up to jump on me and murder me, I felt bad for her and felt a need to reassure her, or at least clean the air. "Maybe we can do this again sometime?" I said with a broad smile.

She glared at me ferociously, the anger evident in her eyes.

"Okay," I ducked back out of the bedroom, worried I had kick-started her rage. "Well, it was nice meeting you."

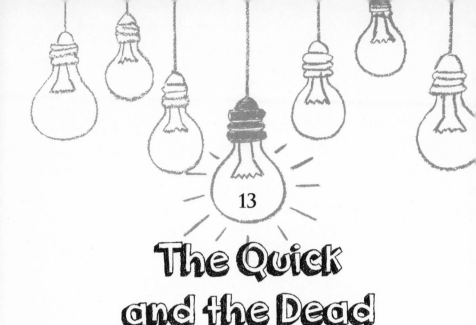

13

The Quick and the Dead

"Speed dating!"

It had been three weeks since my night with Katie, the flame-haired athlete-come-dominatrix. It had been three days since Matthew was able to make it an hour without bringing up the night in question and laughing hysterically.

"Speed dating?"

He was onto step two of his master plan to get me laid by as many women as possible, and as usual, I had no idea what he was talking about.

"Speed dating!" Matthew repeated, his eyes ablaze with euphoria.

"What is that?" I asked.

"It's exactly what it sounds like," Matthew exclaimed.

"It sounds like your dream come true."

Matthew beamed, fluttering a number of leaflets he held under his chin, as if to cool his excitement in case he swooned. "Exactly," he said, thrusting one of the leaflets at me.

"'A room full of single women, thirty minutes to see them all,'" I said, reading a random passage from the brightly colored leaflet. "Is this like an orgy?"

"I wish," Matthew said, his eyes drifting upward for a moment as his mind conjured and then stored that wish for later. "It's this new American thing; you rush through a couple dozen dates in an hour or so. It's like the ultimate blind date, cause if you don't like 'em, it doesn't matter; you only have to put up with 'em for five minutes."

"Five minutes?" I said, already feeling anxious. Most of the time it took me more than five minutes to tell a girl my name. "That doesn't seem like enough time at all."

Matthew shrugged this off. "If you like them you can swap numbers at the end, if you don't, *meh*," he shrugged again. "What's five minutes of your life?"

"It sounds demeaning."

"I don't—"

"For them," I quickly added.

"They'll love it, I'm sure. If not, then why would they show up?"

"Maybe they're desperate?"

I saw the glint appear in Matthew's eye and couldn't help but smile.

"Fair enough," I said. "I'll give it a shot."

I was nervous about meeting a succession of women in such a short time so I knocked back a few bottles of beer before the event. The alcohol did little to ease those nerves.

"You're not going to chicken out on me, are you?" Matthew warned with a quizzical raise of his right eyebrow.

"No, I'll go," I said truthfully. "I just don't feel comfortable with it."

Matthew took something out of his pocket. "I had a feeling you'd be like this," he told me. "So I brought these, just in case." He hovered his hand above mine, I opened my palm and he dropped two small blue tablets onto my sweaty flesh.

"What are they?"

"Valium. Sedatives. They'll calm you down, be right as rain."

I looked at him suspiciously, he grinned back.

"What you doing with sedatives?"

He shrugged impassively. "You remember that dancer girl I was with?"

"Jennifer?"

"June or Jessica."

"It was Jennifer."

"Whatever, it's beside the point. She was loud, right? Annoying really, never shut up. Hyper little bitch as well." An affected look crossed his face as he recalled his two-week relationship with the hyperactive dancer.

"I remember," I said slowly.

He looked at the Valium in my hand and gently shrugged his shoulders. "Well . . ."

"You drugged her!" I blurted.

He took a step back, pretended to look insulted. "I didn't. Honestly." He held up his hands. "I mean, I thought about it. . . ."

"You're disturbed."

He grinned. "I agree." He checked his watch. "Now come on, pop the pills, we gotta get going."

"You sure they're legit?"

"I got them from my doctor. I told some lies, said I had some psychological shit going on."

"And what were the lies?"

He feigned a mocking laugh. "Funny fucker, pop the pills, let's go."

The speed dating event was held in the back room of a large local club, a room that usually catered for bingo nights and birthday parties.

A number of two-seater tables—differing in sizes, colors and wood, suggesting more than a few had been borrowed for the event—decorated the middle of the room. Each table had a small glass vase placed in its center and two chairs tucked underneath its sides.

A fully stocked bar ran the full stretch of the left side of the room while the right was bare except for one large table, operated by a peppy middle-aged man and woman.

The middle-aged twosome gave Matthew and me a form, a pen, and a smile.

"Have you done anything like this before?" the woman asked, her eyes flicking between us.

"Has *anything* like this been done before?" I wondered, scanning the form. It was a list of womens' names with an empty box by each.

"Well, there have been a few events," the man butted in, his smile just as wide and genuine as the woman. It was creepy. "We met at one of these just last year," he said proudly, putting a gentle arm around the woman's shoulders. "We fell for each other straight away, exchanged numbers, and were married five months later."

She snuggled into the crook of his arm and wrapped her own arms around him, squeezing tightly and then quickly letting go.

"Isn't that sweet," Matthew said, the sarcasm not evident in his voice but clear in the look he gave me.

She leaned across and gave her husband a kiss on the temple. "He was number six. He was the perfect man. Tall, dark and so, so, so *incredibly* handsome . . ." She trailed off longingly, staring into his eyes.

"Handsome? What happened?" Matthew asked, ever the one to kill the moment.

The man looked at him unsurely for a moment and then slowly found a laugh. "Ah, you Brits and your humor," he said.

"You had much success with this speed dating over here?" I asked, keen to change the subject in case Matthew tried another, more successful insult.

"We've only done two events before this," the woman declared, finally moving out of her husband's loving grasp to pass a form and a smile to another aspiring speed dater. "The first wasn't as popular as we had hoped, but we learned our lesson, spread the word a bit more, and managed to pull off a very successful night second time around. A lot of people came; everyone had a lot of fun."

"And there are even more people here tonight," the man added. "It should be a floozy."

"Indeed," Matthew said, grinning at the choice of language. "So when does it start? Do we just jump right in now?" he wondered, looking across at a large gathering of anxious woman on the far side of the room.

"Oh no, you can't talk to the single ladies yet," she said, checking her watch. "The event begins in five minutes, take your seat now. I'll call you when it's time."

We did as instructed and found two tables next to each other, the chairs less than a foot apart.

Ten minutes later, the American woman stood, rang a bell to attract attention, and then declared, "Every man please take a seat. One to a table; there are enough tables for everyone."

A short bustling followed as eager males filed into the chairs.

"You will get five minutes with each of our gorgeous single ladies," she continued, gesturing toward the women and to a small stopwatch around her neck. "After the bell rings—" she held up a silver bell, jangling gently in her bony fingers, "—I want you to switch seats, moving clockwise around the room. No dallying please, we need to keep things going. I'm sure our lovely men will demand your attention but you need to move on. At the end, all forms will be handed in. Once the votes have been counted on both sides we'll see how many matches we have and you can exchange those telephone numbers! Are we ready to speed date?"

The crowd mumbled in reply.

The women moved like a swarm, smiles of expectation on their faces, glasses of wine in their hands.

There was a moment of silence, an eerie peace that blanketed the room after the sound of the bell, and then the women began to seat themselves and the room erupted in a cacophony of awkward greetings, rehearsed one-liners, and feigned laughter.

"Hello, my name is Cassy."

My first date: tall, blonde, tanned, a fresh yellow flower in her golden hair; a hint of an Aussie accent on her bright red lips.

"Hello."

I didn't know whether to go for a handshake or a kiss on the cheek. I decided for the handshake. I reached over the table and offered my hand, confident I would headbutt her if I tried to kiss her.

She clasped it and shook gently. My palm slipped in hers. I could feel the wetness of my own hand. I could sense the sweat as it transferred from me to her.

"I'm sorry," I said, withdrawing the appendage and wiping it on my trousers. "I didn't mean to, I mean I didn't know—"

"It's okay," she said genuinely.

"I washed my hands," I assured her. "I mean it's not dirty, it's not urine or anything. It's just sweat; I mean that probably sounds just as bad, well, certainly *bad*, perhaps not *as* bad."

She looked away shyly. I paused, cleared my throat awkwardly, and drained the last dregs from my bottle of beer.

"I mean it could have been perspiration from the bottle." I told her, glancing at the smeared glass. "Is it perspiration or is it condensation? Is there even a difference?"

I heard a loud cough and turned around to see Matthew glaring at me.

I stared at the empty bottle and fingered the sticker, peeling and picking away at the adhesive.

"They say this is a sign of sexual frustration," I said absently. "I never quite understood that. If you were *that* sexually frustrated and your hands were *that* idle, wouldn't it be easier just to have a wan—"

The bell sounded and the Australian girl sprang like a tightly wound jack-in-the-box. She flashed me a brief smile—the excitement and wonder in her face having faded somewhat—and disappeared without saying a word.

Number two looked like a man. It had short, dark hair, thick bushy eyebrows, a prominent brow, and a monstrous set of teeth that poked through an underbite with the jagged uncertainty of broken piano keys.

"Hi, my name is Ashley," it said in a voice that could have passed for a slightly feminine man or a slightly butch woman.

Despite many flaws, Ashley had a powerful set of green eyes that would suit any supermodel. They glistened at me from across the table, catching the light of the halogen bulbs above.

"I'm Kieran," I said.

This time I decided not to offer my hand, even though the sweat had now mostly dried or had been transferred onto my jeans or the hand of the Australian girl.

"You know, you have amazing eyes. I know that's a corny pickup line but I didn't mean it like that," I said. "Not like I wouldn't want to pick you up," I quickly corrected. "I mean you're a beautiful ma—woman." The inflection was a little higher than I had anticipated, it shot to the heights of helium abuse and I was forced to cough it away and pretend it hadn't happened by adding more base to the next few syllables. "*You are*, don't get me wrong. I just don't do pickup lines."

Ashley stared deeply at me, as if trying to figure something out.

"So . . ." I looked down at my fingers as I danced them absently on the table. "Do you come here often?"

The bell sounded again. The sound of chairs being shoved by eager backsides immediately followed.

Matthew leaned over before the third woman sat down.

"What the fuck are you playing at?" he asked in an angry whisper.

"I don't know, I really don't. I'm blabbering; I told you this was a bad idea. I'm still nervous; I don't think the pills are working."

"Calm down," he said in softer tones. "Let them do the talking."

Number three was a plump, middle-aged woman with a bubbly smile emanating from a face flushed with red, either through nerves, alcohol, or excitement.

I did as Matthew said and let her talk. I didn't even need an opening; she attacked the silence after our introduction like a dog attacking a piece of meat. She ate up the sentences like they were made of cake.

I pretended to listen to every word she spoke. If my brief experiences with women have told me one thing, it's that they not only like to talk but they like other people to listen. So I played the listener.

She stopped talking after she had munched through a handful of sentences. She had a look of expectation on her face.

"So?" she said, prolonging the word so it sounded like *soo-oooo*.

I had been thinking about something else, anything else; *everything* other than what this woman was saying to me.

"Sorry," I said, "I drifted off there. I didn't hear—"

"Am I boring you?" she quickly interrupted. Those sweet bubbly features now turning sour.

"No, not boring as such."

"*As such?*" I had flashbacks to my childhood and to Kerry Newsome—the same angry tone, the same questioning glare. I was sure that if she was standing, she would have her hands on her hips right now.

"It was interesting, honestly." I plastered a smile on my face; even *I* knew it looked disingenuous. "I'm just tired. Distant. Maybe a little drunk." I held up the empty bottle as if it were concrete proof.

"Don't patronize me." Her sour face looked prepared to spit. She seemed to be having an internal battle, perhaps deciding if she should empty her glass of wine on me or not. In the end the bell made her mind up for her, and she stood, distastefully muttered, "typical man," and departed.

"Three and out?" Matthew whispered across.

"She's got issues," I said. "She has some Jekyll and Hyde thing going on. I dodged a bullet there. Not my type anyway."

"I told you, tonight your type is female, end of. And even then we can make exceptions."

The eyes of number four were on me before she sat down and they never left me when she lowered a trim backside, fitted in tight formal pants, onto the seat. She was attractive, stunning actually, her features set with a film star glow reminiscent of a decade long dead. A charm nestled in her eyes, a beauty in the small lines at the corner of her mouth, a touch of class in her demeanor.

Like the previous single woman, she was about twenty years older than me, and before I could stop myself I made a point of mentioning it.

"You look a lot like my mother," I said it with a smile and good intentions, but my heart sank when I heard those words leave my lips.

The woman with the film star looks didn't react how I would have expected. She didn't frown, she didn't look away, she didn't slap me. There was a touch of indecision there, but nothing malignant.

"I'm so sorry," I said, covering my mouth, as if I could force the words back in. "I meant that as a compliment, honestly. I heard myself saying it . . . it didn't sound like a compliment, I know, but . . . I'm so sorry, I'm not very good at this."

"You have a tendency to speak before you think," she said, her voice soft, reassuring. I thought motherly, but quickly forced that thought out of my head in case it did any more damage.

"You don't know the half of it," I said, somewhat relieved she hadn't hit me yet. "I don't mean anything bad by it, I just can't help myself. I talked to the first girl too much, the last one talked to *me* too much—I didn't listen to a word—and the second, well, I'm not even sure that was a girl at all."

"Well, you haven't scared me away yet." A genuine warm smile curled at the corners of her mouth, as reassuring as her voice. "I'm Ally."

"Kieran."

"So Kieran, what brings you here?"

I glanced at Matthew. He was leaning across the table and listening intently to a woman who had yet to visit me. "A friend," I said, looking back at her. "He said it would be fun."

"Has it been?"

"It's been eventful I guess."

"You label offending three women as eventful?" Ally asked with a cheeky grin.

I smiled, suddenly overcome with shyness. "Just three? So you're not including yourself in that?"

"It's impossible to offend me," she said confidently.

"I'm sure I'd manage."

She seemed to ponder this. "Is that a challenge?"

I grinned. I sensed things were finally going my way. Then the bell rang.

Ally stood with an apologetic shrug. I watched grimly as she backed away from the table.

"That looked better," Matthew whispered across. "She was smiling, always a good sign."

"I liked her," I said, leaving space for a disappointed *but*.

"How did you blow it?"

"Why do you assume that I blew it?"

The next round of girls sat down and ended the hushed conversation.

Number five waited patiently for me to greet her, but I did so with such a lack of enthusiasm that I set the tone for five minutes of awkward coughing, throat clearing, and small talk.

I could feel the onset of the Valium, a wave of warmth that had started in my toes was now tingling its way through my thighs and my groin.

My inhibitions began to ebb away. I could feel my anxieties and my worries departing.

Number six was an anxious blonde; she didn't look much older than nineteen. Under the increasingly enchanting spell of the sedative, I felt a desire to connect with her; a oneness with my fellow human beings. But this newly found social desire translated into five minutes of blank staring and smiling, hereby increasing her anxieties while my own dissolved.

With number seven I made a good early start on the conversation, but it turned ugly, very quickly.

"So, have you been single long?"

"What is that supposed to mean?"

"I'm . . . nothing. I was just—"

"Why are you smiling like that?"

"I'm smiling? Am I smiling?"

"You don't know that you're smiling?"

"I do now, or at least I think that I know that I *am* smiling now, otherwise why would you have asked such a thing?"

"What?"

The five minutes couldn't have been up sooner for number seven; she nearly tripped over the chair as she scuttled onto the next table.

The steadily increasing warmth of the Valium continued to suck my inhibitions away by the minute, but during the eighth date that warmth exploded into an unimaginable heat.

Number eight was a small Asian woman with delicate features and a thin smile. She introduced herself, I gave my name, and then I insulted her. Another blip, another blabber. But this time I didn't react with a sinking heart; it was like watching a DVD of my life,

the impact moment had been played, but I was able to pause, hold
the scene and contemplate.

I was looking for the rewind button when she retaliated.

"What do you mean, 'We'll all be speaking Chinese in a few
years?'" She was no longer smiling but I was. I hadn't meant to say
what I said—it slipped out as so many careless words do—but I
didn't mind. The Valium took care of that.

"I didn't mean anything bad by it. I'm not racist or anything," I
assured her. "Or is it xenophobic?"

She didn't answer. She glared.

"If I don't object to the color of your skin but I hate your country, that's xenophobia, right?" I shrugged my own nonchalant reply.
"Anyway, I have no issue with you people."

"*You people?*"

"That sounded bad, didn't it?"

"Uh-huh." I could practically see the steam blowing out of her ears.

"I used to work with a guy who was Chinese," I said, trying to
sound serious but unable to brush off the simpleton smile still plastered over my face.

"Really?" she said, in a displeased monotone.

"Well, he was Korean, but it's the same thing, ain't it?"

She grunted a noise that didn't sound human, looked around the
table in fleeting aggression, and then shot upward, throwing her
chair backward with the force of her calf muscles. "You're despicable," she spat, her voice infused with rising octaves of frustration.

She stormed straight out of the room, her hair billowing behind
her as she strode through the doors and allowed them to slam shut
in her wake. A few people looked my way, a mixture of disgrace and
wonder on their faces.

Sober, I would have sunk my head ashamedly, or followed my disgraced date out of the room with a flushed color decorating my cheeks, but under the influence of sedatives, I returned each stare with a smile that said *isn't this wonderful?*

And I generally believed that, because at that moment I felt wonderful. After that moment, with the benefit of hindsight, I would have stopped myself. I would have gagged myself or kicked myself out of that room and into the street.

But I didn't have the benefit of sober hindsight and Matthew became too engrossed in the event to save me from myself.

First it was the turn of a pleasant, albeit obese, woman who shifted the table with her stomach when she sat down.

"God, you're a big girl, aren't you?" I said.

She saw the smile on my face and assumed it was either a cruel joke or I was mentally handicapped and had no power over what I said. Halfway through the date, she seemed to decide upon the latter (partially true in this case) after listening to a dialogue that ranged from the bathroom habits of Britain's fattest man to the economical upsides of anorexia.

After the bell, she retired, barely having spoken two words. She was replaced by a woman with dark hair, everywhere. The strong features of number ten were on the attractive side of plain, but were warped by a unibrow, a partially bleached mustache, and thin wisps of black on her cheeks.

We introduced ourselves and I watched with eager eyes—my face resting on upturned hands, my elbows on the table—as she told me about her hobbies and her job. I interrupted her after a minute or two, having not heard a word she said.

"You're very hairy, aren't you?"

Huffing like she was trying to blow my house down, she stood up, glared at me momentarily, and then spent the next four minutes of the date standing by the table, staring the other way. Her arms were crossed over her chest, her foot tapping monotonous rhythms on the floor.

I tried to engage her again, telling her I thought hair was sexy and even offering to help her wax, but I received nothing more than an annoyed grunt in reply.

The rest of the night went the same way. I didn't get much out of number eleven but sensed that I had annoyed her somehow, while number twelve made her annoyance clear by walking away after a passing comment I made about only coming to this event to look for sex with easy women.

The Valium was in full flow when the event was over, and I was disappointed when the final bell tolled and the call was made for everyone to hand in their forms. I filled my form out with gusto (generous with those I disliked, knowing that it didn't matter since they hated me) and handed it in.

I had enjoyed my time with Ally, the smart-looking woman in her forties who I had likened to my mother. I gave her the maximum score, not expecting anything in return. After the results were tallied I was delighted to learn that Ally had also rated me highly.

"So what happens now?" I asked the event organizers.

"We'll return the cards with your matches in half an hour or so. In the meantime, go and mingle!"

The men and women were mingling at the bar area and some had drifted into the other rooms in the pub, but I saw too many angry faces when I looked into the clutches of singles. I had no intention of joining in, regardless of my intoxication.

"Can I just leave my number with you?" I asked her. "If there is a match with anyone, *anyone*," I clarified with a sweep of my sedated hand, "Tell them to ring me; I'd be happy to take them out. But I have to go now."

"Are you sure?"

"Positive."

"And what about you?" she wondered, turning to Matthew.

"He's coming with me," I said, butting in.

Apologetic about the Valium, eager to learn the nature of my dates, and happy to divulge the nature of his, Matthew took me for a coffee and tried to force some sobriety and energy into my sedated bones.

The warmth of the drug faded after an hour and I grew lethargic. I had expected a pleasant fatigue, but it felt more like I had been hit over the head with a sledgehammer. I didn't trust my ability to stay awake, feeling the presence of sleep looming threateningly over me, so I called a taxi.

I arrived home just an hour and a half after the event. I scrambled to the bed, drudged out of my clothes, and fell flat onto the mattress. I was asleep before my face sunk into the sheets.

I woke around noon the next day, having slept for fourteen hours.

I remembered waking sometime in the night and stumbling to the toilet with a desperately full bladder, but I couldn't recall anything else. The phone had sounded a few times, but other than its impact on a surreal dream, the noise did little to disturb me.

Hoping to wash an arid dryness from my mouth and brush a foul smell from my tongue, I stumbled into the bathroom again and bore witness to my nighttime struggles.

"Oh, my dear god," the words seemed to grate out of my throat, crackling like a cooked pig.

I had lived in the house long enough for my instincts to guide me to the toilet in the dark, and I have urinated enough times in my life for my body to do the rest, but it seemed that no amount of instinct or experience could tell me whether the toilet seat was up or down.

The jets of urine had crashed against the closed lid and sprayed around the bathroom like water from a sprinkler.

The disgusting droplets ran down the front of an amusing gorilla poster, decorating the poor primate with yellow tears. A bar of sweet-smelling soap on the sink was now soured with the stench of ammonia and, worryingly, Cocoa Puffs. An aftershave bottle glistened like freshly sprayed apples in a grocer's window. A hand-towel was stained and damp; a bath-towel was soaked. An unlucky fly had been caught in the B-Movie horror show, having spent the night avoiding the streams of piss, it had eventually given up and taken an eternal swim in a stagnating pool on the windowsill.

The bristles of an electric toothbrush seemed to have avoided the spray but, if not tainted by proximity, would stand forever with the question of *what if* hanging over its use.

I picked my way through the bathroom with a pinched nose, regretting not putting on any slippers after taking my third step.

Despite my sleep, I was still feeling fatigued and was in no mood to clean up the mess. After managing to urinate without redecorating the bathroom, I quickly retired to the kitchen sink to wash my hands and feet with untainted soap and towels.

A digital display on the answering machine awaited me when I moved into the living room to wake myself up with a cup of coffee and some tedious daytime television.

It told me I had six messages. There had been none when I left the house last night.

The first was from the organizer of the speed dating event. Hearing her voice immediately sent me back to last night, flashing the memories through my mind like a slideshow tutorial on how to insult and upset people.

"Good evening, Mr. McCall, I hope I'm not phoning you too late but I wanted to give you the good news as soon as possible! I have given your number to two of our beautiful girls. They both liked you and rated you higher than anyone else at the event, isn't that something?" she said this like she was asking something else, something like *how the hell did that happen?* "Anyway, just thought I'd let you know!"

My spirits rose somewhat. The tiredness hanging over my head and the disaster-area waiting for me in the bathroom were now a distant part of my day. Two people liked me. I had no idea how I had managed to impress as many as that, but it felt good.

The second message, sent late last night, helped to further lift my morning:

"Hello, Kieran, right? I hope so, I hate using these things and if this is the wrong number . . ." The voice was soft, pleasant, and familiar. "This is Ally, I met you at the speed dating. I'm sure you'll remember, I'm the one who looks like your mother. The little American woman gave me your number so I thought I'd give you a call, and considering you're not in, I'll leave you my number and pretend to play it cool while I wait for you to call." She reeled off her number and hung up. She didn't seem as cool or confident as she had last night, but I was still drawn to her.

11:30

Still last night, the messages coming through while I drifted into a drug-induced temporary coma.

"Hello, Kieran, sweetie," The voice was also female and no doubt from the second woman that the organizer had said was interested, but it wasn't familiar. "Just thought I'd drop you a line, see how you were, what you were doing, ya know . . . so . . . ring me back!"

11:45

"Me again!" So peppy, so happy, but not filled with the pleasant tones that Ally's voice was. Something else lurked behind those high-pitched, exclamation-riddled syllables. "So, you haven't called yet, that's okay. I wasn't sure you'd got my last message or not, just wanted to make sure you got this one! Have a good night!"

12:03

"Just to let you know I'm going to bed now." A touch of sadness had crept into the voice. "I'll phone you tomorrow, or you phone me, either way . . . just don't phone tonight. Unless you really want to! Goodnight."

01:03

I cringed, expecting another call from the strange woman. It was Matthew, drunk and trying to order a pizza from the automated voice on my answer machine.

08:05

"Good morning." It was her again. "Silly me, I just realized that I didn't give you my number last night—"

She began to give her number; I ended the message, having no desire to hear anymore. I had to prepare for Ally. I had to clean, dress, eat. I had to clear my head and phone her, have a conversation that didn't begin with me comparing her to my mother. I needed to ask her out, book a rest—

The phone rang again. I assumed it was Ally, probably because she had been on my mind when it rang. I wasn't awake enough to remember I wasn't psychic.

I picked it up on the second ring.

It wasn't Ally.

"Good morning, Kieran!" the voice came through like the greeting of a Prozac-pumped morning radio DJ. I suddenly felt an urge to request "It's Raining Men" and jump in the shower.

"Good—" I cleared my throat of a particularly restrictive clump of phlegm. "*Good* morning."

"You sound ill," the excited tones mellowed into sympathy.

"Just a little worse for wear," I said, allowing my voice to dip into the threshold of influenza.

"Oh, poor you."

"Poor me." I feigned a small cough, the action grated my throat.

"Why don't I come around and make you some chicken soup?"

"You know where I live?"

"Of course not."

Good, I thought, allowing my heart rate to settle a little.

"Oh, okay. I thought I'd told you. Never mind," I backtracked, keen not to offend. "So, what are you up to today?"

"Housework, daytime television, you know, the usual. I have the week off and this is how I spend it! Pathetic, huh?"

I laughed unsurely. "Where do you work? I can't remember if you told me," I said, still unsure about anything she had said or even who she was.

"I *didn't* tell you. I'm a model. Just magazines, stuff for the Internet, some company stuff. Nothing too fancy."

I racked my brain for anyone at the speed dating event who could have passed for a model. Ally was certainly one of them, with her film star looks and her radiant charm. She was a little too old for glamour work and too full-figured for catwalks, but could easily replicate the smiling faces you saw in stock photographs.

The Australian girl had been pretty, but there was no hint of an Aussie accent here. The Chinese woman had been very cute and had an English accent, but she hated me. If she was masochistic enough to want to date me, she would have surely mentioned the xenophobic remarks from last night.

I vaguely recalled two younger women who had both been attractive and devoid of personality—two traits common in the modeling field—but neither had shown even a remote interest.

"Are you okay?"

She was still talking. I had drifted off.

"I'm fine," I said abruptly.

"You went quiet on me."

"I'm sorry, I'm a little tired."

Was it possible I had been so wasted that I had forgotten one of the dates? Had I managed to charm this woman while in a fugue state, only to completely forget about her?

"Why don't you go get some rest, sweetie," she said.

Is she so forward because I started something with her last night? Did I already go on a date with her?

Can't be, I thought. *Surely not.*

Maybe I'm losing my mind.

"Will do," I said.

"Give me a ring when you feel better, we can arrange something then."

"Arrange something?"

She giggled, "A date, silly! Our *first* date. Our first *proper* date that is. So we can get to know each other properly. You know, technically I've only known you for five minutes, but I feel like I've known you for a lifetime."

"Okay." I didn't know what else to say. "See you later then."

I hung up and sunk into the couch.

I had destroyed my bathroom in a trance but I hadn't gone on an extended date in one. She was just forward, *very* forward. She was also a model and she liked me, and as much as I liked Ally and preferred the idea of spending time with her, I still wanted to see where things went with the unnamed girl. I had to keep my options open.

I'm dating two women, I thought with a grin. *Matthew would be so proud of me.*

The Film Star and the Model

I tried phoning Ally but her phone rang out. I showered, dressed, poured a large cup of coffee down my throat, and tried again; it was still ringing out.

I didn't want to leave a message on her answering machine. I didn't trust myself in the silence; I would end up embarrassed and she would end up with an extended monologue.

Hoping to clear my head, I went into town.

The day was bright and the wind was cool enough to freshen me up as I walked head-on into it, down a busy midmorning high street. The speed dating hadn't gone as well as I had hoped and I still cringed a little when I recalled my efforts to impress, but the fact that I had managed to win over two women cheered me up to no end. I walked with my head held high, a proud smile on my face.

In the street, I smiled at everyone I passed, happy to share my good mood with the world. A permanent whistle pushed through my pursed lips.

I didn't doubt that there was still a sense of sedation in my bloodstream aiding my happiness but, artificial or not, I was happy to be happy. Few others shared my mood. The majority looked back with glum, disinterested faces, as if they couldn't be bothered to face the day with a smile and wondered what gave me the right to do so.

A couple of faces did return my smile, and I was overjoyed to see that one of them was Ally.

I was peering in through the window of an electronics shop at the time, eyeing up a display of computer games. I had seen her from behind, but without recognition. Her long silky hair draped between her shoulder blades, the faint arches of which were hidden underneath a glorious white jacket. I had glanced, admired, wondered if she was pretty, and then concentrated on a poster over her shoulder.

When she turned to look at me, my eyes were already on hers. She looked a little confused at first—somewhat surprised to see me standing there staring—but eventually she curiously ambled out of the shop, leaving a perplexed friend to study a row of portable televisions.

"Kieran, hey!" she said. "What are you doing here?"

Her attire matched the confident woman I had met yesterday. Underneath the short, padded jacket she wore a thin, billowy white blouse, latticed all the way across the neck and between the buttons, barely a stitch out of place. Her face was lightly made-up, just enough to accentuate her natural beauty, her hair neatly aligned behind her neck, catching the glare from the sun above.

She placed her hands gently on my shoulders, leaned in close and kissed me on the right cheek, then she pulled back; she smelled of expensive perfume and coconut shampoo.

"I don't know," I said with a shrug, my mood increased tenfold having seen her. "Just fancied a walk I guess."

"Oh, okay." She didn't look too sure.

"It's a good thing I ran into you actually," I told her. "I tried phoning you earlier, you weren't in."

The smile sagged partially as she peered back into the shop. "No, I've been out all morning," she said.

"Well I know that now," I laughed a little, and she offered an awkward smile. "I was just wondering if you'd like to get to know each other a little better."

"What, now?"

She didn't look as confident as last night, when she had been so assured of herself and her surroundings. She was wobbling gently as she stood, her eyes flicking around almost impatiently.

"No," I said, shaking my head. "Well, unless you want to?"

She didn't seem impressed. She glanced at her feet unsurely, then looked back at me, a half-smile etched onto her elegant face. "Tonight maybe."

"Tonight sounds great. Do you want to come to mine, or . . ."

"A restaurant," she said quickly.

"Okay."

"I'm sure your place is great," she was quick to add, a defensive tone in her words. "But I know this great place, great food. Vegetarian as well," she said, seeming to effortlessly regain her ease.

"Vegetarian? You mean like salads and—"

"It's *sooo* good," she exclaimed.

"—bread?"

"What?"

"Nothing," I beamed. "Vegetarian it is."

She gave me the details and scurried off, back to her friend. I saw them talking, their faces close together, their words hushed. Her friend looked over at me a few times, quickly turning away when she saw me looking.

I tried to force my happiness to return, but it was flagged by a weight of uncertainty. I didn't know quite what to think about Ally. The run-in had been a little odd, certainly more so than last night. She still possessed the same untouchable beauty, but there was something else there.

That night, on my date with Ally, I ordered the stuffed mushrooms for starters. Ally recommended them. I didn't really like mushrooms but she seemed enthusiastic about the recommendation so I didn't object.

They came piled high with an assortment of weeds—the spotty waiter had given them a fancy name, but they were definitely weeds. The mushroom sat underneath the foliage, suffocated by garlic-infused cheese that dripped over the sides like pus from a putrefied pimple. The base of the mushroom squeaked and shifted on the plate when I dug my fork into it, bleeding black oil onto the ceramic with every movement.

"They look so tasty," Ally said. I noticed she was picking up a habit of lying.

I ate them with feigned gusto and was glad when my plate was clean, the contents diminished to an inky, oily pool.

"Lovely," I told Ally afterward.

She was thrilled that she had chosen well. "Didn't I tell you?" she said.

She hadn't ordered the stuffed mushrooms. It didn't feel right for her to make a pushy recommendation, wait for me to order, and then order something entirely different for herself, but I didn't say anything; it was our first date, I could let that one slide.

"You did," I said with a smile, taking note never to listen to her again.

The main course was an amalgamation of vegetables chopped and boiled into a pate and served on another section of the Amazon Rainforest. I picked at it with my fork, hoping to weed out the bugs before I dove in.

"So, how long have you been a vegetarian?" I asked.

"I'm not," she said simply.

I looked at her in horror.

She noted my reaction and laughed softly. "I know, I'm sorry, but it's nice, right? You like it?"

I decided not to dignify that with a response.

She smiled and took a sip of wine, peeking at me above the rim as the red liquid swished around below her nose. "I used to come here with my husband," she told me softly, looking down at her plate in silent contemplation.

I had been inspecting a soppy piece of greenery, wondering if I was supposed to eat it or if it was decorative. I dropped it back onto my plate.

"Husband?"

"Don't worry." She looked back up at me, a forced smile breaking out. "Not anymore, we broke up awhile back."

"Oh," I softened. "That's okay; I don't want to go down that road again."

"Again?"

"Never mind." I picked the greenery back up and decided to risk it. It went into my mouth and then popped out again; it tasted like a dead dandelion. "What happened with you two?" I wondered, trying to talk the taste of deceased weeds out of my mouth.

Ally had retreated from her confident stance, slipping into reticence and bashfulness. I watched her with intrigue, wondering what was going on inside her head.

She took a long drink of wine. "He was a *bastard*, that's all. Best not to talk about it."

I didn't really want to hear about it, not if it was going to diminish the confident side of her that I admired, but I sensed she wanted to talk about it regardless of what she said.

"Are you sure? I don't mind if you—"

"He was a dick," she blurted out, suddenly showing me a third side of her personality, a bitter and resentful side. "He cheated on me." She pointed a fork at me as she spoke; a smudge of avocado dripped off the prong and fell onto the tablecloth. "*Three times!*"

"I'm sorry," I said, not sure how else to react and genuinely feeling apologetic under her accusing glare.

"I finished with him and he had the nerve to *stalk me*! Can you believe it?"

"No," I said. "I'm sorry."

"He was a pitiful man. A lying, cheating—" She shook her head. "—*bastard*," she reiterated, letting the word fall out of her mouth like a clump of bad tasting bile.

"I see." I looked as thoughtful as I could. "I'm sorry."

She laughed a little and shook the anger out. "No, I'm sorry," she said, repositioning herself on the seat as Hyde departed and Dr. Jekyll returned. "I was getting started then, every time I *think* about him or *talk* about—" she shivered. "Let's just leave it."

We did, and I was thankful for it. Ally turned back into the cool, confident sophisticate she had initially appeared to be. After the main course, we talked about the speed dating event, she told me she had met a sleazy guy who reminded her of her husband, she said he tried to talk his way into her pants and would have probably gotten there if not for her experience with scum-of-the-earth like him. I kept quiet. I knew she was talking about Matthew; it seemed wise to pretend I didn't know him.

After a light, green-free dessert, I paid up and we left the restaurant. Outside Ally told me she had a wonderful time, beaming proudly as she said it. She kissed me softly and compassionately on the cheek, said a pleasant goodbye, and then walked off down the street.

She left me standing there, perhaps presuming I would walk straight ahead into a taxi, or veer off in the other direction. She didn't realize I lived in the same direction and I didn't want to tell her. We had already done the goodnight dance and it had gone well. In a life of awkward embarrassment, it was good to have one occasion that I didn't mess up.

Instead I pretended to tie my shoe in case she looked back. I waited around a minute for her to get a good distance away, and then I followed.

I put my head down as my mind pondered the night and the three sides of Ally I had encountered. Matthew had told me to be careful of divorced women, especially those above forty. "If they've been married for a long time," he'd said once, 'they've had all the life and enjoyment sucked out of them, and once the divorce comes in, that all gets replaced with bitterness. They'll act nice and polite, but only because they know how to fake it. Shag them and then try to leave them in the morning and they'll slice open your scrotum with their high heels."

Matthew's advice usually came from experience; I could only assume the same applied to those words of wisdom. His balls had taken a lot of abuse.

I walked with a twisted smile on my face thinking about Matthew and his tendencies toward the sadomasochists of the world. That smile was still there when Ally called my name.

I looked up to see her standing just a few feet ahead of me, a look of worrisome curiosity on her face. She was leaning against a wall that marked the perimeter to a nearby garden; in her hand, she held a high-heel shoe. She had clearly stopped to pick stones or gum from the sole, but a lump stuck in my throat when I saw the malevolent footwear.

"What are you doing?" she asked with raised eyebrows.

I stopped, hesitated. "I'm going for a walk," I said innocently, not wanting to reveal the awkwardness of the initial goodbye. "I didn't know you'd gone this way."

Yes, you did. I said to myself. *You watched her; she* watched *you* watch *her.*

"I mean, I did," I clarified. "I just wasn't really looking."

That makes no sense.

I tried again: "I *looked*, but, well, I guess I got lost."

She slipped the shoe back on and took a couple steps back. "We had a good night, Kieran." I detected a slight tremble in her voice. I stepped forward to reassure her, but that only forced her back a few more steps. "Why don't we leave it at that for tonight?" she spoke slowly.

I shrugged. "Sounds fine."

She turned and hotfooted it away into the darkness. I waited for a few more minutes and then set off again, keeping an eye on the path ahead of me and walking like a disabled turtle.

When I arrived back home, I wasn't surprised to see that the unnamed, unknown model had left a message for me on my answering machine. The red flashing light clawed at me in the darkness:

"Kieran, just wanted to see how you were. You feeling any better? Ready for our date yet? I know I said I'd wait for your call, but *well,* I couldn't wait!"

The message was followed by a mixture of awkward laughter and repeated throat clearing. It cut off after several cringeworthy seconds.

I didn't want to let the woman down. I also wanted to redeem myself after screwing up a good date with Ally, a girl who now probably assumed I was stalking her.

I phoned the unnamed girl back that night. She was as hyper and awkward as she had been on the answering machine, but after a few minutes she relaxed. I wasn't so apprehensive about arranging a date at that point so I agreed to a dinner date the following weekend.

As the week progressed and the date grew near, the apprehension returned with bite. It worried me that I was going on a potentially one-sided blind date. I sought out Matthew's advice to see if he could help me determine who she was. He didn't have a clue but he did suggest I meet her and sleep with her.

I waited for her outside the restaurant with a rapid heart. I tried to act casual, to lean back on a lamppost, foot up, eyes down, but I never could pull off cool and casual. I looked like a rapist on the prowl.

I caught the eyes of a couple beautiful women coming toward me on the street, and I prayed that she was one of them, that they had been there on the speed date, that I had completely forgotten about them and now I was going to have a night to remember with one of them.

When a taxi pulled up a few feet away and she climbed out, I remembered her instantly. She hadn't slipped my memory at all. I even remembered her name.

"Hey, Ashley," I said, putting on my best smile and walking toward her.

She clambered out of the car with the decorum of a lemming. She paid the driver and then joined me on the pavement.

She wore a long black dress, but not very well. It was loose around the shoulders, the straps slipped off repeatedly. It hung over her figure like a football uniform.

Her eyes were as mesmerizing as I remembered, the brightest green I had ever seen, but the rest of her was also as I remembered.

She was far from attractive and looked like a man in loose-fitting drag. I didn't want to let her sense my disappointment, though. I felt guilty for thinking those thoughts about her, especially since I had agreed to go on the date. I knew I would just have to battle through, get to the end of the night, and then calmly and politely brush her off.

In the restaurant, I drank my way through a bottle of wine before the main course arrived. Ashley noted my thirst and didn't seem to mind. She joined me and we got through another three bottles before dessert. It began as a way to get through the evening, but when the alcohol started flowing, I enjoyed myself.

She was a little boring, tedious, and awkward, but I was more than content to stare into her eyes and listen to her recall her life story. By the time the night was out, and I had drank a few bourbons to finish the meal, I had even convinced myself that she was an incredibly beautiful woman, who, now I had gotten to know her, was just the girl I was looking for.

The rest of the night went by in a blur. The walk home, the kiss, the invitation inside, the sex. It all sped by in a drunken haze.

The next morning I woke up in a strange bed, in a strange house. I was naked and clammy, thin bedsheets stuck to my body. Ashley was naked next to me.

My head rang with a relentless ache. My breath was dry and smelled of stale wine and bourbon. My body also ached, partially from dehydration, but also from the deep scratches that Ashley had carved into my back the previous night, some of which had bled onto the cream sheets and were already healing into painful scabs.

The events of the previous night flooded back. I threw the sheets off my fatigued body and brushed my hands against my face to restore some vigor, removing the sleep that had wedged into my eyelashes and the corners of my eyes.

The first memory to bite my fatigued, tender brain was her voice: she had insisted on talking about everything, no matter how mundane, in every detail. It gave me a headache just remembering it. I had listened to and ignored more information about her then I could have ever hoped to hear.

Then came the memories of the awkward, sloppy kissing: she had a way of using her tongue long before our lips met, like she was lubricating them in preparation. More than once I had taken a break to surreptitiously wipe my mouth on the back of my hand.

Then the end of the night: after a stumbling walk home, hand in hand, arm in arm, there had been the violent, demanding, strange, and aggressive sex. Not only did she scratch my back, claw my buttocks, and play my stomach like a bass drum, but at some point she forced her finger into my anus and then tried to get me to lick the contaminated appendage. Thankfully I hadn't been that drunk, but unfortunately I didn't remember much more.

I shivered at the flashbacks of what I remembered and winced at the thoughts of what I didn't. I turned to see Ashley lying next to me; she was snoring silently and making sporadic gurgling sounds. Her left hand was tucked under her cheek, and her fingers and the pillowcase were moist with drool.

Then I remembered her leg.

She had removed it during sex.

I looked down at her body under the covers and, sure enough, her silhouetted form was short of a right leg, the imprint under the covers stopped halfway up the thigh. I saw the missing prosthetic limb on the floor, over by the other side of the bed.

I clambered out of the bed. My clothes—all of them, even my socks—were on the other side as well, her side. That was Ashley's doing; she had insisted I let her strip me completely when we scrambled onto the bed.

I tiptoed around the bottom of the bed, maneuvering around the jutting mattress atop the solid wooden bedframe. My foot creaked on a loose floorboard. I panicked and stood still.

Ashley continued to snore, oblivious. Content, I ambled forward carelessly. I jammed my toes against the bottom leg of the bed and screamed as the tiny digits parted against the wood construct.

That was enough to wake her.

She looked at me with questioning morning eyes—beautiful green eyes, even more radiant in the first light of the day.

"Where you going?" She thrust herself up onto her elbows and glared at me. I expected a morning greeting, maybe some light questioning, but she was already in full accusative mode. This wasn't the first time someone had run out on her.

"I'm going home," I said honestly, too tired and dehydrated to lie.

I made a move for my clothes, ignoring the throbbing pain in my toe, but she dove out of bed and grabbed them, bringing the bundle to her chest and pulling them back into the bed with her.

I pulled myself back upright, the simple action tiring me out. "What are you doing?" I asked breathlessly.

"You're not going anywhere," she said defiantly, hugging my clothes like a child with a confiscated toy.

I watched her eyes dip from my face to my naked body. She surveyed it quickly with a lustfully sly grin.

"Look, last night was a mistake," I told her, ignoring the suggestive looks. "I hope I didn't give you the wrong impression, but I don't think this will work out."

"The wrong impression?" she spat. "You mean when you fucked me?"

"Well, yeah."

She made a loud groaning noise and then she shoved the clothes underneath the blanket. I could see the bulge over her stomach and leg.

I sighed deeply and slumped my tired, aching head to my chest. I could see her clothes on the floor, clumped into a ball near where mine had been. A skimpy G-string and a long dress that would probably fit me better than it did her.

"Don't you dare!" she snapped, seeing my intentions. She swung out of the bed again, leaving my clothes nestled between her leg and stump. She picked up her dress and underwear and pulled them back to the bed with a pendulum swing.

"What do you want from me?" I wondered, arms out.

"Come back to bed," she insisted.

"I told you—"

"We can make it work. We just need to spend some more time together."

"But—"

"You had a good time last night, didn't you?" she asked.

"Well yes, but—"

"Then come back to bed."

I stared at her and thought about giving in. She did have the most mesmerizing eyes—

I couldn't give in. I couldn't let her eyes lure me like the song of a sickly siren.

I saw her leg on the floor, discarded toward the far wall, out of reach of the bed. I waddled over to it and picked it up. "I'll take this then," I told her, thrusting it angrily toward her.

She shrugged apathetically.

"You need it more than I need my clothes," I told her, waving it around triumphantly.

"Nah. I'll be fine," she said, trying some reverse psychology.

"I'll leave," I said. "And I'll take it with me, then what?"

She smiled. "Then you'll be naked, carrying a prosthetic leg down the street. Are you that desperate to get away from me?"

I thought about that for a moment. I *was* that desperate. I gave her an ultimatum: "Give me my clothes back or I walk out of here, and you never will."

"You don't have the balls."

In the heat of the moment, feeling temperamental from the hangover and annoyed with the persistent woman in front of me, I felt like I didn't have any other choice. I stormed out of the bedroom and out of the house, cradling the leg in my right arm.

I heard her call after me, but I ignored her. I was angry, I was tired. I wanted to get home and sleep without the one-legged beast drooling next to me.

I slipped on my shoes, which had been left near the front door. The reality of my nakedness hit me when I stepped out into the street. A chill wind saturated the air and brushed across my flesh like a cold seductress.

I stayed at the front door for a while, surveying my surroundings. She lived in a quiet slice of suburbia; semi-detached houses littered the street ahead. A high perimeter hedge obscured the views to the left and the right, stopping the next door neighbors from seeing my dangling humility.

I was going to turn around; I had come to my senses and realized I didn't want the world to see my bits blowing in the wind, but then I heard Ashley. She had hobbled out of bed and hopped to the bedroom window. She was shouting down at me.

"You finished with your games yet?" she called down. "I'm bored and horny. Come back up here and fuck me."

I cringed and shivered. It was difficult and traumatic sleeping with her drunk—there was no way I could manage it sober.

I clambered onward, waving my arms around in a marching walk. I slowed down at the head of the garden, giving her a clear view of my retreating cheeks as I opened the gate and disappeared into the street.

I was happy to see there was no one else in the street, but it crossed my mind that there was sure to be a lot of people between here and my house—a good twenty-minute walk through estates and busy roads.

I hadn't brought a mobile phone, and if I had I certainly wouldn't have stored it in my anal cavity. If I did have a phone, I could have called Matthew, who would have relished such a situation, but could have saved me from embarrassment.

I walked on with my head down, not knowing where to go or what to do. I knew that the last thing I wanted to do was walk all the way home looking like this, but I walked on regardless.

I passed a number of houses and saw curtains twitch out of the corner of my eye. I was using the prosthetic leg to preserve my dignity, but I doubted that would absolve the moment of any absurdity.

I stopped. I turned around.

I had left on an impulse, a moment of anger and desperation. That moment had passed in the cold, moist air. Now I felt ashamed and exposed.

Ashley's house was visible, but I had already walked a couple of hundred yards. I didn't want to have to walk all the way back to her, not when the prize was having to face her again.

Swallowing what little pride I had and ignoring all the voices in my head that screamed against it, I headed to the nearest house.

It was an unorthodox method, but I was sure I could find someone to help me. Someone who would let me use their phone or give me something that would hide my nudity better than Ashley's leg.

I knocked on the door, hung my head, and waited. It was going to be awkward, but it had to be done. I imagined a small child answering the door and then his or her father beating me up and accusing me of pedophilia, but I pushed that to the back of my mind.

I heard someone approaching the door. They fiddled with the lock. I heard the small device click.

The door swung open. I slowly lifted my head.

"Ally!" I said merrily.

The woman with the film star looks and the interchangeable personalities was standing in the open doorway with an appalled and worried look on her face. Her eyes moved up and down over my naked body a few times before settling on my face.

She still had her hand on the doorframe; I saw her flesh squeeze as she gripped it hard, ready to swing it shut in my face.

"I'm so glad to see you," I said, releasing all my anxieties in a long breath. "Can you give me a hand?"

She looked down at the leg, and I followed her eyes.

"Or a leg," I added, laughing meekly. She didn't look amused. "It's okay, just ignore it." I stood the leg up by the side of the house; it fell over, apparently not used to standing without the weight of a human attached to it. I repositioned it steadily, it fell again, and I ignored it. "I need your help," I told her.

She tried to say something, but she was speechless. She cowered backward, the door edged closer to the jamb.

I raised my hands, stepped forward. "Please, it's not what it looks like. I'm not really sure *what* it looks like, but I'm sure it looks odd. I just need to use your phone."

"My phone?" her voice crackled.

"Just to call a friend, or a taxi."

"I can do that for you," she said unsurely.

I clapped my hands together joyfully. "Excellent," I proclaimed. "I can give you the number—"

The door slammed shut.

"Or you could just phone a taxi!" I shouted through the sealed wood.

I leaned forward, trying to peer through the glass. I could see a smeared form on the other side of the door. It appeared to be hunched over, something pinned to its ear.

I smiled and took a step back, admiring the house and keeping an eye on the street for any passers-by.

I gave Ally enough time to finish the call and then peered through the door again, but she had gone. I hopped onto the front garden, crossed the small lawn and peered through the front window. She had the curtains drawn and I couldn't see beyond the thick material. I tapped on the glass and waited to see if she shifted the curtains, but she didn't.

"Some clothes would be nice," I called through. "Maybe a drink, I'm really thirsty." I waited with my face against the glass, but she didn't respond.

I was cold. The alcohol had done a number on my body and now it needed sustenance. I hopped up and down in the middle of the lawn, rubbing my hands together. My bouncing balls would no doubt be an amusing sight to any passing neighbors, but it helped to keep me warm.

After a few minutes of waiting, I heard a car pull up outside the house, obscured slightly by the hedge that ran around the perimeter. I walked down the path, opened the gate, and peered out.

Two policemen were striding quickly toward me. They started and stiffened when they saw me and then, almost simultaneously, they pounced.

"No," I objected, standing back. "It's not what it looks like."

They grabbed me and pulled me away from the gate and out into the street. Before I knew what was happening, one of them had strapped my hands behind my back with a pair of handcuffs.

"This is a misunderstanding," I said when my rights had been read.

"Like to wobble your bits for the ladies eh, loverboy?" one mocked as they escorted me back to the car.

"It's not what it looks like!"

They opened the back door to the car; I felt a hand on the back of my head as they pushed me under the roof and into the back seat.

"Try not to mess up the seat," the other said, his face twisted in disgust.

"Wait!" I called, before he slammed the door shut on me. He dipped back inside, sneering at me. "I forgot my leg. Can you go get it for me?"

They exchanged amused grins, then one of them reluctantly went back to the house to have a few words with Ally. When he returned a few minutes later, he was carrying Ashley's leg and looking perplexed.

He slid into the passenger seat with the prosthetic between his legs. "You want to explain this?" he asked, looking at me over his shoulder.

"Not really," I replied timidly.

15

Doctor Peterson

They took me to the police station, recorded my name and address, told me I would be questioned, and then led me to a cell. They didn't have the decency to give me anything to cover my nakedness, and they took away the leg. They also took away my shoes.

"Seriously?" I argued with the woman whose job it was to remove the offending sneakers.

"It's the rules," she said sternly. "No shoes."

"Why? New carpets?"

She glanced up at me to show she wasn't impressed and then continued to remove the shoes. When she had finished, she put them to one side and grabbed my elbow, which seemed to be the only place any of them were willing to touch; it wasn't anywhere near my ass or my penis, the perfect safe zone for them.

"You think I'm going to use them to escape?" I asked her as she guided me down a dim, cold corridor. "Because I'm not that smart, I don't think anyone is."

"It's so you don't harm yourself."

"With *shoes?*"

"You could use the laces to hang yourself," she said matter-of-factly.

I stopped walking, she stopped with me. "Are you having me on?" I wondered softly.

She shook her head.

"You think I'm going to hang myself with shoelaces?"

She nodded her head slowly.

I looked into her eyes for a moment, shrugged, and continued walking. It wasn't worth the argument.

She led me to a windowless cell. A bed rested against the right side, a thin foam mattress lying on top, a cold sheet draped over. On the other side was a steel toilet with no base and no lid. It looked foreboding and cold. I was happy I didn't need to use it and hopeful that I wouldn't.

Inside she released my elbow, stepped back, and closed the door. The jangle of keys rattled down the empty corridor as she locked the door. She said a mocking goodbye and then I heard her footsteps pounding the cold corridor floor.

They left me alone in that cell for a couple hours. When they finally came to collect me, I was wrapped in the bedsheet and curled up on the bed.

They took me to a small interview room and gave me a very brief and confusing interview. The officer conducting it looked like he wanted to be somewhere else. He rarely looked at me, seemed annoyed when I spoke, and rushed through a series of questions like he was presenting a quiz show.

I could have put his behavior down to my nakedness and a potential for shy reserve, but I was wrapped tightly in the bedsheet—having brought it with me—and he didn't look like the reserved type.

After the short session he exited the room without explanation.

I was left alone to ponder what had just happened and in the silence I decided I was going to give him a lecture on human rights and police brutality when he came back. It wasn't strictly brutality, but it was very mean nonetheless and he needed telling.

I prepared a little speech in my head, but when the door finally opened and someone stepped inside, that speech vanished, as did every other thought.

The woman who walked in was not wearing a police uniform, nor was she wearing the smarmy smile that they had all possessed after witnessing me walking naked down their halls. She had a soft face. She was smiling. She was beautiful.

She had blonde hair, locks of which strayed on her face; dark eyes that caught the light and held a deep intensity; a porcelain face with such neat and small features, encapsulated by a tiny upturned nose and whisper thin lips that arched artistically into cupid's bow.

I was mesmerized, awestruck.

She held out a hand and offered a smile. "Doctor Peterson," she said.

I mumbled something, snapped out of my trance, and said, "Kieran," suddenly not entirely sure that was my name.

She sat down opposite me and took a folder out from a bag she had carried in with her. I studied her intently.

"So, Kieran," she spoke slowly. "What brings you here?"

She was joking, but I answered her anyway. "Two guys claiming to be police officers. You?"

"A naked guy carrying a wooden leg."

I nodded. I relaxed a little in her presence, but was still all too aware of how nervous and awkward her beauty, and my current vulnerability, made me feel.

"It wasn't wooden," I explained. "I think they call them *prosthetics*."

She smiled and nodded. Then something clicked for me.

"You said *Doctor?*" I noted, leaning forward.

She nodded, almost apologetically. "That's right."

"And I'm guessing you don't have a stethoscope in there?" I gestured toward the bag, which was now on the floor.

"Actually I do, but only for personal reasons," she smiled; I glared. "Only joking," she clarified.

"Oh."

"I'm a psychiatrist."

"*Ohhhh.*"

"How does that make you feel?"

"What?"

"I'm sorry, I'm messing with you," she laughed softly. She took a piece of paper out of a brown folder and studied it.

I shifted uncomfortably, pulling the sheet tighter around my torso.

She looked up at me. The smile had faded; something serious and sinister entered her face. "We can't seem to find any record of you, Mr. McCall."

"I exist, I can assure you."

She was looking at me but she didn't seem to hear me. "No police records, no health records to speak of."

"I think I had my tonsils out when I was a kid."

She frowned. "You *think?*"

"It may have been my appendix."

She looked at me intensely for a moment as if she was trying to figure me out, then she blinked and turned away. "No psychiatric record is what I mean," she clarified.

"Never seen a psychiatrist before," I told her. "You're my first." I thought about winking, but I didn't think she was the sort to be impressed by euphemisms.

She skim-read a few more papers from the folder, turning them over hastily. "I see," she drummed her fingers against the table top; her nails clicked a scattered tune on the dull surface. She finished reading, the last of the papers tucked neatly into the folder. "So, do you want to tell me what happened?"

"It was all a misunderstanding," I began, happy that someone was finally going to listen to my side of the story. "I slept with—" I paused, hesitated. I slumped back into my chair again. "Why am I seeing a psychiatrist anyway?" I asked.

"I'm just here to help move things along."

"What's that supposed to mean?"

"What do you think it means?"

"You like to ask questions, don't you?"

"Do I?"

I frowned; she grinned.

"You're checking to see if I'm insane, right?" I asked.

She shrugged. She didn't want to admit it but I was right.

"And if I'm not?"

"Honestly?" She looked around, cautiously. The room was small, and it was obvious no one else was there; it was also obvious that we were being filmed by a whirring camera in the corner and her movements were for dramatic effect. "You'll probably get a slap on the wrist and will be out in no time."

"And if I *am* insane?"

She leaned back, stretched herself out on the chair, and shrugged impassively.

"I have to keep seeing you?" I wondered.

She didn't reply, but I sensed a *yes* in her eyes. She pulled herself forward again, rested her elbows on the table tiredly, and looked deep into my eyes. "So, are you going to tell me what happened?"

I wanted to see her again, but I knew I couldn't bring myself to ask her out right now. I was naked but for a government-issued sheet, she was supposed to be interviewing me, and we were both in a police station; it was terrible timing and I didn't feel up for it. I decided to lie, but tried to play it cool. There was a fine line between being insane enough to continue seeing her and being a crazy stalker who had a tendency to harass women and show up naked at their houses.

I tripped over that line a few words in.

I told her that I had obsessed over Ally since the speed date and gone out of my way to instantly find out more about her, following her home that night and then following her from her house the following morning. I tried to stress the part where I won Ally over with my charm, but it was lost in the insanity of following her to the street to arrange a date.

"She phoned you though," she jumped in at that point. "Why didn't you just wait until she was in and give her a ring back? Did you *have* to follow her?"

I shrugged. "I guess I wanted to see her sooner."

"You were keen."

"Very much so."

I told her about the date, how great it had been, how much *fun* Ally had, how much she enjoyed *my* company.

"Ally already gave the police a report," she cut in.

"Oh."

"She said you tried to follow her home that night."

I was glad I wasn't telling the truth; I was too tired to explain what really happened. "I did."

"You couldn't bear to be without her?"

"Either that or I wanted to attack her and rape her," I joked softly.

She raised her eyebrows.

"I was joking."

"I see."

It wasn't going well so I quickly moved on. I explained that this morning I showed up naked at her house in an attempt to impress her. I hinted that I had a lot to impress with, which was also a lie, but I didn't think they had recorded penis size on the reports.

"Where did you leave your clothes?" she asked.

I hadn't anticipated that one. "A friend's house," I said unsurely. "He lives just up the road."

"He knew about your plan?"

"He's on vacation. Ibiza. Italy. I was watering his plants."

"Ibiza is in Spain."

"I know, but *he's* in Italy."

She frowned and stared at me for a while. I didn't flinch.

"And the leg?" she asked.

"A present," I said, in lieu of anything else.

She nodded, as if she knew. "Where did you acquire it?"

Where do people buy legs? I wondered. *Debenhams? Boots?*

"I got it from my grandmother," I said hesitantly. "She has a prosthetic leg as well."

Perfect. I proudly told myself.

"As well?"

Shit.

"Yes," I nodded surely. I didn't know how else to respond.

"As well *as*?"

I nodded again. "Yes."

She put her pen down and looked at me sternly.

"Do you know somebody *else* who only has one leg?" she inquired.

I plastered a look of bewilderment on my face. "Of course not," I assured her. "What makes you think that?"

She opened her mouth to reply, then promptly closed it. "Never mind," she said, picking up the pen again.

I ran over what had been said and realized I sounded mad, but not *insane*. Mine were the actions of a socially clueless, lonely idiot, not of a man who needed psychiatric help. I decided to kick it up a notch.

"You see, I've been feeling really down lately," I lowered my head as if in contemplation of my own intolerable suffering. "Things just seem, pointless, you know?"

"How long have you been feeling like this?" she inquired.

"I don't know, a few years maybe," I mumbled into my chest.

"Have you ever thought about harming yourself?"

"All the time," I said, perhaps a little too cheerily. "*All the time*," I repeated in a slightly deeper tone.

"I see."

I peeked up and noted she was writing something down with a somber and interested look on her face. I smiled and ducked back into my chest when she finished.

"Do you take any medication; recreational drugs?"

"No."

"Have you ever?

"No." I paused, lifted my head. "Yes," I amended. "I took ecstasy once."

She nodded as if she understood. "To help you feel and connect, right?"

"Yes," I said meekly.

I was at a friend's house, I had a headache, and I thought it was aspirin, but I liked her answer better.

"Are you a heavy drinker?"

"Only when the pain gets too much to bear." I was on a roll.

"Do you have any compulsive habits? Gambling? Sex?"

I didn't want to push it. "No."

"Do you hear any strange voices, or noises?"

I opened my mouth to repeat the negative, but quickly decided against it. "Yes," I said confidently.

She wrote this down. I was onto something.

"What do they say?"

"I—I—I—" I stammered, hoping a spark would ignite in my mind. It didn't. "I'd rather not talk about it," I finished.

"Do they say helpful things?"

"No."

"I see."

"No, wait," I stopped her before her flurrying pencil scribbled more rapid words. "That was a lie."

She paused, raised her eyebrows. "You don't hear voices?"

"Not at all." I shifted in my seat again, and the sheet nearly fell, so I clasped it and pulled it tightly. "I just wanted to sound more interesting."

She placed the pen down carefully. "I see."

"Yes, you say that a lot."

She smiled and shook the comment off. "Do you often find yourself lying to make you sound more interesting, Mr. McCall?"

I shrugged a weak *yes*.

"Maybe you think more people will pay attention to you if you lie?"

"You're right," I said, feigning a mask of depression.

She seemed delighted with this. She picked the pencil back up and jotted more words down. It took her awhile. Halfway through, she glanced at her watch and then hurriedly finished the rest, turning the paper, jotting something on the flip-side, and then stashing it away in a sparsely occupied folder.

She greeted me with a smile when she finished.

"Is that it?" I wondered.

"For now."

"Does that mean I have to see you again?"

"I'm afraid so."

A little voice inside me screamed in jubilation.

"Can I go home now then?"

She was putting the folders back in the bag, but she stopped. She looked at me sympathetically. "I'm afraid not."

"They're keeping me in here?"

"Not here, no." She lowered the bag again, caught my stare in hers. "I think it would be best for everyone if you came with me."

I loved that idea; I was already standing up, moving forward to join her. "Where?" I asked happily.

"The hospital. St. Peter's."

I sat down sharply, suddenly glum. I knew that hospital, I had heard stories, everyone had. "The loony bin?"

St. Peter's Psychiatric Hospital was on the outskirts of town; it sat imposingly on the top of a steady incline and could be seen for a mile in every direction. It was shut off from the world and completely self-contained.

Necessities could be bought at a small local shop, owned and run by a family that had catered for the hospital for more than fifty years. They sold everything from newspapers and magazines to candy and bread.

There was small onsite café attached to the back end of one of the wards, and it was run by a small number of select patients. It catered for visitors and those patients with an equally loose rein as those cooking the food and operating the till.

For those who didn't like the idea of the inmates running the kitchen, there was a small, sleek, newly built restaurant just over the road, where a sane chef served expensive meals to customers who weren't due back on the wards after they paid their check.

The hospital was also staffed with its own doctor and dentist, it had its own team of security guards who monitored the grounds and controlled any aggressive patients, and it had more recreational rooms and activities than the average town.

As a child, I had heard many horror stories about the complex and stayed well away. It was the stuff of nightmares, campfire stories, and games of truth-and-dare, which I never fully committed to. As a teenager I had taken a school trip to the onsite facilities to learn more about the history and sociology of the hospital. I had retained a sense of childhood apprehension and had been somewhat disappointed to discover that not only was the hospital not run by a team of sick, sadistic doctors who tortured murderous, insane patients on a daily basis, but the entire complex was actually a fresh and enjoyable place. I had even mentioned that I could imagine myself living there, and, as it turned out, as an adult, it became my temporary home.

The police were polite enough to take me home to pack a few belongings and put some clothes on. Then they took me to the psychiatric hospital and left me in the care of a friendly male nurse who, when showing me to my room, gave me a happy soliloquy about the hospital.

I had never knowingly encountered anyone suffering from a mental illness; therefore, visions of the mentally ill had come from television and films. I imaged these to be false and prepared myself to ignore any preconceptions they might bring, but Donald came right out of a Hollywood script.

He was standing in the center of the room when I saw him; I froze in the doorway, surprised. He grinned at me with the wide-eyed stare of a stimulated drug user. Both of his hands were pressed to his face, the palm of his left firmly on his cheek, the fingers of his right in his mouth, rapidly being chewed.

He was dressed in a blue dressing gown that trailed the floor around his feet; it was open down the center and exposed loose-fitting pajamas. His penis was hanging out of the fly in his pajama bottoms. He either hadn't noticed or didn't care.

"Donald," the friendly nurse spoke quietly. Donald's attention darted across to him. "This is your new roommate." He laid a hand gently on my back, gesturing me inside.

I took a step forward and offered my new roommate a meek smile. "Hello, Donald," I replicated the nurse's soft tone, wondering if anything higher would spark a fit of aggression.

I held out my hand, but he didn't take it.

His eyes bore into mine and he didn't blink. "What's your name?" he asked, lifting his fingers temporarily out of his mouth; a thin line of drool trickled down his chin and soaked into the collar of his dressing gown.

"Kie—" I tried to reply, but the nurse startled me.

"Donald!" he said abruptly and sharply. "If I've told you once, I've told you a million times: Put. Your. Penis. Away."

Donald looked down and grinned at the dangling member. He was well endowed, no doubt part of the reason for his cheeky smile or his insistence on letting it hang out.

"Keith. Maybe Keith. Likes it. I thought," he replied, his words were quick and stuttered. "Keith. I thought Keith would want to see. Keith may not have a big one. Keith's may be small. Mrs. Embleton says I have a big one. I should be proud."

"It doesn't mean you should wave it around for everyone to see."

He reached down and grabbed it like a wild snake. "Keith. Want to see?" he said, pointing it at me like a curious question mark.

It took me a few seconds to realize he was talking about me, and a few more to reply. "I—I—" I realized I was staring, wondering why he seemed so intent on twisting it like it wasn't attached to his body and wasn't an incredibly sensitive organ. "It's lovely," I said, feeling like a parent praising a child's scribble; glad I didn't have to pin it to the fridge. "Very nice."

"He's seen it, now put it away."

He tucked it into his pants like he was stuffing a scrap of paper into his pocket. Then he beamed at me. "Keith. Show Keith's penis now."

I didn't show Donald my dick. Nor did I hang around so he could try to talk me into it.

I went on a walk, taking a small tour of the hospital. After a few laps around the sterilized hallways, passing a number of dole-faced patients who flashed meek smiles, and equally sour-faced staff that didn't, I decided that the place wasn't so bad. It had everything I could possibly need and more. There were snooker tables, dartboards, a fully stocked library, a television room, a computer room, and outside, in the expansive grounds, I was informed there was everything from tennis courts and a soccer net to a trampoline.

I was going to be well looked after by qualified nurses. I would be fed three square meals a day and I had a comfortable bed to sleep in. It would be like a vacation—one which didn't cost me a penny.

I contemplated this while I dug into the final meal of the day. They had served up roast beef with all the trimmings; I ate it like the starving man I was. It felt so good to finally get some food into my stomach and I instantly felt better, the remnants of the hangover and the atrocities that had followed dissipated.

I spent the evening talking to two young men in the television room. They seemed normal enough, certainly more so than Donald, and I got on well with them. I went to bed that night delighted that I had made two new friends on this exciting new vacation of mine.

That night things soured slightly with Donald. He talked at me for three hours straight. He mentioned my name, or what he thought was my name, more than three hundred and sixty times in the first hour. After that I stopped counting and tried to turn off my brain. That night I dreamed that a man called Keith was attacking me with a six-foot penis.

The following day I showered in the communal area, changed into a new pair of clothes, and went to my second appointment with the beautiful Dr. Peterson.

"I believe you may be suffering from a case of autophobia," Dr. Peterson said plainly. She raised her eyebrows questionably, gauging my reaction and understanding.

"Fear of cars?"

"Fear of *yourself*."

"Oh," I nodded slowly, hoping to give the images some time to sink in, "you mean like mirrors and stuff?"

"It's more of a personal thing," she explained, shifting in her seat and looking at her lap momentarily, hiding a grin with the tilt of her head. "A fear of loneliness, of abandonment. I think that is why you refused to let Ally go after your dates, why you went to extremes to win her back when you thought you had lost her."

"That makes sense."

It did make sense and I was amazed and a little impressed by her reasoning. It was completely wrong, of course, but it was impressive nonetheless.

She looked happy with herself; I was happy for her.

"I think—inadvertently, admittedly—I may have done the best thing for you by bringing you here. I think this place can do you a world of good."

I was a little less impressed now. I had only been here one night and already, after the penis dream, I was feeling far more insane than when I entered. "What do you mean?"

"This place is full of life! There's no place to hide in here, no place to run!"

She was intelligent and good at her job, but she wasn't very reassuring.

"There is no cure *per se*," she continued. "And we can't really keep you here for more than a week. I don't think you pose a threat to yourself or anyone else." She paused and tapped her pencil against her teeth; the vibrant white enamel gleamed underneath her dark red lipstick. "As for the stalking incident, well, I'm sure that was a one-off. You have no history, you didn't intend to do harm, and I don't think you would do it again, am I right?"

I thought about this: saying no might have given me an extended stay, but probably not. I reasoned that I didn't need it anyway; a week was probably long enough for me to work up the courage to ask the doctor out. If I did it at the end of the week, I would also be signing off as her patient, thus ridding her of any moral or legal doctor/patient obligations she had.

"That's right."

"Excellent, I thought so. So I want you to treat this like a vacation."

I couldn't help but smile.

"Go out there and enjoy yourself, kick back. We'll keep an eye on you and I'll be here if you need me. But the best thing for you would be to forget about your troubles, forget about Ally." She wiped a hand across the air as if to wipe Ally out of existence. "Go and relax! Try not to think about your life back home, about anything that has gone on in the past or about anything that might happen in the future. This is a vacation of complete relaxation, funded by the taxpayer. So I order you to go out there and relax!"

I smiled and stood. I offered her my hand and she shook it merrily, her face still alight with joy that she hoped would transfer to me. It did. "Thank you, Doctor."

She winked at me. "You're welcome." She was getting carried away with herself now. I felt a little embarrassed for her but retained the smile and turned to leave.

"Oh, and Mr. McCall?" she called.

I turned around, still smiling. She was scribbling something down on a prescription pad. I sensed what was coming and really hoped I was wrong, I didn't want her to ruin a successful moment and devalue herself in my eyes.

She ripped off the top sheet and handed it to me.

"To be taken every day," she stated tritely.

I looked at the pad, unable to hide my disappointment. The word relaxation was scribbled in messy doctors' script; it was even properly signed and came with a suggested dosage.

And it had been going so well, I told myself.

I sighed inwardly and forced the smile back to my face.

"Thank you, Doc," I said, holding it up. "Will do."

In the cold light of a sober day, after an awkward meeting with a woman I realized wasn't perfection personified, I realized that getting myself locked up in a psychiatric hospital probably wasn't the best thing to do.

Like most psychiatrists, Dr. Peterson had found the perfect solution to a problem that didn't actually exist, but in a way, she was right. I did feel like I needed a break, not because my life had been particularly stressful—I hadn't worked in over two years and had spent my spare time chatting up women with Matthew—but because I needed a vacation in general. The last time I had been on anything that qualified as a vacation was the trip to the campground when I was fifteen.

Stuck in a state of ambivalence, I waddled back to my room and found that Donald was awake and waiting for me again.

"Lovely," I told him as I brushed by. "But I saw it yesterday."

"Keith. Where's Keith's?"

"You wouldn't like mine." I ducked and slid into the bottom bunk. It had been disconcerting having Donald on top of me all night and may have contributed to my threatening penis dreams, but there was also a degree of comfort to it. The walls and ceilings were sterilized, dull, and spacious. It was good to have them shrouded in darkness or blocked from view.

"Keith. What's wrong with Keith's?"

I sighed deeply. Donald had turned toward me now, and, as the monstrous member swung from side to side a mere four inches from my face, I realized why lying down on the bottom bunk wasn't the best place to be right now.

I sat up with a start, wiped imagined penis juice from my face, and slid out from under the bed.

"Keith, penis now? Donald wants to see Keith's penis."

I left the room without replying, not quite sure how I was supposed to reply to such a statement.

A short walk down an empty corridor brought me to a small door that flushed with bright light from a clear day. I pushed it open, expecting it to be locked like a tempting mirage in the desert. It wasn't.

The door led out into the grounds. The day was warm, bright and fresh.

The outside area was fenced off, but the fence was a few hundred feet ahead and stretched around an expanse of grass, concrete, gardens, and recreational areas.

Within minutes, I was smiling again and enjoying a walk in and around a garden. The flowers were all in bloom. The hedges neatly trimmed and well-manicured. The lawn crisp. The gravel chips that wove paths between flower beds and patches of grass were neatly confined within cylindrical wooden borders.

At the end of the path, around the corner from a bloom of wild poppies, I stepped onto an island of the gravel. The cylindrical lattice wrapped a spherical border all around. Flowers sprung up behind it, gravel sat patiently before it.

A two-seater chair rested at the nearest end of the gravel island, sitting in the shade of a tall tree. A young woman, about the same age as me, sat on its center. She was smiling at me; she had a warm and reassuring smile.

I walked over to her, drawn by her beauty and kind features. She had jet black hair, which flowed behind her head and disappeared into the shade. Her bright face was alive with a fresh smile, which I gladly returned.

"Hello," I said.

"Hiya."

I stuffed my hands in my pockets. She moved aside on the chair and gestured for me to sit, so I did. Despite the foot or two between us, I could sense her warmth and smell her perfume.

I sat in silence for a while, contemplating the peace and beauty of the little garden paradise. Birds sang in the distance; insects busied themselves; patients squabbled far off; but here, away from the hospital and tucked neatly in this man-made Eden, it felt like perfect silence.

"This place is lovely," I said, after a while.

"It is, isn't it?" she replied.

I turned to look at her and caught her eye. She smiled back. At that point, I would have usually looked away in awkward shyness, but I felt comfortable, at ease. The garden had such a calming effect on me.

It was also possible they were spiking my tea with sedatives, but I didn't entertain that idea for long. They didn't think anything was wrong with me, and a sedate man wouldn't have run out on Donald and his repetitive ramblings.

Why Keith anyway? I thought to myself. *And why so much? So many times. Keith. Keith. Keith. Keith. Keith.*

The woman turned to me, a pleasant smile still plastered on her pretty face. "What's your name?"

"Keith," I said calmly, looking deep into her blue eyes, slightly grayed by the shade of the tree. "What's yours?"

"Beth."

"Nice to meet you, Beth," I said, extending a hand.

"Nice to meet *you*, Keith."

We smiled and shook, and she giggled a little. Then it sunk in. *Keith?* I thought dismally. *I didn't, did I? Shit.*

16

Keith and Beth

My obsession with Dr. Peterson, a woman whose first name I didn't know, faded as quickly as it began. She was a beautiful woman and I hadn't seen anyone quite as beautiful, but she intimidated me, she seemed self-absorbed, and if I admitted it to myself—which I only allowed myself to do when I lost interest—there was no chance we could ever be together.

Now I had a new love interest; my dad was right, the perfect woman for me really was a patient in a psychiatric hospital.

My first meeting with Beth lasted for an hour, from noon till one. We didn't speak much but we didn't need to. I didn't feel awkward in the silence and it seemed that neither did she.

We talked briefly about the garden; she told me that it was tended to perfection by a patient who had spent his life in the hospital after being institutionalized at an early age. Along with a couple of helpers and students, he had created the perfect space where once there had been nothing but grass and soil.

When she departed, I watched her. She disappeared around the back, toward a different block, a different ward. I was a little disappointed to see she wasn't on the same ward as I was, but I knew I would see her again.

She told me she was in the garden every day at the same time, so the following day I arrived ten minutes early and waited.

In the silence of the garden, I heard approaching footsteps as they crunched along the gravel path. They slowed when they reached the opening, which would bring them into my eye-line and me into theirs. There were a few crunches of apprehension; I stared, waited, and then she appeared. She was looking straight at me.

I grinned, she smiled back.

"Hello again," she said happily.

I patted the seat for her to sit down. She did so with a soft sigh, planting her buttocks down an inch or so closer than they had been yesterday.

"Are you stealing my relaxation spot?" she asked, her eyebrows arched in mock inquiry.

"It's lovely out here," I said indifferently. "Nothing else to do."

"Nothing else?" She looked shocked and pretended to be insulted. "There's *everything* to do here. You can play soccer, tennis, cricket—"

"Can't kick a ball; can't hit a ball."

"There's a swimming pool."

"Can't swim."

She frowned, leaning forward on the chair slightly and looking back at me. "How can you not swim in this day and age?"

"I haven't been able to swim for twenty-one years," I told her bluntly.

She laughed. She was still leaning forward but I was sure she shifted closer to me. "It seems we have something in common."

"You can't swim either?" I wondered. "Bit hypocritical of you then."

She laughed again. It wasn't an awkward laugh but it wasn't entirely natural. I thought, and I hoped, its intentions were flirtatious. "I mean, I'm twenty-one as well."

"Ah, gotcha."

"And anyway," she leaned back, looking at me sideways now, a sly twinkle in her eyes, "you can always just splash around in the shallow end."

"I don't look good in trunks."

She pondered this momentarily, either thinking about me in trunks or mentally dressing me in a bathing suit instead. "There's a gym."

I shook my head. "Working out embarrasses me."

"*Embarrasses* you?"

"Yeah. Half-naked people sweating and grunting in a small confined space. No one talks and men seem to get more out of it than women; it's like sex, only a lot less fun."

"Fair enough."

"What about you?" I wondered. "Why are you out here staring at the scenery when you could be inside those depressing walls playing tennis?"

"The tennis courts are outside," she said without fault.

"You know what I mean."

She shrugged again. "I like it here, it's peaceful. I like the silence; I like having the time to think."

She looked into the middle distance, as though to emphasise what she said. A mellow breath escaped her lungs. I followed her gaze.

It occurred to me that I was ruining her peace; I was spoiling her thinking time. But I reasoned that if she minded, she would have said something. She certainly wouldn't have hinted to me to come back here today, nor would she have been pleased to see me.

In the distance I could hear the sound of a disgruntled patient, the noises filtered through the chirping crickets like a foghorn in the darkness. The patient was shouting obscenities and screaming as he ran away, his voice growing fainter and fainter.

I waited for the silence to return and thought about mentioning something to Beth, but she hadn't reacted. She was still looking ahead contemplatively. I decided against ruining her mood.

"It *is* very peaceful out here," I said, anticlimactically.

She laughed. Her face was alight when she turned to me. "That happens every now and then," she said, referring to the crazy outburst. "You get used to it."

I wondered how long she had taken to get used to it, how long she had been locked away in this remote part of town, discarded at the top of a hill inside a busy complex, where her unassuming nature sought out the quietest and remotest part.

I didn't want to delve into the reasons she was here; I didn't want to scare her away. If she was going to tell me, she would do so in her own time.

I also didn't want to have to tell her my story. I didn't know which one to give her. I didn't want to tell her I had stripped naked and stalked a girl I had only just met, but I equally didn't want to admit I had walked the streets naked with a stolen leg and lied to a psychiatrist because I fancied her.

An hour after she sat down, Beth stood up to leave. This time she stalled before walking away and we exchanged stares; she tapped me gently on the shoulder and said, "See you tomorrow?"

It wasn't a kiss, but it was contact, intent.

The following day, I was twenty minutes early, eager to see her and equally eager to get away from Donald who had been waving his penis around like it was the rubber end of a skipping rope.

She came on time—her footsteps coinciding with the twelve bells from a distant, unseen clocktower—and she brought food.

We had a mini-picnic under the shade of the tree. The day darkened quickly and a chill cut through the garden, but neither of us mentioned it. We ate in silence and then talked about anything that came to mind. It was easy to talk to her and I had never experienced that ease with any female—there had always been a degree of forced conversation.

It was different with Melissa, of course, but only after we had been going out for several weeks. And even then the conversation was tinged with a feeling that Melissa wanted to be somewhere else, talking with some*body* else.

Beth told me about her family. We had a few things in common.

She had no brothers and sisters. Her mother was overprotective and wore the pants in their family, and her dad was a lovable embarrassment to her as a child.

"I remember when I had my first girlfriend," I began to tell her, looking beyond her eyes in recollection. "I reluctantly let her meet my parents, they had to drive us somewhere. I think I cringed and gritted my teeth the entire journey. He had this whole thing about mentioning *girlfriend* in every sentence, *every* few seconds." I smiled and looked across. She looked at me in surprise, quickly turning her head to face me. Something seemed to be forming in her mind, but she quickly shrugged it off, the smile returned.

"In the first hour, I think he mentioned it over a hundred times, he also managed to fit in half a dozen quips about thinking I was gay. I seem to recall him telling her if she knew what I got up to alone in my bedroom, she would think twice about shaking my hand, let alone being my girlfriend." I grinned. "He has a way with words."

Beth nodded in recognition. "I've heard it before. I think all dads are the same. For *boys* anyway," she clarified. "With girls they're more protective. My dad never took his eye off my boyfriends—he insisted they were all after one thing and he didn't want any of them getting that, *ever*."

"To be fair, most teenagers *are* just after one thing, and if my teens are anything to go by, we don't get very much of it."

She grinned, a flicker of pity in her eyes. "When I was seventeen," she continued, "he found a pack of condoms in my boyfriend's coat pocket and he lost it. He pinned him up against the wall and shouted at him for half an hour."

The air had grown thin and cold. She wrapped her arms across herself and instinctively moved closer to me on the seat. We were touching now, but only just. I thought about putting my arm around her but dismissed it—the moment didn't seem right. Not yet.

"Poor kid was blubbering by the end," she recalled. "No sympathy from my dad though. He kicked his sobbing ass out of the house."

I smiled and made a mental note to bring presents if I ever met her dad. "What did you do during this?"

Beth shrugged. "I let him. I wasn't sexually active, he said he wasn't either. At the time I figured he was sleeping with someone else, so I guess a part of me enjoyed watching my dad shout at him." She laughed and then let a look of shame spread across her face. She turned to me. "Disturbing huh?"

"Not in the least," I told her. "*Was* he sleeping with someone else?"

"Probably, you know what teenage boys are like." She winked and gave me a gentle shove with her shoulder. "Most of them anyway," she added with a mocking grin.

"I got my fair share," I affirmed.

"I'm sure you did, stud."

"There just wasn't much sex involved," I finished.

She grinned; a soft laugh escaped her lips. She looked down at her folded arms, eyeing up her watch. "I better get going," she said reluctantly. "Tomorrow?"

"Of course."

We met in that little piece of heaven every day for the rest of the week. We sat side by side, closer and closer.

On the sixth day, we went for a walk because she said she wanted to show me around the grounds. We walked arm in arm around the building, bypassing a flurry of nurses, patients, and activity. A few patients knew her and called to her, she merely smiled back; I didn't probe any deeper.

When I had established she liked me and there was potential for a relationship, I couldn't stop thinking about her illness, about what had driven her to stay in the hospital. How long was she in for? Would I have to remain a patient just to be with her?

On the seventh day, we kissed. It was brief, and nothing more than a soft peck on the lips, but it was the most rewarding kiss I ever had. It wasn't a kiss leading to awkward, submissive, or cheapened sex; it was something softer, something with meaning.

That day I planned to tell her that I was due to leave the following morning. I was going to ask her why she was in the hospital and whether I would be able to visit, but the kiss changed everything; it melted my mind and I watched her leave without saying a word.

We arranged to meet again the following day. I planned to make sure I'd be there for the meeting.

I was short of options and time, so I decided to go with what had brought me to the hospital in the first place.

In my room, I stripped naked, much to the delight of Donald, who began comparing penis sizes. He won.

"Keith. Mine is much bigger, Keith."

I was sitting on the edge of the bed, trying to work up the courage. It was going to be harder than when I stormed out of Ashley's house. There was no immediate desperation to get away from a scary woman for one thing, there was also little chance of being tackled to the floor and sedated by an army of angry nurses.

I wasn't devoid of motivation though. If I didn't commit to my half-assed plan, there was a good chance I would never see Beth again, foregoing some future mental breakdown—which, admittedly, was a possibility.

"You'll be hard-pressed to find one bigger, Donald."

Donald beamed brightly.

I took in a deep breath, walked to the threshold, gave myself a few moments to clear my head, and then ran into the hallway. My bare feet slapped the cold corridor floors and soaked an instant and chilling cold from their clammy surfaces; my genitalia swung freely in the sterilized air.

I hadn't asked Donald to strip naked, but he had done so when I did. It was so natural for him that I didn't object. I also hadn't asked him to join me on my naked jog, but after a half dozen strides, he was pacing merrily by my side.

We passed a confused patient with a sedated look on his face. An exasperated female nurse who wanted to do something but didn't know what, and a strapping male nurse who did know what to do—chased us.

I picked up the pace and Donald kept in stride. Behind us another two nurses joined the chase, their voices bellowing angrily at us, simultaneously issuing orders to other staff. Before long, an alarm was raised, a throbbing sound of flashing alert rang violently throughout the thin, lifeless corridors, alerting everyone in the vicinity.

I took turn after turn down the winding hallways, which seemed to stretch forever. I was convinced I could keep the chase up for a while, grab the attention of the entire hospital, and annoy them enough to want to keep me inside the walls indefinitely, but that plan didn't work.

We entered a long stretch of corridor, the goal of a large double door at its tip, but in front of the door, jumping into life and realization, were two more nurses; their statures juxtaposed in Laurel and Hardy fashion.

They ran toward us, their footsteps thudded into the solid floor, adding to the cacophony of noise. One of them shouted something, but I ignored them.

A door ahead was ajar. The shadows of activity beyond sprinkled into the hallway.

Donald was still running enthusiastically by my side, striding exaggerated and merry strides like Forrest Gump, his mammoth penis swinging back and forth.

I grabbed his elbow and pulled him toward me. I shouldered the door open. It swung, clattered into the stopper, and sprang back. On the other side, I forced it shut and gestured for Donald to get up against it with me.

Only then did I turn around to look into the room; a sea of horrified faces looked back. All of them were staring in our direction, but none of their eyes were directed at me.

I heard a few of them muttering above the angry calls and footfalls from the security guards and nurses outside.

"Oh my god, it's huge."

"You mean you've never seen it before?"

I felt the handle twist down, the tip of the cold metal brushed against the small of my back; they applied a small force to the door as they tested the resistance. This was followed by a short pause, some instructions, and then a mighty shove. The door opened a few inches, sliding me and Donald over the carpeted floor, before it slammed heavily back into its frame.

More instructions. Someone warned against further shoves, another voice called for backup, a third prepared to negotiate a way inside.

I relaxed a little.

Ahead of me, spreading across the entire side of the room, were four large windows. Through the glass, which had been smeared with dust and heat, I could see the distant garden where I had spent so much time with Beth.

The walls at the back of the room were lined with crude canvases. The middle of the floor was littered with easels, fresh canvases, and a dozen surprised faces.

"I'm sorry," I told all the expectant faces, pulling some of their attention away from the giant penis currently swinging inches from my leg, while my own tottered about inconspicuously. "We'll be finished in a mo—"

I paused. The teacher was standing at the front. I had seen her briefly in my periphery but hadn't taken anything in. I cursed inwardly and felt my heart sink.

"Beth?"

She was standing rigidly, shocked like the others, her attention on my face and not Donald's dick.

"Wh—wh—what are you doing here?"

"I work here," she said slowly. "This is my class."

She looked around the class as though to emphasize. I followed her gaze. At the back, one of the students was still painting. He either hadn't noticed the naked ambush or didn't care. His tongue tickled the corner of his mouth as his hand worked painstakingly on the canvas.

I turned back to face her, waited for her eyes to meet mine. "You're a teacher?"

She nodded and shrugged, as if to say, *what did you think I was?*

"But—but—but. Ah, fuck."

"Please step away from the door, Mr. McCall."

They tested the door again, pushing it slightly. It remained solid in the frame.

"Fuck. Fuck."

My penis didn't attract anyone's attention but my outburst certainly did. I slumped against the door and threw my hands to my head. I peeked at Beth through the gap between splayed digits.

"I'm so sorry," I told her softly.

"For what?" she looked concerned. I couldn't work out if it was for her safety or for my sudden misery.

"Please step away from the door!"

Again they tried to push; again they failed.

"Donald," I said, turning to my roommate, who was still smiling, happier than ever. "It's done, we're finished here."

He looked disappointed, but then he shrugged and stepped away.

They tried the door again; it gave way against my weight. They sensed victory, pushed harder. I stepped away and it flung open, sending Laurel and Hardy bounding into the room.

They stopped themselves from hitting the deck, and both of them slowly turned their faces toward me. They looked ready to pounce.

I held up my hands. "This has all been a misunderstanding."

True to form, Hardy seemed the most aggressive of the pair, his face set with a permanent scowl. He made a dive for me, groaning as he shifted his heavy stature forward.

I side-stepped around a canvas and threw the easel at his feet. It clattered harmlessly against his polished black shoes. The incomprehensible painting tore against his knee.

I shifted behind another wooden obstacle.

"A misunderstanding?" he spat. "How you gonna explain that, huh?"

I looked at him, shrugged. "I fancied a run?"

They both dove for me, taking me from each side. They had me in a flash, their hands grabbing my arms tightly, their fingers pressing deeply into my flesh.

Donald went with less of a struggle, immediately giving himself up to the nurses waiting just beyond the threshold of the room.

I glanced at Beth before I left, so sure that it would be the last time I was going to see her. If she worked at the hospital then maybe she assumed I did as well—no doubt she would be put off if I was a patient there—and if not then she would have certainly been put off by my storming into her classroom naked.

The two nurses dragged me out of the room and eased their aggressive hold on my arm once they realized I wasn't going to try anything. They paraded me down the long corridor. Donald was led by another nurse in front of me, a fourth waited behind with a syringe, prepared to sedate either of us if we tried to struggle or run.

"I had too much coffee this morning," I told them, as my mind failed to think of a better excuse.

"Really?" Laurel replied disinterestedly.

"Maybe someone slipped something in it," I offered.

"And what, now it's worn off?"

I thought about this for a moment. "Could have been decaf."

They led us back to our room and watched as we changed. Someone remained to watch over Donald while I was escorted to the psychiatrist's room. Laurel and Hardy stood on guard behind me as I sat in the chair in front of Dr. Peterson's desk.

"So much for relaxation," she said seriously.

She looked a little tired, worn out. Eyes that had once been mesmerizing and unthinkably beautiful were now clouded with tiny blotches of red running through them and heavy black bags underneath.

"I'm sorry." I caught her eyes and put on my best pleading face. "I'm not insane, really I'm not. I liked it here, I wanted to stay longer, that's all." I leaned back, content, then shot forward again. "But, now I don't. I want to go home."

She looked perplexed.

I pushed on. "Can't we just forget this ever happened? Go back to where we were before."

"And what changed your mind?" she asked, her eyes tiredly flicking away. She looked like she couldn't be bothered to deal with me right now.

"I can't really say, I mean I *could*, but I'm not sure I *can*. If that makes sense."

"Not in the slightest."

I didn't want to tell her about Beth in case she was breaking a moral code. She wasn't a nurse or a doctor, but she did work for the hospital and I was still a patient. I didn't want to take a chance.

"Look," I pleaded. "I can prove to you that I'm sane."

She sighed heavily and glanced lazily at her watch. "I'll be honest with you, Mr. McCall." She reached forward with a sagging breath; I slumped back expecting the worst. "This is not a private hospital; we don't have the time, the money, or the staff to cater to everyone who walks through our doors."

"What does that mean?" I wondered.

She casually shrugged her shoulders. "You can leave."

"I can leave?"

"You can leave," she affirmed with a nod.

I couldn't quite believe what she was saying. I began to push my luck. "But, I just ran naked through your corridors."

She shrugged again.

"It took half a dozen nurses to stop me."

She didn't seem impressed.

"I thought that—"

"You're free to go, Mr. McCall," she butted in.

I opened my mouth, thought about arguing with her, and then left the room before she changed her mind.

I thought I would need to plead my case; I thought I would need to get in touch with Ashley to corroborate the story of the stolen leg and the naked walk. I didn't, and I was glad, but I was also a little surprised. They weren't letting me go because they saw through my charade; as it turned out, the hospital cared more about free beds than uninhibited flashers. I had escaped, regardless. I was on my way home, but I had no intention of leaving without a definitive answer from Beth.

I searched for her in the art class and was escorted out of the room by Hardy; he seemed angry and annoyed at the sight of me and didn't take too kindly to being asked where his comedic partner was. In the ensuing argument, I sneaked a look over his shoulder, into the class. It was empty.

I asked a female nurse on a station near the entrance. She didn't seem to know who I was talking about and wasn't interested in a prolonged discussion regarding the matter. I left the hospital with my hopes still high and decided to wait for Beth in our little Eden.

Noon came and went, but she didn't show. I had already been discharged and had no right to be on the hospital grounds for long, but I was prepared to wait all day for Beth before conceding defeat.

I heard approaching footsteps after an hour. I straightened up on the seat, brushed clean my jacket, pulled taut my shirt. I allowed a smile of relief to spread across my face and I turned it toward the entrance, toward Beth.

It wasn't her.

A man met my gaze but refused to smile. He carried a pair of shears and a watering can. He set to work on trimming and maintaining the flower beds as I watched with one eye on my watch.

More footsteps sounded ten minutes later. I prepared again, receiving a curious glance from the gardener when I began to breathe into my hand and smell the resulting odor.

I turned to smile at the approacher and again was greeted with a sullen grimace. Another gardener, an equally unresponsive man who knelt by his friend's side as the pair began to work in synchronized silence.

I deflated. I sank down on the seat until my legs stretched beyond the base and my lower back rested awkwardly on the varnished wood. It pressed deep into my spine, squeezing my skin against the vulnerable bone. I didn't move, I didn't care.

The gardeners left after an hour. Neither spoke; neither smiled. The bright morning light was fading to a dull orange, the sun now behind me, laying distorted shades on the freshly trimmed foliage.

A smiling couple came to the garden, their voices so joyous and excited as they trampled the path. Then they saw me, an intruder in a place they assumed would be deserted. Their smiles lost their gleam, but they still looked happy. They held hands and stayed close to one another as they walked a complimentary lap around the garden and then departed, disappointed.

I was certain I had blown the best chance I had with a girl I really liked. I didn't even hear the next set of footsteps behind me; I didn't feel the hand on my shoulder.

"You're not supposed to be here."

It was Hardy again. He looked pissed off.

"It's getting late," he said. "You better leave now."

I didn't want to leave. It didn't seem right that I would have to; I wasn't in the hospital and I wasn't doing anyone any harm, but I was too defeated to argue. I stood without saying a word and began to walk away from the flowery alcove with my head held low.

A breathless voice stopped me.

"Keith!"

I looked up, expectant, hopeful.

It was Beth. Her face was bright red through exertion, her hands on her hips as her body convulsed with staccato breaths. "I'm so glad you're here," she said. She flung her arms around me and in an instant I felt better. I felt vindicated. I thought I was dreaming.

"Come on, sit back down," she gestured.

"I can't," I said, glancing knowingly at the burly nurse who hovered around like an intimidating gooseberry.

Beth followed my gaze, looked at Hardy. "What's the problem?" she asked, her voice ready for the argument that I refused to have.

He placed his hands defiantly on his hips, raised his chin. "The gardens are for patients and staff only," he said sternly.

"Excellent," Beth said mockingly. "Because I work here, and Keith here has only *just* been discharged." She sat down, and I warily followed.

Hardy stood there for a moment, he didn't look like he wanted to leave, but eventually he shrugged his shoulders apathetically and slumped away.

"You waited for me?" Beth asked.

"I—I—" I cleared my throat. "No," I said, playing it cool.

"You did," she gleamed knowingly. "That's how I found you. A colleague came here with her fiancé. She said there was a depressed man pouting on the seat, looking like his dog had died."

"Oh," I nodded. "That could have been anyone."

She laughed. "Chief Wiggum back there heard, even he knew it was you."

"Oh. I guess you've caught me—hold on, was that a *Simpsons* reference—"

She silenced me with a kiss. Our lips stayed locked for what seemed like an eternity. I *wanted* it to be an eternity.

When we finally separated, the evening was setting. The shade of the tree behind the chair blocked what little light was left in the sky and showered us in a gray hue. I watched her face through the light of her eyes.

I decided it was time to explain recent events. I didn't want to, but it seemed crazy to let it hang over us. "Listen, about the whole insanity thing," I began.

"It's not important," she quickly interjected.

"I know, but I just think I need to tell you—"

"It's really not important," she said again.

"—that I'm not insane," I finished.

She frowned.

I shrugged my shoulders nonchalantly. "Had to finish that," I said.

"Fair enough."

"I searched for you, ya know," I told her, changing subject. "I asked one of the nurses, she said she'd never heard of you."

She looked perplexed. "Really?"

"Yeah, then I came here and you weren't here. I figured you were trying to ignore me and had the staff helping."

"Who did you ask?"

I shrugged. "Short, frumpy, fairly mean-faced."

"Sandy?"

"Probably."

"I've known her for years and there are only three art teachers. What did you ask?"

"I said I was looking for Bethany—"

"Bethany!" she laughed a little, then her face creased with bemusement as she temporarily wondered if I really was insane. "Who's Bethany?"

"I thought Beth was short for Bethany."

"No, *Eliza*beth," she said matter-of-factly.

"Oh."

She looked a little relieved. "I used to get Lizzie," she explained, turning away. "Then at about sixteen, I decided it was too childish, so I told everyone to call me Beth."

"Lizzie?" I was a little awestruck. Something had sunk in—it didn't seem possible.

"Yeah. My Nan prefers Liz, sounds a little too old if you ask me."

"Lizzie," I said softly, running the name over and over in my head. The images of the Lizzie I knew. The beautiful, soft face. The reassuring voice. The friendly smile.

Beth nodded. I could feel her slightly bewildered stare on the side of my face as I pondered into the middle distance.

I felt so comfortable with her. *Her*, not the garden. She was the one doing this to me; she was the one making me so at ease, making me so comfortable. Just like Lizzie. I turned to her, the bewilderment on her face changed into a smile.

My memories of Lizzie's face had been so strong, so deeply ingrained, but over the years they had faded, dissipated to the ideals of Lizzie, to the memories of the time we spent and the nature of her personality. If anything, her beauty had been forgotten and then turned into a legend, but was it possible that the girl before me was her? The suggestion of such a thing seemed insane; maybe the hospital was rubbing off on me.

"This may sound a little strange," I began. "My name isn't Keith," I said bluntly.

She drew back a little. "Okay," she said with a nod, waiting for more.

"There's this crazy guy called Donald, you know him, saw him with me, it looks like his leg is wrestling a snake. Anyway, he keeps calling me Keith, he thinks that's my name and he has this *thing* with names."

"Okay." Beth was still waiting for an explanation.

"Anyway, he implanted that into me. The Keith thing. When you asked, I didn't realize I told you, and when I did, well," I shrugged. "I didn't want to backtrack and have you think I was weird."

I smiled. She laughed a little.

"As opposed to letting me think your name was Keith," she said. "Which is not weird at all."

"Exactly."

"So, what is your real name?"

I held her eyes, waiting to gauge her reaction. "Kieran."

There it was: a sparkle of recognition behind the blue orbs. A subconscious flick of the eye muscle, a slight raising of the eyebrows.

"Kieran?" she repeated, her voice slightly softer now.

"It's you, isn't it?" I said, leaning forward slightly, so sure it was. "From the campground? I didn't recognize you, I mean not at first, your hair, I mean you dyed it ob—"

"I don't know what you're talking about," she said abruptly.

I stalled, my mouth open in shock. I pulled back. "I'm sorry," I said, feeling stupid and disappointed. "I thought you—"

Before I could say another word, she kissed me hard, pressing the life from me. Then she pulled back, leaving me shocked, breathless, and confused. "That's for not meeting me and not phoning me back all those years ago," she said.

At that, the smile returned, wider than it had been before, wider than it had ever been.

Epilogue

"Everything will be fine, trust me."

I smiled at Matthew; I didn't trust him, not in the slightest. He was my best friend, and today he was my best man; I loved him like a brother, but I didn't trust him.

"Uncle Matthew is here to make sure all is well," he winked, grabbed at the top of my tie, straightened it, tightened it, gave me a sharp slap on the back for good measure.

"Will you stop calling yourself Uncle Matthew?"

"I didn't know you two were related."

In the corner of the room, Max was fiddling with his cravat, looking stiff and awkward as he stood near the door, holding it open like a penguin doorstopper.

"Where did you get this guy?" Matthew whispered.

"Told you, childhood friend, couldn't *not* invite him."

Matthew sighed and turned to help Max. When he finished, Max stood like a stiffened model, displaying himself with a smile of childish pride.

"Very nice, Max," I told him.

"You look *lovely*," Matthew mocked.

"Thank you," Max beamed proudly and left the room.

Matthew shut the door behind him, making sure to glance down the corridor first.

"That guy is a fucking numpty," he said bluntly.

"That may be so, but that guy also pulls in more money than me and you combined."

Matthew shook his head in disbelief and disgust. "*How* though? It beggars belief."

"Damned if I know. He's a good lad, though, probably deserves it."

"Maybe," Matthew sulked.

I stood in front of the full-length mirror and studied myself. I had never looked so neat and tidy, never felt so awkward in my own skin.

"I'm shitting myself," I told Matthew. "I never thought I'd get married like this, I always imagined it'd be cheap and accidental."

Matthew stood by my side, looking at himself admiringly in the mirror. "Don't worry, mate," he slung an arm around my shoulder. "If I can do it, you can do it."

I shook my head, still refusing to believe Matthew was married. The man who couldn't bear to be with the same girl for more than one night. A man who insisted monogamy was for people who had given up.

I had been his best man, but I still couldn't believe the day had happened. I gave my speech expecting the crew from a candid camera show to pop out of the cake. Matthew had turned into a one-woman man overnight; he had never cheated on his wife and had not been with anyone else since their first date. It was sweet, but it was out of character and very surprising. What was also surprising was that he stopped being my unsolicited wingman; he stopped trying to hook me up with random girls for casual and awkward one-night stands.

There was a reason for that though. I hadn't been single for a long time. I had been with my fiancée for as long as Matthew had been with his wife; there had been no need to set me up with other women. There wasn't another woman in the world I would have preferred to the one I was about to marry.

"You ready?" Matthew said, squeezing my shoulder and meeting my gaze through the mirror.

I straightened my tie an unnecessary quarter inch. Took a deep breath. "Come on then."

At the head of the church, I looked over a sea of expectant faces and contemplated running. They made me nervous, their eyes seemed to be saying: *We've come all this way, we've given up our weekend and we've dressed nicely. You better impress us, dickhead.* as they prepared pitchforks, rotten vegetables, and enough gossip to sustain the town's small-talkers for generations.

There were a few smiling faces amongst them. My parents sat patiently in the front row. My grinning mother, telling everyone how handsome I looked. My proud father, hiding his feelings and telling everyone not to drink too much in the pub because he was footing the bill.

Max was also smiling; he sat alongside a few distant cousins who, until recently, I wouldn't have been able to pick out of a crowded room. He seemed to have the attentions of an attractive pair of twins—three places removed on my mother's side, or two on my father's, it was hard to keep track. They were impressed with whatever Max was telling them. There was only two things that Max could impress women with: his action figure collection and his money, and the girls didn't look like sci-fi fans.

Also at the head of the congregation, sitting on the other side of the aisle from my parents, were the mother and father of the bride. I started when I saw them, almost tripping over backward. They were both glaring at me. The mother warning me of her disappointment should I run out on her daughter, the father threatening to beat me up regardless.

"You look nervous, mate."

Matthew was standing next to me; I felt his elbow nudge mine.

"I'm shitting myself," I whispered. "I don't think I can do this."

"Calm down, it'll be fine."

"I don't think it will be." I turned to look at the vicar, dressed in full garb. He was holding a book, preparing the vows. I wondered how many of them I would mess up, how many I would get wrong.

Matthew's hand reached around my back, his fingers tight on my skin. "You'll be fine, trust me."

Then the music started. The Bridal Chorus. I felt my heart sink. There was nowhere to run, she was coming. If I wanted to leave, I would have to do so when she was here, scarring her for life just before her father did the same to me.

I gulped down a thick glob of resistant phlegm and squeezed my eyes shut.

I heard the sound of activity as everyone turned to see the blushing bride. I heard a few gasps. Some mumbling. Some whispers.

I opened my eyes slowly.

Elizabeth was gliding down the aisle. My breath caught in my throat when I saw her. She was stunning; she looked like an angel, floating above the ground, the bright white dress lapping at the floor around her feet.

I could see her blue eyes through the veil. She was staring at me. Smiling. I returned the smile. The anxiety vanished, the fear was gone. She had cut a line of ease through the judging congregation, softening them all in my eyes. My heart was still beating like a techno drum, but for different reasons. I wasn't worried anymore. I didn't have cold feet.

When she stood in front of me, I told her how beautiful she looked. I told her I loved her, and then, minutes later, I said two words that meant more than those compliments combined.

After the wedding dinner, I received congratulations and admiration from people I knew and loved, and people I wasn't sure I had ever met. Elizabeth's father had a little too much champagne with his meal and before he began eating dessert he was telling me I was the perfect person for his daughter while warning me not to hurt her in equal measures.

It was a long day, but it was a happy day. Elizabeth was by my side the entire time. We relaxed at the evening party. The music was playing, the crowd was mingling, everyone had a little to drink and we were counting the seconds until we could leave for the hotel.

"I'm still not sure if your dad likes me," I told Elizabeth, cradling her in my arms as we moved gently to a fast song, the rest of the dance floor jumping and swinging to the beat.

"He does, trust me. *I* like you, so *he* likes you."

"I like that logic. I don't *believe* it, but I like it."

The song finished, and I escorted her off the dance floor, hand in hand.

I kissed her lightly on the cheek and wove my hand further down her body. Over her breasts, voluptuously pressing against the silky soft material, and her stomach, also protruding against the dress.

My hand stopped on the curvature under her navel. I dropped to one knee, pressed my face close. Elizabeth giggled softly. "And how's my little boy?" I asked the small bump.

"Tired."

"Oh, and he's talking now!"

Elizabeth laughed, running her hands down to meet mine, her manicured fingernails brushing against my skin. "I"m tired as well," she noted. "I can't wait to get back to the hotel."

I looked up and winked at her. "I can't wait to get back either," I said suggestively.

"Oh, you must be ready for bed as well then."

We walked to the buffet table where Matthew waited with his wife, his arm casually thrown across her bare shoulders. She was an attractive woman, a former model, just his type. But she was also nearly a decade older than him and had more PhDs than he had GCSEs.

Behind them, Max was busying himself on the buffet table, his back to them and us as we approached. I walked with protective arms around Elizabeth, one over her shoulder, the other firmly planted on her stomach.

"You thought of a name yet?" Matthew quizzed, nodding toward the semi-bulge.

I exchanged looks with Elizabeth and shrugged. She had thought of a few, but I had knocked them back. I had thought of dozens, and she had rejected every single one.

"I quite like Maximilian," she said, with a furtive glance at Max.

Max beamed and showed his teeth, wedged with flakes of pastry and bits of meat. A shower of crumbs rained down his jacket, but he ignored them.

"Like me!" he declared, firing pastry fireballs at Matthew's shoulder.

Matthew groaned and rubbed his shoulder down, then he stared at me. A warning stare. I looked right back.

"No," we both spat in perfect harmony.

Max sagged slightly, he closed his mouth, a sliver of spinach clung to his lip for dear life.

"Nothing personal," I lied.

He cheered up a bit and turned around to concentrate on further filling his face and dirtying his suit.

"Just a thought," Elizabeth said calmly.

"We have plenty of time to think of a name." I wrapped my arms around her, kissed her on the forehead, the cheek, the lips. Then I released, lowered, and planted a kiss on her stomach. "No rush," I added softly.

Before I departed to the hotel, I escorted everyone out of the building. I had already seen and heard from everyone, but now they were lubed up with alcohol, the day was almost over, and they all wanted to offer more congratulations. Elizabeth retired early, using her condition as an excuse, so I waited by the exit alone as streams of drunken revelers left via the door behind me.

After I thought everyone had departed, my dad came through from the main room. His eyes puffy, his tie pulled loose and shoved over his shoulder. I thought he might go for a hug to match the occasion; he didn't. He shook my hand.

"I'm still amazed you married her," he told me. I saw a glint of genuine pride and elation in his eyes. He tried to hide it but it was there.

"I know," I huffed. "The first girl I ever fancied, my *first* girl-friend, then a decade later: my *wife*."

"No, I mean I always thought you batted for the other side."

I slumped my shoulders and glared at him disapprovingly.

He shrugged, as if to say that he couldn't help it. He slapped a heavy hand on my shoulder, "You did well, kiddo."

"Thanks, Dad."

He looked tearful, but he brushed passed me and left before those tears developed.

My mother came next. She didn't restrain herself; she was already crying on her approach. The tears rolled down her face in streams, her whole face a picture of distress. She looked like she had been out in a storm.

She threw her arms around me, her tears soaking into my shirt and dampening my skin. She mumbled a heartfelt and extended conversation into my shoulder, but I couldn't understand a word. Then she pulled back, gargled something profound, fluttered her eyelids forlornly and then withdrew.

I trudged back into the main room to check there were no stragglers.

Throughout the night, the room had been lit by small lights embedded in the walls and around the dance floor like a sparkling border. Fluorescent lights in the ceiling now bore down onto a floor littered with party streamers, scraps of food, and carelessly dropped paper plates and plastic pint glasses.

Tables that had once been so neatly and immaculately arranged were scattered and disjointed; perfectly pressed white tablecloths hung from their wooden tops like dusty, lopsided hats. Chairs that began the night under repressed backsides had lost their formality in the midst of alcohol and joviality and were now strewn around the room.

It was a war zone, but at least the war had been won.

I lifted my hand to the light, looking one last time at the large banner that ran a tacky line across the top wall, its colorful plastic coating slightly peeled in places and leaking lines down to the buffet table beneath. The adhesive in the top right had lost its hold and the corner flopped miserably. The entire banner sagged in the middle, a few hours and a few feet from drooping into the punch bowl.

It was still readable though, still prominent. I let the image burn into my head and snapped off the light. In the immediate darkness, I could still see those bright red letters, my name, her name, *our* surname, and then: happily married. And we were, and I knew it would last.

Acknowledgments

First, I should thank the person to whom this book is dedicated. She might not have been the one to bring it to press, but I'm sure that, without her, this book would not exist. My life as a struggling writer was made considerably easier with her by my side, so from the bottom of my cold, repressed, British heart, I thank you, and I love you. I should also thank my family because they put up with my shit for just as long. So, to my mother, father, my brother Gary and his wife Adelle—as well as the three children, Leah, Aiden, and Harry, who make their lives both a joy and a living nightmare—thanks for your support.

There are a few family members who supported me and never lived to see this day. To those, I can only apologize for taking so long.

I offer a wealth of sincere gratitude to my in-laws, my Greek family. To Tasos, a man who embraced me, even after I took his daughter from him; a man for whom the words "I'm full" initiates a look of bewilderment and an offering of more food. To Pamela, to Vanya, and to Nancy. In fact, to everyone in Greece and Cyprus, friends and family alike, who have done their best to treat this strange little English boy as if he were their own.

I would like to thank my agent, Peter. His knowledge, experience, and reassurances have been crucial to this whole process. I also owe a debt of gratitude to my editor, Nicole Frail, who has made this a painless exercise, and to everyone else at Skyhorse Publishing.

For reasons that I don't want to explain here, I also want to thank Alan Fraser, Gary, and Carl. They will understand why, and I hope this message finds them well.

This has been a long road, and to thank everyone who has helped in some way or another would require more pages than I am allowed. Needless to say, if you have been there for me, and if you're not a prick, then I extend my gratitude.